Coalitions

Coalitions

David Rounds

OUTERBRIDGE & DIENSTFREY
New York

Distributed by
E.P. Dutton & Company

For My Father, Stowell Rounds

Library of Congress number 76-126584
First published in the United States of America
in 1970
Copyright © 1970 by David Rounds. All rights
reserved including the right of reproduction in
whole or in part in any form.

Design: Anne Hallowell

Outerbridge & Dienstfrey
200 West 72 Street New York 10023

Coalitions

i

Amarantha dried her hands on her dress. "So where's this supposed thunderstorm?" She plucked a brush from the dresser and tugged it through her hair. "It's going to pass over, because that's what you deserve." With the brush held up she whirled towards a knock on the door: "Okay, who's that?"

"Amarantha?" The door opened. "Are you nearly ready for—"

She interrupted, "Amarantha's a peach, okay? Get out of here."

The woman stepped out. "That's all right, dear."

She hurled the hair brush at the closing door and then ran after it while it clattered. She opened to the hall. "Mrs. Linton? Mrs. Linton?"

"I'm just over here, Amarantha."

"Oh I know but—well—"

"Dinner's very soon. Finish brushing your hair."

"Well—"

She turned back inside her room and closed the door. Jumping up onto the bed, she called through the transom, "I'm sorry, I'm sorry—"

Her dress rustled, and she stepped down and advanced to the window against a warm wind. "Because it is going to rain." She leaned out the window into city air. Pigeons on the fire escape slapped their wings and whirred while a sound truck brayed suddenly beneath her: "Confront the racist unions now! Join our peaceful demonstr—"

She yelled down: "Get out!" and added, grinning, "They're going to be flooded out in two minutes." Engines and rainclouds rumbled in her ears. She sat up on the fire escape and leaning back yelled: "That's right and listen up there you, none of these peaceful demonstrations because I want a crunching riot—"

A shatter of thunder unzipped the air. Nodding briskly, "Okay then," she slithered back through the casement and in the middle of her room stood wrenching clothes from a chair and whirling them round her head. "Shoes? Shoes!" She struggled. "Coat. And hat. And furthermore cane." She scuttled out the door and backed quickly down the stairs as she heard:

"Amarantha? You aren't going out?"

She called, "Yes I am, you guessed her, Chester."

"Dinner's in five minutes."

"Eat it—" she banged the street door open and stamped down the steps into the rain.

"Honk screech er-er-er crunch, get them, rain, rat-tat-tat psshh—" A battalion of raindrops thumped the truck tops, rapped the cars, drummed the trash cans, lashed onward to the fleeing feet that splattered past her on the sidewalk; "Gug-gug-gug—" Water filled her mouth as she stretched out her arms and, stamping out a puddle, spun slowly round faceup to the storm. "Tuh. Squish foot. This puddle's finished." Damped shouts struggled against the roar; wheels swashed, wipers whined, horns brayed. "So what's down this street?" Clothes clinging, skin needling, she walked on as her mind chased drips that scudded down her belly and away.

The sound of racing footsteps swooped at her. A woman shouted: "Look out!" and crashed into her shoulder. Amarantha staggered against a parked car. Her cane skittered down the sidewalk as the woman ran on calling "Sorry!"—the quick heels clacked beneath the roar into silence.

She pushed from the car and listened. "Cane went over here I think—" she bent to rub her knee as she walked. "The fat old bitch"—she crouched and patted the sidewalk with her palms. "This is impossible." She jumped up. "Hey, someone?"—snarled "Thanks," as the steps splashed by. Turning then and touching a car hood, she sidled out and leaned into the avenue and waved, "Hey! Hey!" A horn stabbed the air and hissing wheels sprayed her as she leapt back. "Jesus Christ." She squat by the gutter, her fingers scrabbled in mush. "Except I think it went—oh good, someone? Wait! Wait!" Steps slapped from the rush and spattered out again. She yelled: "I hope you slip and fall and get crushed by a truck—" She pressed her ear to the concrete; heard only the rumble of underground trains as chill grit gathered in her hair. Rising, her back inched along cars and her hands patted the dripping steel. "I think I turned, though—oh, disgusting." She stopped to peel sodden paper from her palm; she shook out her hand. "Yecch. Attack, rain. No wait I didn't turn though—no, I did that's the thing—"

"Watch out, John!"

An opening car door nudged her and she leapt aside. The door closed quickly. As the window rolled down, she yelled at it, "You watch because you're the one it's going to attack."

"Sorry, I didn't see you, did I bruise you with that?" The door creaked and she backed cringing along the cars. The man called as he got out: "Look, are you all right?"

"Yes."

The man's steps neared. "Listen, my wife and I'd be happy to drive you home if—"

3

"No." She clutched her throat and gurgled. "Sorry—sorry—sorry—"

"Stop that." Quicker steps approached while she backed, thudding her fists on the cool steel. "Okay—okay, what's happening."

"Yes, go ahead, Marian."

"I can hear because Amarantha's a peach, okay she's a peach—"

"I'm on my way over to you, honey—" the woman's hand fell gently on her shoulder; she pushed from a fender and ran. "Amarantha yourself! Amarantha yourself!" Feet splashed after her. The man shouted, "Turn left!" She staggered and turned right and slammed into a car. Her knees crumpled. The man dragged her up; she clawed him and kicked. "Get out! Get out!" He held her wrists down hard. "Be still, Amarantha." She caught breath in a gasp; she unclenched her fists, frowned, and was still. She rested her forehead on his chest.

"Mister, I—" pausing and backing away: "You don't have to hold now." He let her go. She said to his silence, "If you'd—I mean I'm sorry to have got you drenched and everything but if you'd find my—cane, I dropped it down the street a little ways and—"

Beside them, the woman interrupted, "Come inside first though won't you, till the rain stops? We live right here— Aramantha is it?"

"No wait, because maybe it'll stop—" the rain held its breath; it spat on the sidewalk again and she shivered. "Well it isn't—"

The man said, his voice disappearing as he walked, "It'll rain all night."

"Come on, Aramantha." Soaked fingers fell on her arm.

"I don't know who you are, though."

4

"We're Marian and John Morrison, and we live right here. Steps coming up now."

"Yes, but I have to get back to dinner and besides I—"

"Dinner waits," the man said. A lock clicked. "I ought to have a look at that knee."

"You what?" she stopped. "All right, no doctors thanks a bunch." She tossed away the woman's hand and turned and walked down the stairs.

"Honey, please will you—"

"Get in, Marian." He said then, "I'm tired of this. The stairs are in front of you."

"I know where they are."

"Climb them." His steps faded and she climbed, muttering, "It will, though, it will too." He said: "Turn right, Amarantha." She turned right and patted the doorway with her toe; stepped in. The door thudded out the roar of the rain.

She whispered silently to herself, "Now what, though." Wet clothes swished from bodies and splatted on the floor in the dark. "Hey, right in the public hallway for God's sake? because maybe they're crazy, that's not just coats they're taking off—" Space whirred in rooms beyond. "You think it's some kind of sin-den society? Sure because their accent? Wait a second."

The man was speaking. "I don't imagine Gaylord will come now."

"Oh the fourth. It's an orgy. That's what I'm for."

"Yeah, well I never thought he would anyway."

She said aloud: "Who's Gaylord?"

"A friend of ours, honey."

The man said sharply: "One who apparently doesn't bother to honor invitations."

"Come on, John. He's had a way of failing to show since as long as I remember him."

The man said, "It's perfectly obvious that he's been avoiding us."

"It isn't obvious to me," she said.

"That's simply because you don't much care for him any more if the truth be known. It is obvious, Marian, and I tell you it's part and parcel of the whole sweep of things—"

The woman spoke sharply also: "I'm not going to talk about this now, John, hear me? hear?" Her voice turned to Amarantha: "Do you want to go into the john and get your wet clothes off, and I'll put them on the radiator? Come on, I'll give you a robe."

"Well I don't think I'd better, thank you, but—" She reached to touch the woman's nearing shoulder; it was bare. She pulled away. "I've got to get my cane."

"Only person want to steal it isn't going to see it, far as I can tell."

"Yes, well I suppose—oh, I've got it." She paused, sniffing; she nodded. "Like this isn't a building, it's a house. Yours."

"Mm-hm—"

"Because I couldn't figure out why you were taking off your clothes in the hallway." Both her hosts laughed and she added: "Be quiet."

"We're just taking off our coats and shoes, honey."

"*I* know. Where's the john because I'm cold." She spread her hand on the woman's back as they walked. She thought: Goosebumps, feel? Skin. Stairs croaked. The woman said: "Up now, Aramantha."

"It's Amarantha." She thought: You watch because as soon as they get me into the bathroom and out of the way, blam-blam he's going to give her twenty-seven blows about the face arms and neck, and as soon as she starts babbling, whop and he's on top of her in two seconds. There's a zoo in these stairs. Everything smells old.

The woman said: "Here's the door. You take your time." A towel butted her hand. "Be all right?"

"Yes I think—you sure? It's very nice of you, Marian."

The bare feet receded. "Any time."

"Since this is how a bathroom ought to smell. Stupid zipper, dammit"—She bumped the door closed, pared off her soaked dress. "Well if you have your own house of course. Whop he's going to. Mm. You just give in. Of course if you're married. Quite routine, you know. I'm not sure if I'd want to be, though, wasn't it terrible the way they—Terrific this. Underwear out please? How long's the room." Hunching her shoulders, she whipped out her bra and hurled it; it whirred a moment and whacked. "I'd have my bathroom a little longer. I think. I knew right away from their accent, couldn't you tell? I ought to call up Mrs. Bellylinton and get back to the halfway house. No screw it because what's down here." Waving her hand before her and fretting the towel on her hair with the other, she walked down the wooden floor until her fingers rapped the high lip of a bathtub. "Well what, on legs?" She stooped. "Claws. That I'll have." She stepped in and slapped a shower spout. "Modern conveniences. Soak the patient. They won't mind? Double terrific. Losing my cane has got to be developed." She flung the towel down the room and squeaked the knobs; pipes honked and gurgled. "Come on, well come on then?" Pulsing sighs mounted in the shower, heaved, popped out with a burble, dribbled on her brow. "Well what kind of man are you for God's sake? I'm not that ugly." She reached and beat the pipe; water burst down. "Okay he's got one—Jesus Christ more hot—no less hot, ouch—yes I'm talking to you—okay—okay okay!" The heat crept down her like a tongue. She thought: Now this is a man for you.

Soap? Yes I think it's time to   Why shouldn't I? Use the soap   Where is it then? Maybe they don't wash? They'll throw me out of course   So what   He's a doctor   I've a certain clinical interest don't I? Hmmmm very interesting case   Kook   Shut up Well soap in the washbasin? I knew it. It might as well be one of the hands on the farm since we're on the subject   No because this shower hasn't got any hands No that's just a word   Shut up   I'm lending him my hands anyway   All over   All over   Yes I know and I think I'm what's-her-name Marian   Her husband has too many patients   Too many integration committees and human rights commissions   Like he gets up at six and in at midnight and she's had it   Hot afternoon   She's lolling in bed with nothing on   Click   The knob turns   This strange man's in the doorway   He's Jimmy   The tall one   The build he had   Six kids   He strolls over   Rips the sheet off   Stares at her   A slow insolent smile   She's pants on just   He reaches and he rips them off her Drops his own   Jesus   Black   Whop   Blam Hands   Mouth   Yes I know and it's the most disgusting thing   He's over her   Both his hands are absolutely pulling me apart   You hear about these girls well I don't know how they live with themselves She's begging practically screaming while   These people who can't wait, they just turn everything to filth   It's like my father says   It's like the corn If you pick it before it's ready and fitting to pick it then where's all your toil and trouble gone to

"Get out get out get out will you get out"—she slammed the soap against the wall and clutched the towel rack, half-choking, half-laughing. "Watcher, I said get out—"

She whirled round. "Hey what—" she heard the door close, wafting cool air. "Marian?" Her arms

8

flailed through the water, trembling, to grip the knobs, which blared into silence and uncovered the drumming of the rain. "Marian? You aren't here?" She flung the curtain over her shoulder, "Marian?"—she inched a leg down, walked through steam to the door. "She could have seen—dry—" Her breathing slowed. One after the other onto the seat she hoisted her legs and toweled. "All right, watcher. Because I'm going to rat on you tomorrow for butting in like this, since that's twice today? Try and stop me from telling him, and I'll ask for the shocks again, you watch. Sure because you can't stand that—bzzt-bzzzt." Cupping the back of her skull with one palm, she rubbed the towel on her hair. She muttered, "As far as I'm concerned they can drill in and slice your stupid eyes completely out of me and I don't care if I'm a turnip afterwards.

"Absolutely clean more or less dry Amarantha.

"Oh good." She listened. "I figured she'd leave. Wait, my arms." She rubbed. "Anything to avoid the nasty electrodes. Zap-bzzzt—" She sat down, her face in her hands. "Look, she's going to be dead, she's going to leave me alone, all right?" She shoved the water from her chest. "Sure. Next winter maybe. Christ, *I* don't know." Drips from the shower slowed and failed; there was laughter below. They're dressed now, come on come on, they didn't hear anything, she didn't see anything   The shower curtain   It's not at me—Christ she's lent me clothes too   I think I'm settling in this part of town   I will so put them on, they're clean, aren't they? She held the clothes to her face and sniffed. Of soap because her skin doesn't feel any different, did you notice? Well I must say Crooking her arms behind her: a rather ample lady this Marian. Because I don't believe any of that stuff about Negroes, it's garbage.

Look out! Sorry! Ivory-voiced that bitch was   Not

to speak of the rest of them   This John is too
You can just hear a hint in him. Well obviously I'm
hippy enough   Besides considering she's maybe four
inches taller   Well we farm girls   I thought that was
supposed to be attractive? I bet I wouldn't have
guessed without hearing Marian though. Dress please.
Stuffs himself with education   Revamps his diction
Makes a pile   Gets a white friend to purchase his
house because a dermatologist he's obviously   Treats
the high-born ladies's aging   Growl-voices   Spurns
them   Marries back home   Stick to your own kind
Wait, a comb on the shelf I bet?   This doesn't
happen back in Kansas let me tell you.

Shepherd's pie down there—

She tugged a steel comb through her hair. Because
their friend's not coming   Gaylord   I knew one
home   He's white of course   The chief obstetrician
on the floor   The supposed friend of our Negro
dermatologist because our Negro dermatologist is
feeling extremely paranoid tonight   His wife hates
that   Since did you notice who flared up the most at
the end, mm-hm? What she really wants to know is
why he even bothers with these white friends. Well I
know why. It means an extra portion tonight. For me.

Rain keep going

Okay.

She yanked at a snarl. Because you're not going to
bust in, all right, watcher? Okay you're not? Like
what, you think they're planning on doing some
experiments on me or something? Sado-glitter behind
her honeys? She smiled and drew the comb from her
hip and stabbed the air. "Bzzzt." The comb tinkled in
the basin. She clenched the dress and wiggled. "Kook
sails out to land a dinner. Evil Doctor. Black Magic.
Food."

ii

Gaylord lay like a stone. The morning sun shouted through his window and stung his vision as it splayed over his body and sent up the smell of him. Shading his eyes, he tucked back his chin and surveyed in wry stupor the several hairs upon his chest. He observed in a cracked morning voice: "Negritude."

"Yessir, sweet Negritude." He pommeled his belly gently. "Rich deep proud, superb impure, insuperable thunderous Negritude." He slung his head over the bedside to let the blood rush, and bawled to the dark beneath the springs: "BRUTAL Negritude."

He spilled to the floor in a tangle of bedclothes, and ground his knuckles into his eyes. "Up." He smiled at the sunlight that cavorted on his knees; he disbursed the tangle and rose.

At the basin with dropped jaw: "Aahhhh?"—his eyes examined themselves in the mirror. "Good, good, not the faintest trace of abuse or debauch. Too bad I can't say the same for a certain thirtyish female." He croaked the faucet, blubbered water over his face. In the mirror he was framed by his empty bed. "Hey, Lascivia?"

"Lasciviaaaa. . . . " Eyes clenched in watery discomfort he reached for a towel. "Ah. Now where's that cat of mine? Lascivia!" He dried his face. "Out getting drilled I suppose. Parading amongst the trash with Lord Estrus. I swallow my words." A white cat padded in primly, with each step bouncing out little questions to her master. "Brrpp-bpp?" he mimicked her—"Hello Lasciv'. Yas, brrpp-bpp." The cat sat on its haunches and meowed. "Yeah, well she isn't here and she ain't going to be. Now drink." Again he twirled the faucet and the cat soared onto the basin, lapped, twitched a wetted paw, yawned. Pointing to the sun, he said to her: "Now, it don't care; dig?"

Horsemeat splat upon a saucer and winged in his hand to the floor before her. He flipped on fire beneath a pot of water, while addressing her: "What you want with Martha anyways? You always were mine instead of hers, even if you were from me to her at the wedding, she never accepted you any more than a present you open and leave on a shelf, and you took it lying down, you going to deny that? I should've known by that what was coming if by nothing else. Except this kind of thing, you don't even believe what you know." He gazed at her chomp and purr, at the dogings of the lavender flame; padded to the closet, mused into his clothes.

"So meanwhile what the hell we going to invent to kill off today with and avoid thinking about it, tell me that, Lasciv'? Inspiration!"—he shot up his arms to the ceiling—"Trickle down the pants leg of the air!" The cat was weaving at his ankles, tonguing her jowls. She prattled off, swiping at the dancing shadows. The water ticked on the fire. "Ah."

He fetched the pot to balance it on the basin's edge, and he brought out his razor, his shaving soap, his brush. He hummed "My Country 'Tis of Thee" as he wet them and scribbled the brush in the soap. "These bantambreasted items, they don't have their roles straight anyways." He screwed his gaze to the handle of his shaving brush: "Fully Guaranteed Pure Bristle of Badger—like did I ever tell you the time, Christ she—hey. Hey, dig this."

12

A mottled elipse of yellow light, in a sudden mischievous apparition, winked on the wall by his mirror. It was the sun's reflection glancing from the razor in his hand. He reached to touch it, but his hand by moving flipped it to the ceiling, where it trembled while it looked down on him as if in silent laughter. He twirled the handle of the razor against his palm and the shape of light whipped round the four walls in a frenzy, then stopped short where it had begun by the mirror, as if ready to sprint off again at his bidding. "Yeah but the funny thing is the sun don't usually get over here. Except didn't I notice it before? Wait a sec." He peered at a loud clock on his dresser. "Ain't but five-thirty A.M., hear that? I thought it was eight at least. That's what you get for going to bed early. This is going to be splendid." He walked to the window, where on the sill the curled cat cleaned paws. He tugged at the golden shade. Outside, lost within its own diffusion of white cool glare, the sun was topping the roof of a brownstone across St. Botolph's Street. Gaylord leaned out over the sidewalk, where no step sounded beneath the blinded windows. Sea salt rode through the still city on the June air. As the secret sun clambered onto the roofs across the way, its light advanced against the shadow on the roadway in a diagonal line, undraping the street before his eyes. While he gazed, the light shimmered on the brown puddles of the past night's rain; glanced in the fluttering newspapers, glittered on the chrome of parked cars, sparkled on the mush of scraps in the drains. "Think it likes what it sees, Lasciv'?" Think so?" The cat purred. "See what this is, is an everyday enterprise of the dawn light checking out on us, snooping around, see, uncovering everything while we're asleep, catching your shape and picking your dreams, a kind of celestial FBI, ain't that a fine notion? Think so? Like it writes down all the sins it sees, good and bad, as it creeps around the earth, and then sends it all back along the nerves of the sun to the high residence of the gods, to be sifted by thermonuclear brains."

Stroking his cat as she stirred, he watched the light scale the buildings opposite and curve through windows, as it had through his own, to finger the still, sleeping forms. "They got a beautiful dossier on Martha. A most rococo set of data. Whole hot side of Mercury devoted to storing it. We aren't talking of her. Hey, Lasciv'." With a leap, as the sun overcame a water tower opposite, its light captured the nearby intersection. "Snipping out the heinous flimflams and other sundry floppy odia been weeding up the place since yesterday—tell me, for example, how many of those poor souls out there but didn't commit just last night—" he bared his teeth—"FRIGHTFUL perfectly frightful mortals and venals of o-mission, co-mission, e-mission, and Protestant mission? See what I'm saying? And over there in whiteytown, just picture to yourself, Lasciv', the awesome compendium of vicious squirmy nigglings, and oak-paneled broad-beamed shafts and outrages, and star-spangled barred-and-striped bell-towered fission-powered hideums, that tolled last night over there, Lasciv', amongst the graceful and the lovely?"

He rubbed his hands. "I'm getting back in shape now we've severed a certain connection." He looked round. There, in his own room, where no surface was free from the light's examination, he watched shadows retreat and the light slither and peer over him and his cat and the manufactured things of their lives. "The system works, see—you can't bribe the inspector, because as far as he's concerned every one of these things he's inspecting is perfectly meaningless, don't matter what memory the thing might be brimming with to us, he couldn't tell which to light up and which to leave in the shadow; far as he can see every object in the room could as easily be itself or something else or nothing at all, he could be peeping under Martha's steaming bedclothes, he could be looking into Jesus Christ, he wouldn't understand a thing; all he digs is the arbitrariness of everything in the world."

The wind rose, the shade flapped. The light, its mission done, scattered into scores of bright children. He looked round as they chattered in a game of patternmaking; crazy quilts of light fluttered over his feet, over the walls and the floor. "Now the thing about these is—I'll have it for you in a second—hey." In a sudden instant the patterns were gone; the room was in shadow. "What's this?" He looked out: a cloud was creeping its darkness down the open roadway. "The inquisition of St. Botolph's Street is done." The shadow advanced, the light sunk into the railbed beyond, glinted once on the steel road, and leapt over the wall to saunter deeper down the deep slums.

"What do we got?" He crouched down and rested his elbows on the sill, rubbing his cheek, still puffed with lather, against the warmth of his sleeping cat. "Obviously, baby, what we got is something to invent for today and carry us at least until noon, maybe, namely a call-to-action, a sermon, of course, and conceivably a mass running and screaming through the streets—only possible thing under the circumstances. I mean here we are, the residents of St. Botolph's Street, and the whole citizenry of Boston, Afro and Europ alike, fouling up the general ambience with our offals, positively wrecking the place with divers turpitudes, and we all being written down every morning in exhausting detail without our knowing it—except—" he held up a forefinger and smiled—"*you *and I know it.* Now with all this, are we to allow a mere pantsful to be saved from the dry ice and fire, without a warning? How could you suggest it?"

"Nosir." He swept her off the sill, swung out the door into the hall with her, set her down; he tramped, she padded down the still stairs. They burst out the door into the morning. She meowed in question as they crossed the roadway, which was cleared once again of shadow and bare to the sun. "You're going to see, little girl. We're going to set up a royal semicircle of drums and broadcast the facts in a stately manner. Know those jungle-type shows they put on in them African holes-in-the-wall? The heritage, my dear, the heritage." His voice was alone against the morning. "You're going to see." He hemmed and sang in tenor nasal;

"My country, tiiiiis of thee"

as he began to overturn trash barrels with careful quietness before a scabrous brownstone.

"Sweet land of liiiiiberty"

Bloody meat papers and buckled tin cans flooded to the pavement.

"Of thee I sing."

The cat snuffed about the trash, purring loudly, while Gaylord puffed as he arranged the upside-down trash barrels in a tight semicircle before him.

"Land where my faaaathers fried"

He leaned his ear

"Blood-dee with fraaaatricide"

to the upended bottom of each barrel in turn, rapping them softly to test their resonance. "Splendid. Wait." He tipped up another barrel

"Now war-hungerrrr's astride"

and set it within the semicircle of the others. "That's my drummer's stool. C'mon here, Lasciv'. Got to keep track of you in case of upsettables." He snatched her up by her midriff. "Brrpp? Yas." He scuttled her under the newest barrel, set it down again with her trapped inside, and sat upon it, shouting,

"Waa-atch freedom cringe." He beat thrice with his fists on his trash-barrel drums.

"Wake up, you blackskinned terriblesinned mother-violators of St. Botolph's Street!" *B'doom bam!* "Repent!" *B'doom bam boom!* "You're being IN-QUISITATED!" *B'doom doom bam boom.*

The light flashed on his drums as their dull gray clang raped the street's stillness and thundered against the tenement walls. The cat scratched and yowled; a drinking glass hurled from a window popped on the pavement and splashed about her prison and his heels: "Quiet, Lasciv'." He yelled: "Wake up!" He drummed: *B'dam boom.* A contralto bawl replied from a window:

"I already am awake you crazy drunk, now are you going to shut up?"

Gaylord called, grinning, "They're writing down every one of your sins, mamma—"

"Then they need just as much sleep as me," she shouted, slamming her window down, as a hoarse male voice bellowed:

"You're shutting your ass or I'm breaking it, brother—"

"Go home!"

"Shut up!"

"Repent!"

Doom doom.

Sudden automobile brakes uttered on corners; a siren spiralled up into the air. Gaylord, seated still, kicked at his drums and they bumped and deafeningly tumbled into the street. He massaged his forehead and frowned a moment; his opening eyes spied a woman's stocking on the pied ruckle of junk; he smiled and rubbed his hands. He swiped up the stocking and tugged it down over his nose. His hands pattered quietly over the barrel beneath him as he whispered: "Get ready, Lasciv'." Through the stocking's beige gauze he watched the squad car swing up to the sidewalk, sweep around the pails, glide to a halt before him. The man in the car looked out with a smile.

Then the siren gurgled and swallowed into silence; the rolling pails rumbled their last, turned once as weary animals and settled together in the roadway; night-clad men and women gathered in the doorways, watching in the stillness. Gaylord and the cop stared at each other, motionless. The cop cleared his throat.

"Going to get up off of that barrel, nigger?"

Gaylord scratched thoroughly the inside of his left nostril. "Where's your friend? I thought cops always traveled two in a pie?"

"Get up, faggot."

Frowning and looking down, Gaylord tipped up the barrel as he slipped off it backwards. The cat shot hair-raised from under with a shattering shriek. For a moment the cop looked at her, and Gaylord raised the barrel over his head and hurled it at the squad car. The pail crashed into the door. Gaylord ran and the cat streaked after, and the street blared again with the thuddings of the barrel, the cheers from the doorways, and the summons and curses of the cop as he struggled his arm through the smashed door. Gaylord ran while warning gunshots snapped and bullets sung over his head. He yelled; the squad car pursued. His footsteps slapped on the pavement. "Lasciv'!" He looked about; the cat was disappearing into an alleyway ahead. Gaylord followed her and made a game of stepping on his toes through strewn glass. He vaulted a fence and turned round. The shots rang. "C'mon Lasciv'—" The cat squatted before the

18

fence, whining. "C'mon!" She leapt, scrabbled at the fence, fell back; "C'mon!" She leapt again and he reached down and wrenched her up and over as the cop pulled even, not in good aim because the alleyway curved, but firing as Gaylord turned to run, and the bullet bounced screaming from the wall of the alley and bored through his arm and into the cat's haunch as he held her. She screeched and clawed. Wincing, he clenched her to him while he fled down the alley, down another and a third, down a street, into a wide avenue. He bent and flexed his searing arm, raised his elbow, tore the stocking off his scalp, and flung it to the silence of the morning.

He trotted, slowed, walked beside still buildings. "It's just the muscle, hey, ain't it Lasciv'?" She was quiet, blinking; one hind leg dangled slightly. "Hey, baby? You all right?" He stroked her: "Just a couple muscle wounds, there's my Lasciv', there's my fine wicked infinitely horrible Lasciv' . . . Cop ain't got no idea where we've gone to, baby—should've left you upstairs, Christ—I've got to understand you can't take a chick along on these things or I'm never going to succeed in keeping one. I'm sorry, little one, I didn't figure he'd shoot with all that audience—I got a problem with audiences—you all right?" He stroked her and gazed up the hill to where the road met the bright sky.

He said to soothe her, "Used to love this street in the old days, when I was small and we'd first come North, used to think them trucks grand the way they'd bolt trash in them revolving grinders like the mouth of a demented man, used to watch cats parading down the street with white chicks on their arm and think: there's freedom, why right over this hill coming up I'm going to find the new Jerusalem my mother'd always be talking about, poor pea pod

19

she was, poor little rail—here they come, Lasciv'." He skipped ahead and turned to crouch in a shadowed doorway as a fleet of police cars droned over the hill and wailed by. "Real nice of them to announce theirselves." They screeched and turned, scattering wastepaper. "Now that's done, we got to get moving, we obviously going to have to get over to John's place. He's going to know a vet that'll keep his mouth shut—EEYOW! watch that arm, will you?" He shifted her and rolled his red-blotched shirt to his shoulder: he blinked at the wound in his upper arm. "Ain't too bad, ain't too bad. . . . John'll fix it up easy, it ain't too bad. . . . "

He walked quickly with her along the sidewalk as the avenue awoke. Vehicles thickened; early workers clustered at bus stops; litter men swung off their gliding trucks and grappled grunting with gloved hands at the barrels, shouting curses and their jargon. Walking faster, he muttered, "Of course it had to be this, I ain't seen John in six, eight months, since Martha left anyways, and they asked me over for last night—you ain't got no right to not feel up to seeing him. He was right about her and there's nothing else to be said on it. You're going to tell him so, brother. Steady cat like him, won't be no problem if you talk about it. You plan to let her keep on between you now she's gone? Lasciv'? You okay now?" He furrowed her coat with his fingertips while she lay still against his chest along his good arm; for a moment she murmured and purred. "Going to be all right—"

He stood at the brow of the hill. Boston was before him, puffing and glinting beneath the morning sun, pushing its flesh down to the Charles River Basin's shores. The water shimmered in the warm wind. Over the bridge the trickle of cars was gaining to a stream, and he said to her, "It's getting late, baby, be a traffic cop here soon and a squad after, and there isn't one spot to hide on that bridge if they come by, we're going to have to swim it if we're getting to John's house"—He stood still, looking down at the glittering waves. "They don't care, see baby, anything bucks them, they just wind right around it, they don't take it to heart because they got no heart, like there ain't no reason for me to have been the same place same time as Martha yesterday, just dead forces pushing us any which ways, you should've seen what grounds for divorce she's walking with now I'm telling you, all Afro-done and Continental sandals and Appoloniac fire in his gaze—on their way to a picture gallery like as not I suppose—well she always did yearn for the beautiful people—what we going to think about, hey, Lasciv'? Hey little bolster, what we going to think about?" She lay still in his arms. "Lasciv'?" Suddenly he became aware, along the good arm she had been lying on, of a hot stickiness. Dread rushed into him and sent him running across the street and stumbling down wobbling wooden steps to the river's shore. He sat down on the concrete shelf underneath the bridge's first arch, and lay her out on her side in his lap. Her breathing caught; she gurgled. Blood was seeping from her belly quietly. "Don't Lasciv'—" Her eyes opened and she blinked at him. "Don't, will you? Don't?"

Stroking her, he gazed down the shore to the highway at the river's edge, thundering at last with a rush of cars, and to the buildings piled beyond. He looked for the morning light, captive now, another tool merely, the city it had owned now man's. He watched his kind rewind its habits and scurry again among its rectilinear creations. He walked to the edge of the waves; the sun soundlessly shone. "I should've split when the cop came, I shouldn't have brought you downstairs at all, I shouldn't've done any of it except the inquisitor story—"

"It's the first one I've told in a long time though,

baby, you got to remember that, I feel better in a way—after seeing the thing stark like that last night."—The cat moaned. "Be all right, Lasciv', John's place is just the other side—"

He waded to his waist in the brown water. "Be all right"—he lowered the surface of her back gently against the wetness. She snarled her surprise and bit him. He clenched his teeth and said to her, "You have to, little girl—" He lowered her again, half-immersing her this time, cupping her head and her hauch in his palms to keep them dry. On the touch of the water she yowled, and she twisted out of his hands, ripped her claws along his wounded arm, leapt into the water, flailed to the shore. She turned to him and hissed with arched back and slitted hatred in her eyes. She crumpled on the sand.

"Lasciv'—" He rushed to her and crouched; he pressed his ear against her chest. He said after a moment: "Yeah, I suppose." He picked her up and cradled her again, and waded once more into the river. For a long time he stood in the shadow of the bridge as it rumbled and trembled above him; the water circled warmly round his knees. He watched the waste foam gather at the shore and the ripples disengage the foam, sluice it aside, then fling it up once more, while the river lay down beneath a sheet of light in a warm sleep, only to shiver at the advancing wind and shatter into a thousand suns. He let her go to the current. She curved round an arch and was gone.

iii

"Wait!"

John rushed out of sleep and sitting up whipped his gaze around the room. "What?"

The house was in stillness. "I had a feeling that I—Marian?"—Murmuring, she tugged the sheet and curled away, her breathing slowing. He stood and walked quickly to the window and fingered the shade aside: the brilliance of summer sun blinded his eyes. "Perhaps we'll march in decent weather for once." On the bed table a glass of water stood beside pills; he walked and drank half, thinking: fill it. What did Pereira give her? He turned the bottle around: well he knows what he's doing, I imagine. Your wife is a woman. Yes I gather that's meant to be obvious.

Turning, he walked to the door; his hand halted on the latch. Oh that girl's out there. He reached clothes from a chair, muttering: "I don't see why we couldn't have driven her home after dinner and had done with her—Marian has to do all this mothering. I suppose. The tepid days she spends now. I thought we felt a little closer last night with that girl here though—What in hell she finds so damned humiliating about adopting a child I can't see." A shade snapped and he looked up: sunlight reached in, with square fingers making free with his wife while she lay unconscious and uncovered but for twists of linen, putting off time with tossed dreams. He cleared his throat as his eyes traveled on her dark skin. Lust touched him; like rapture, it departed when he noticed what it was. He cursed and turned away, pulling trousers. What's wrong, I thought you were getting over that? I detest being in the position of envying my wife's admirers instead of being jealous of them. They have no fear of her.

Where's that stupid thing. On the dresser. He straightened from fumbling with his shoes and winced at a typescript that lay among Marian's creams. His eyes caught phrases as he buttoned:

Brothers and Sisters, I want to tell you why I, as a white man, am joining this demonstration . . .

His forehead heated with annoyance. Cut the Brothers-and-Sisters, will you? Do I have to prattle this at them? If black power is going to be the way of the Committee then it's going halfway having me speak. Being polite to me for old times's sake, no they're not. I'm their ace in the hole, in case inter-racialism turns out to be the way after all. Apparently that long chance is not influencing my friend Gaylord. What does that say about where I am? He punched the speech into his pocket. Well, John, I'm real glad you asked me that question.

How *much* is that whiiite man-in-the-window?

The one with the shaggy brown guilt

He laughed; Marian stirred. As she turned over, gently snoring, her narrow hip rose as a hill in shadow against the windowed sky. "If it were our own child though." Walking round, he knelt beside their bed, lay down his cheek beside her fisted hand. I wouldn't feel such a stranger down there now, you see? His hand, remaining in the air an inch from her body as if her skin might burn him, ran back and forth along the length of her, to land at last on her hair. "Marian?" His voice emerged from a whisper: "Marian, I—" Her mouth was formless in slumber. Stupor gathered in

24

him as he murmured, "It's early yet—get some air—"
He rose and walked out and down, stepping on the
quietest portion of each stair. That girl not up yet,
then.

Youth.

Outside, into the morning, across the street through
chattering shadows, a thought landed and he started:
Christ, it's lucky I remembered and that's why I woke
up so suddenly of course as if I'd been tempted to
sleep through it—Well at least I'm not so hackneyed as
to forget our anniversary, I got her that object—the
wrong thing I suppose, after all my preaching—let it
pass—I can exchange it—

Twelve years

He leaned against a poplar that grew from the
sidewalk; tugged the speech from his pocket, stared at
it, not reading; chuckling. He remembered waking
from unconsciousness on a city street, and there
settling into his vision blood, buildings, a woman's
face: Marian's. "You breathing all right now? Lord, I
thought he going to kill you, way he sinking his boots
in you—" With the tail of her blouse she had wiped
his temple dry while a fold in her belly loomed. He
had said: "I bit him. I think on the buttock. He went
"Aargh!" Leaning back, her laughter: "What do you call
yourself, *daddy*?" The crackle of a bullhorn had covered
his name. "Think we'd better move?" Routed marchers,
shouts, hooves. "Yes, help me."

ACCUSE COPS PUMMEL YOUNG
WHITE CIVIL-RIGHTS G.P.

Everyone in Roxbury furious and delighted.

He moved down the sidewalk, speaking aloud to
himself: "*Daddy* we called each other.

"Talk, talk. Out with it: tears. And then the hands,
the eyes, the hair, the mouths: langour and arrogance.
We knew all the answers, didn't we? having no

25

questions. So what happens?" He laughed again and beat the roof of a parked car. "Tell me what happens?"

He scratched the crown of his head with the typescript. "The politics of bullshit, I won't read this. It won't bring it back. 'Why I, as a white man,' is not the issue. *I* am no issue, can I get that straight? Stick to business; picket the union. Jobs first, brotherhood afterward. We get to feed first, afterwards for morals. Can I get that through my head? Do I have to need the limelight? Shall I accept what decade this is?"

I can't.

He crossed the street again, rubbing the back of his neck. You abdicated up there this morning, you realize that?

Talk to her—His feet splashed and soaked in a puddle. "Hey, damm it"—Cool wetness seeped among his toes. He pulled off his shoes and dumped drips from them as he gazed along patterns of rain flow down the roadway. "We'd better have sun tomorrow. We had a thunderstorm the last march and snow the one before—I take it Nature's to the right of center." Smiling, he raised both arms above his head, his hands dangling shoes. "Then civilize! Civilize!"

"No, man. That's a drag."

"What?"

Gaylord shoved his jaw up to John's startled face and whispered loudly, "Mind telling me who the bitch is in the window?"

"Christ you scared me." John dropped his shoes and looked up to the guest room as Amarantha's face disappeared. He circled a pointed finger round his ear and mouthed to his friend: "Nuts." He added: "I thought that was against your philosophy anyway?"

"What's my philosophy? Hold on a minute." He rolled up his sleeve and exhibited his red upper arm.

"I'm in need of professional services."

"What did you do, cut yourself?" John gripped Gaylord's elbow and squinted up close at the wound. "Listen, is this what it looks like?"

"Yeah but don't breathe a word on it."

"Of course not but who the hell's after you?"

"I ain't a suspect. I was lawfully protesting my fate of being born for the sole and express purpose of driving delivery for Cadillac Cleaners, Inc., five days weekly."

John said, not looking at him: "Another little—?"

"A scene, baby. A gentle tweaking of the community wattles. And no problem this time."

John plucked at Gaylord's sodden shirt: "This smells like the river?"

"I swam for it."

"We'd better get cracking. How've you been otherwise?"

"I'm all right."

They tramped inside to the kitchen. "Can you move it?"

"Yeah but don't ask me."

John drilled water in a pot, set it to boil and pointed. "Wash and get those clothes off. I'll lend you some. You'll need a mess of shots. I'll get my bag." He disappeared into the hall.

"Hey, John?" Gaylord's voice came through his shirt. "Hey dig this, I saw Martha last night in a liquor store."

John called after a moment: "Oh?"

"Don't worry, baby. She isn't getting into my house again."

John returned, saying as Gaylord's soaked clothes splat to the floor, "I'd get rid of those if I were you. I can do it. So what did you say to Martha."

"Nothing much, see; I don't want her to know I'm

planning to get the goods on her. Point is, it was the first time I'd actually seen her with another cat who she was obviously making it with, and seeing it bald like that, know what I mean? Of course you never had that problem but—" He stood naked in the laundry tub and dusted detergent over himself. "There was a beautiful lot of turds in that stream." He squatted and blubbered under the tap. "Funny thing is, John, I haven't had one bit of action since she left and before that it wasn't too cordial between us, and the sixty days I served in the shithouse is in there besides, must be near a year since I had a woman, and suddenly now I feel like looking for it, you know? Like I needed to run into her like that, to free it? I'm set to roar through twenty different beds inside a month, of course that ain't my style but—"

John stood silent over a pot of liquid into which he was dunking surgical tools. Gaylord said, looking up: "I'm sorry I didn't show up last night, man."

"It's all right."

"I'd just seen her, you know, and I didn't feel like society for a while—"

John lay out a sheet on the kitchen table. "We got caught in the rainstorm picking up that stray girl you saw, it would've been awkward anyway."

"Yeah, now listen I know Martha fawned on you and all that bullshit—"

"She was all right. A little hostile. Towel and clean clothes are in the hamper there."

"Look, man, I—"

John interrupted: "I don't want to talk of this now, Gaylord. Things change and people can't help it. Groups come together and fall apart. Let's get this done."

"Yeah but I'm trying to tell you, see—"

"Don't bother." John turned his back on him and

began to scrub his hands in the sink. Frowning and smiling, Gaylord rinsed and toweled in silence. John muttered after a minute: "I'm sorry. I haven't been well lately."

"Bullshit."

John cast his eyes upward to the ceiling, toward their bedroom.

Gaylord said softly: "You mean Marian don't know of it? What the hell you got, man?"

John shook his head. "No, you don't understand, I'm in perfectly good physical health."

"Yeah? Well you ain't got a problem with her, John. She's honest. Believe me."

"I do. That isn't the issue. I don't want to talk about it."

Gaylord stepped heavily down from the laundry tub. Phrases of "Clementine" filtered from upstairs. He said after a moment, "We calling down the chick up there for surgeon's assistant? A little pulchritude in the mists of pain?"

"I doubt it. She can't see."

"Oh yeah?"

John said quietly as Gaylord rummaged in the clothes hamper: "I told you she's a bit nuts, though, you'd best not flirt with her."

"Pants: aha. What are you worrying about? I leave miscegenation to the brave and the mad."

"The which?"

"Besides, she's flatchested."

"Excavay-ting for a mine—"

The girl's steps on the stairs ceased. She called, "Hey, John?"

"We're in the kitchen, Amarantha."

"Oh good." She appeared in the doorway. Gaylord said sharply:

"Wait a sec, will you?"

"Why?"

"What do you mean, why? Because it's embarrassing, walking in like that."

"Walking in like what?"

"Walking in on a cat you ain't even met while he's putting his friend's pants on."

"I can't see, though."

"It's still embarrassing."

"All right then, I'll turn around."

She faced away toward the stairway and put her fingers over her eyes. "I hope I'm not interrupting anything."

"You mean you hope you are interrupting something. You aren't, though."

"Oh. Yes but you must be doing something. People do something."

John said: "This is Gaylord Jackson, Amarantha."

"Oh the one last night? Oh really?"

"What's so surprising may I ask?"

"Nothing, but can I turn around? I heard you zip up."

"That a fact?" He climbed onto the kitchen table and lay down on his back.

Turning, she said: "You were the one who was coming to dinner but you didn't, because why not?"

"Yeah, it was raining, see. I got depressed."

"Yes, but didn't you call up? I mean how do you expect John and Marian to feel about it?"

"What are you talking about?"

"I mean, well if you don't mind my asking?"

His voice came louder. "So what's with you anyways?"

"Oh, *I* don't know." There was a long silence. Clinking instruments and breathing scraped against it. John said: "This is minor, Gaylord."

"Yeah, thanks, John."

"Look, would it really be too much to ask if you told me what you're doing?"

John said, "I'm sorry, Amarantha. I didn't think."

"That's all right. So what are you doing?"

"Gaylord cut his arm and I'm putting some stitches in."

"*That's* what." She paused. "Does it hurt though?"

"Naw. Yeah. Come over here a sec, okay?"

"All right."

Gaylord cocked his head back and upside-down watched her pat the counter as she moved. She swished faintly in the stillness. He cleared his throat. "Hold on now. Let me take a look at you."

"Jesus, well you're sort of direct aren't you?"

"Naw. Direct to what?"

She hugged her shoulders and swivelled them back and forth. "Don't get me balled up, I don't like it."

John said: "Don't twitch, Gaylord."

Amarantha, loudly: "Ha, ha."

Another long silence followed. "Listen, are you really blind though? I mean you don't look blind, know what I'm saying? Like none of these funny stares or baby-blue dinguses growing on your eyeball?"

"Well thanks, since what do you think I am, a skoptophile trying to reform or something?"

"You kidding me? What'd you say your name was?"

She shouted: "I said what do you think I am, a skoptophile trying to reform or something?"

"Amarantha, there's some sheeting in the closet over your head."

"Oh—okay." She turned round and reached, slapping cabinet doors. "This one?"

Gaylord said, "Is this for a sling, John? No sling."

John frowned darkly with a smile: Quiet.

"This one though?" she said.

"That's the one."

Pause. "So what's a, what's it, skriptophile? baby? mind telling me?"

"Nope—it's people who watch other people fuck."

Both men started slightly but audibly. Gaylord moaned: "Christ Almighty." The girl faced round, linen in her hand, grinning. "So here's the sheeting."

● ● ●   Twelve years. Twelve Junes, John, one hundred forty-four months and I wouldn't care to figure how many thousands of mornings that sun's come walking in here and turning that shade to gold, feeling around to see if we're alive still, winding up and around, up and around, millions and millions and millions of times, looking at us poor fools tearing about, I don't see how he can bear it, I don't see why he don't just lay down and die.

Marian sat cross-legged on their bed, rocking and grinding her teeth against the cramps. God damn pills they give you aren't no good at all, I'm taking two more and I don't care what he says—She reached for the bottle, threw the white bits into her throat, and swallowed the rest of a standing glass of water that tasted of dust. You'd know it'd have to come on our anniversary, very fitting isn't it. He'll be out all day and half the night with his meetings anyways so what does it matter, he'll want me to come, I'm not going to come. Well, it isn't his fault they decided on tomorrow for the stupid thing—I hope it rains.

Political action   Where'd he get his ideas about political action   Exploit what potential there is for democracy, Marian   We do have the franchise   We got a lot of talk that's what we got   I don't know what makes him think those crooks in the statehouse and the rest of those downtown smooth-ass smileys going to give one damn how many poor black fools walk down Commonwealth Avenue singing hymns and waving signs in Boston of all places You'd get more reaction in Mobile Alabama Greaseball union and blue-eyed Beacon Hill got it all worked out together and they never going to let a black man into that union or into that factory except to clean toilets Every morning this week he's down there walking back and forth What does he think they care

Sometimes I think he's off his nut completely

Bitch bitch bitch bitch that's all you ever do No wonder he don't bother with you

Maybe when the march is over

Yeah and that's what you said the last time.

Our own day and he's already cleared out of this room He's already got a crowd down there—The shade reared and kicked out backward, revealing the warm sky. Such a pretty day too, John, I'd love to shove you in the car and drive up to Ipswich or down to the Cape, get a wine-red bikini to make my husband's eyes pop till he gets all hot to come home again Why we just got here baby And take the first swim of the year and sun And sun, he used to like me when I got real dark, remember, remember that time down the Cape In Wellfleet it was We went down to the beach late at night and a storm It came thundering up, thundering up and no one was there at all not a soul and the dunes flashing in and out of sight with the lightning and we made love standing up in the waves—She shook her head slowly and smiled. All that time gone.

And him white against the moon

You ain't never going to have that kind of thing again. You think that'd happen if you got him to go today, even on our anniversary?

It isn't that of course, it isn't that, you can count

yourself lucky you have it for a memory, I can hardly
see myself getting all lathered up and losing my head
like it used to be anyways, it's been so long, why we
haven't even made the most driest kind of businesslike
love in I don't know how long   He's been so busy
with the march and all, but it isn't that either, you
wouldn't ever find me hopping round from bed to bed
like Gaylord's Martha does   Endless strings of arms
and legs   I don't know how she keeps track of them,
it isn't that   It's just you need a little quiet   A little
being together John, a little I don't know

Something's come up for air in the last year or so

As if he's wary of me   As if he don't know what
to do with me   It isn't as if he doesn't want me
around   He doesn't snap at me   It's just he doesn't
love me any more in the same way he used to and he
don't know how to change to a new way, now that
the old kind of being together has passed us by

He says we need things to do together   I wish he'd
make it clear how addressing envelopes and soliciting
contributions while he sits around talking strategy and
twisting arms is going to make us feel close   He
thinks it'd be better if we had children   Sure it
would I'm ready to try again any time you say   I
can take losing one every once in a while   Once a
year even   But we need a little cooperation on your
part baby

I don't want children if I can't have him   I ain't
that kind of woman   Father told me John'd leave
just like that soon as I got pregnant   Well he didn't
He's still here   He wouldn't leave me   I know he
wouldn't   He wouldn't   I'm sure he wouldn't   You
wouldn't John

Of course I didn't know I couldn't make a child   I
didn't know I was such a freak

He says I'm not   He said we've plenty of chance

still   Ten years at least   He said the difficulty could as easily lie with me as with you Marian, there's no way of determining these things   He's just being kind   No he isn't   He wouldn't lie to me

I'd like to know why I deserve being turned around and dried out   I'd like to know what I done when all these girls ain't been women a year are walking round with their bellies like a watermelon   Yes and I used to snort and look down on them and John spends his time at the risk of jail teaching women and girls how to use the pills the diaphragm the intra-uterine thing   Well we don't break no pope's law here I can tell you that and I don't want to see any pregnant women   I don't want them in my house Seeing their dresses hang   Seeing them smile   I remember my father standing up there preaching out curses   And the women will be barren   He'd roll it out like on a bass drum   And the women will be barren, barren, barren.

Is that what Father prayed the Lord to curse me with because I wouldn't put it past him   Telling me I'm cleaving to the scourge What kind of words is that As if John could help what color he is   There been nothing barren about the sort of love goes on in this house   The way he'd yap-yap about the white blood in our veins   The things he'd waste his breath on   As if it wasn't red

It's been so long now   It seems so natural   I can't even remember what the fuss was all for and I go for months without giving it a thought, I have to think twice now when someone looks at him strangely or at me strangely when we're together which isn't too often these days

Well we forget but no wonder we find it hard now the juice is gone out of our veins because we got nothing in common at all except our house and our no children and the memory of our desire. Lord, he got a set of ideas how to do everything   That's our conditioning, he says to me   *Conditioning* I'm telling you, the words he got to keep himself away from himself   I used to tease him something terrible *Conditioning*   She cocked her head and smiled. I guess I conditioned him something

We jostled out a way of life till we fit   And then we stopped   Nothing happened any more   We stopped without even noticing

Daughter, if you think you're escaping the burden he placed on your shoulders by making you black   No ma'am, you've just begun to feel the weight. I told him no down-home nonsense going be a burden to me Lord, them eyes of his   And I don't know, John, maybe you understand the woman part of me with that doctor's brain of yours, but as for the black part you're as blind as that stray girl and you're a white man, John, I don't care how long you've lived in our world or how much you love being in it like you say you do, you're a white man, and I don't understand a single thing that goes on in that churning head of yours, not a single solitary thing, not even—when you're—inside me—

The cramps wrenched through her again and she doubled over, clutching her belly and twisting her head aside. John I wish—She straightened, slowly looking down along herself. And I wish you wanted me now and then, John, just now and then—I know I ain't a slim filly any more and I know my breasts don't start out like a pair of nails from an old board and I never did have the prettiest face you could find and I'll be thirty-four and someday I'll be sixty but I'm your wife, John, and I hate seeing you sleep next to me and do nothing but grunt when you touch me by mistake—I keep thinking maybe I'm wrong to ask you   Not that I ever say it out loud but you can't tell me you don't know, and I can't help what I want, John, how long do you think we have before we dry up and spread and look in the mirror one day and see a pair of sacks of bones not even able to get angry anymore—Stumbling, she walked to a chair, flung on a robe, pulled at the window shade. As it rose with a crackle, there glided before her a school of sparrows that soared out over the roofs. You're the one who keeps saying we're lucky if we live to be fifty living near a naval base, so why are you always at war with your own self, if the fools are going to bomb us then why don't we leave and reach somewhere for some peace, a little peace?

The door was knocked and opened; he was there, carrying breakfast things. She turned from the window and he said, "Summer's come." She shrugged and did not answer. "You feel all right, Marian?"

"Rotten." She sat down on the bed wearily. "I been railing at you, John." He came around the bed and she held her hand up: "Don't say it. We aren't going to talk about it."

"I was going to kiss you."

"Oh—I'm sorry."

"Now you said it."

She stood and kissed him. "You know I'm such a bitch? You got all these things to worry about and here I'm sitting here knocking at everything."

"So you feel bad, you're supposed to knock things. On the best medical advice." He brought a table to her and set the tray down. "I meant to come right up again but the illustrious Mr. Jackson appeared and that was an end to it."

"Yes, I heard. What'd he come to get out of you? Thanks, baby." She looked up and touched his chest; she browsed at the coffee as he said:

"Well he got mixed up with the cops again."

She snorted. "Man with his brains, what's he spend his time with those imbeciles for?"

"Don't ask me, I'm just a homely internist. Which is lucky for him since he had a bullet wound in his upper arm—happily it was minor."

"Some bright day we're buying flowers for his funeral. They going to get him?" She crunched toast, stroking his back as he sat down next to her.

"I don't know the circumstances. He's on record. They might. You don't know what Martha will drive him to."

"Did he say about last night? This's great jam you got."

"Yes, isn't it?" He shrugged. "He apologized. I was sharp with him, I don't know why. He makes me anxious. There's nothing to talk of any more, except the old times." He stood up. "I don't like to think about it."

"Could be you never could talk to him, really I mean? Since Korea, anyway? You just used to hop each other up, that's all. He was being hip cat digging his paddy boy, and you were being college boy gaping at the down and out. Big deal."

"Stop it, Marian. What you say is correct, but it was a big deal. Particularly for me as you know. Well, it's all past, let's not talk about it."

She looked up at him, frowning a question; she stood. "I'm shutting up." She kissed him shortly as she passed by him, shrugged off her robe onto the chair, and went to the bureau to burrow for clothes. "Thought I heard what's-her-name's voice? I can't get her name straight." She pulled out underwear and began to put it on.

"Yes she was down there watching the proceedings."

"She dig Gaylord?"

"Who can tell what she digs? I told him not to flirt with her, so he enrages her. I should have kept my mouth shut."

"I'll take her out to find that cane of hers before he finds a maniac on his hands. Will you come, John? For a walk? Jesus I haven't got one clean blouse." She was silent for a moment. "Where'd I . . . Will you come though, baby? When do we have to be at headquarters?"

"I'm afraid dammit I have to look in at the hospital this morning. I wish I could, Marian."

"Mm."

"I thought since I have to go to the hospital anyway I'd stop and have a chat with her doctor, whatever his name is. Epstein."

"I forget."

He stepped up beside her, saying: "Forget what day it is too?"

"No baby. You see?" She brought out and held up a red summer halter, smiling.

"I got you a present."

He crouched before the open closet, his eyes flickering as they passed by her bare midriff. She put the halter down on the bureau quietly. He grunted as he pulled, one side then the other, at a heavy carton. "Here."

She bent down; they ripped at the binding. "I wondered what this was." It was revealed; he lifted it out as she beat his shoulder with her fists: a television. "I never ever would've believed it." They stood and she embraced him. "Rot your Marian's mind? Swamp her in lies?" His hands held her under her buttocks as he smiled sheepishly; she stretched up, rubbing against him, kissing his neck and face—she swung away. Over to the window: she whirled the curtains aside, flung up both windows, and turned: the summer air tumbled in.

"John, look!" He came over to her, quizzically smiling. "Look, baby"—she whipped her arm out the window toward the bright sky. "Don't you want to—can't you—"

"What, Marian?"

"John, let's go away—John—" She said quietly, gazing at him, "Let's go away—" She came up before him and put her hands by his arms, working at his shirt, saying to his chest with her head bent down, "John, can't we go away today, it's our anniversary and such a pretty day, John, can't we go to the beach to the Cape to Wellfleet, there won't be anybody hardly at all, and we can swim, and lie in the sun, I bet the room's still there that we had twelve years ago, John, I was thinking this morning, you remember that time in the waves, John, you remember, I know you must remember, baby"—His arms had gone round her as she spoke. "Can't we go, John, can't we go today—"

"You know I remember, Marian, and you know I want to go, and you know we can't go today."

"Why not, John, *why* not—"

"You knew three months ago that the march would be tomorrow, and we'll go next weekend I promise, and we'll go for two weeks in September and maybe more if I can get away—"

"I know, but I'm not asking you to give up the march, we can go back tomorrow morning, but just today, John, just today and tonight, you can tell them you're sick, you can tell them you're sick and make your calls and then we can go—"

"Marian, I can't lie to them, I can't back down now. They're relying on both of us. I ducked out of this morning's picket as it is."

"You duck out for your patients but you won't duck out for your own wedding anniversary—"

"I would have, Marian, but we agreed to pretend it was next weekend, that's not so hard—and as for the patients they're sick. Some of them are dying."

"Yeah well I'm—"

"You're not." She was turning away but he held her shoulders; he smoothed her hair back. "Don't. You're not. Next weekend is only six days from now. I didn't know the time itself meant so much to you, you should have told me, you should tell me these things—"

She went to the bureau; she took up the halter and a pair of summer shorts. She turned to him and stared. "You're so white, John."

He winced at her from the window; he looked down, scratching his hair. "What am I supposed to say to that, Marian. I don't know where that came in from. I'm the man you married."

"The man I married cared less about the Knee-grows and more about the black girl in his bed." She grunted with the halter.

"All right, but—" He walked to her again: "Marian, I wanted you this morning. And last night. I thought things would be better, really I did."

"You wanted me, did you, baby? That's the first I heard of it."

"You're having cramps, or don't you remember? That wasn't my fault or yours either—"

"So I had cramps. So what? If you really wanted me at least you could have asked me—"

"That's not fair! We've never made love when you've been in your period and you know it."

"Yeah but I used to be sure you'd want me the next night so it didn't matter. And that was your decision anyways. Do you think I cared if it hurt me? Where's your psychology, Dr. Freud? You've stood up to the man and the gangs all these years but when it

41

comes to me you walk on eggshells. Don't you know how I loved the way you took that blind girl over in the storm"—she swung her arm and slapped her open hand against the closet door and it slammed; she drawled viciously, "Baby, it satisfied."

"Marian, all right, all right I was wrong but dammit where's your own psychology, you know I can't, you know I can't . . . dammit . . . I don't. . . . "

"You can't get yourself to boss me how I want. We've been through it. So where does that leave us, John? Because maybe it just—"

He interrupted: "Marian, you're bringing up an ancient issue which has nothing to do with what's happening to us now." He turned to her: "Do you know why we felt closer last night and this morning? You know why?"

"No, baby, why was that?"

"You said it yourself; because of last night. Because we did something together for once, dealing with that girl's fugue state or whatever it was—"

"You think so?"

"I know so. I thought about it this morning and I know so."

"She's a substitute for us is that it? a prop? And the television, that a prop, John?"

He kicked it and shouted, "It's a present, don't you want it? Don't you want it?"

"John, yes. I'm sorry yes but—"

"I'm sorry too if I have to use a machine to please you with and so the thing's a prop, what's wrong with that? So the girl's a prop to make us feel like we have a family, what's wrong with that? How long do you expect us to go on without children as props, tell me that, since any couple in their right minds would have adopted by now instead of waiting around for another failure—"

"I won't, John."

"No, you won't. And you're asking me where we are."

"I'm not having a child in this house till we put it in order."

"That's its disorder, Marian."

"You think so, do you?"

"*Yes* I tell you—"

"You think that's all it is, John, shit you really think so?"

"And what's your brilliant idea, if you don't mind telling me?"

She gazed at him coolly, then turned away toward her dresser. He said angrily to her back: "That's a luxury, do you hear? It's a luxury not to talk and then to sit here and think how aggrieved you are and how I don't love you any more, how I don't want you, that I don't have any idea how lonely you've been feeling and all the rest of the maudlin garbage." He slammed his fist on the wall and leaned his forehead against it, saying into the wall, "I'm sorry dammit, I put that too harshly but—I'm not a piece of ice, Marian, I'm not a stone, I feel these things too, you've seemed so dammed far away lately and it's not your fault I'm not saying that, maybe it's all in me but—" he felt her hand on his shoulder and he turned. "Marian anything we can use to bring us closer together again we should use without thinking twice, and if there were a child here, any child, that's all I'm saying, we could make something, there'd be something, living sounds in this house—"

They were facing each other; she took his hand. Saying nothing, she led him across the room, and she sat on the edge of the bed, facing the window; still holding his hand, and looking up to him, she pointed to the floor between her feet. "John, kneel there." He knelt, frowning; he put his hand on her belly. "It's all right, then?" Shaking her head with wide-open eyes, her hands on his cheeks, she said quietly, "No, baby, it's not all right, the cramps just came again, and there's two props downstairs besides." He looked at her desperately. "Later, John, a little later if the cramps go down, or some other time—just kiss me now." She took off the halter, unbuttoned his shirt and spread it off his shoulders, and she pulled his head to her breasts, saying, "Kiss me." He embraced her, shuddering as he began, and for a long time she stroked his blond head as she looked out to the wheeling sparrows and the warm sky.

iv

"Doesn't it hit you when you come out of a store like this, Gaylord? I mean boom, roar, sometimes I think it's going to actually open and the whole city's going to crash through—I don't see what holds it up, is all."

"Don't you now? Well that's an interesting question there."

"You sound fascinated I must say."

"What's that?—Green light, Amarantha. Cross now."

"Oh all right." She trotted after him into the avenue, clutching his elbow. "Look I just meant because it keeps thudding at itself."

"That worry you does it?"

"*Yes*, sort of."

"Curb now."

"Okay—hey this John's an interesting person, I hear he runs a clinic in the poor section?"

"That's right."

"And how does he keep from thinking of himself as some kind of Albert Schweitzer?" Gaylord said nothing, and she went on: "Well what are they, intellectuals? They have all kinds of odd people coming to their house? Painters? Augurers? Eskimo nationalists?"

He turned round to her after a moment: "Hm?—Oh, yeah."

"For Christ's sake then, we won't talk."

Silence resumed. Amarantha muttered to herself in a whisper while she switched back and forth her cane, which they had found earlier on their walk, before Marian had left them. Smiling and surveying himself meanwhile, Gaylord preened with his thumb the lapel of the cordoroy jacket he had just bought. "Too bad you can't see this, baby. It shines." He flapped his new and floral tie at a traffic cop. "Complete with white chick on my arm? They ain't looking for that kind of class."

"So that's what we're taking this walk for."

"What'd you say?"

She repeated loudly: "I said so that's what this walk is for? Because you got into some kind of fight and got your arm cut this morning and the stupid police are looking for you, that it? So getting well dressed and out on a genteel excursion with a white person is just the disguise you need until the heat's off, and I'm so glad to be of use."

He laughed and bowed slightly to her, saying with irony only partly in his voice: "Damn good, and what are you on this walk for now?"

"I thought Marian would stay with us."

"No, baby. You could've begged off by not feeling well same as her and stayed behind at your place along with her."

She did not reply, and he prodded, "Right?"

She shrugged; "As if I had anything better to do."

"Cop-out answer."

She switched her cane, then stopped and caught it up next to her, saying with a smile on half her mouth, "All right, so I was curious."

He said without pleasure: "Oh yeah? On what subject?"

"Oh, *I* don't know."

Traffic receded; they walked on grass beneath chestnut blossoms that touched along the wind. She stopped as mist and clorination seared coolly in her nose. "Wait a minute; a fountain?"

46

"We're in the Boston Common now."

The chittering of children entered the spray. "Whacky statues with water zipping out of indecent places I bet?"

"Naw; turtles. *Boston* Common."

"Oh."

"You want to dig a really spaced location then?"

"Spaced? Sure—"

"We're hitting the statehouse."

"Hm?"

"You'll see," he said. "One of those thuds of yours."

"And then?"

"And then what?"

"And then where are we going?"

He laughed with annoyance. "Don't know, I hadn't thought about it. I thought you had a doctor's appointment."

"Who told you that?" she said.

"Marian did. She asked me to take you where you had to go."

"You do what she says?"

"Look, Amarantha, we'll do what you like, okay?"

"We'll do what you like, okay? Because you've got charge of me till doctor time, is that it?"

He laughed again and looked away. They walked on in silence. He said then: "We're across the Common now and we're going up to the statehouse."

"Won't that be interesting."

"Yeah well, would you like me to tell you about it, how it looks and all?"

"You can fill up what you've figured is the right amount of time in any way you please."

"How about going back then."

He stopped; she said nothing. "You aren't curious any more?"

He waited. "Gimme that." He wrenched free her hand that was nailing into his skin and forced it past his arm; she clutched air as their elbows linked. "I'm not made of leather." He stepped up a stair; she did not follow. "Move those legs, woman. They ain't blind. Nope—you aren't getting away." He reached across his chest and grabbed her wrist, prisoning her tightly as she grunted and struggled.

"I'll go where I want—damn you—damn you—"

"No, baby. Where I want. Now move." He walked up the stairs, dragging her. He turned his head away, saying quietly as she followed perforce, tugging at him, "Now what this statehouse is here Amarantha—it's kind of hard to say exactly—you walking right or you getting one across the mouth, hear me?" She cried out as he twisted her wrist. "Anyway it's this huge-takes-up-more-than-a-block Greek-temple-palace kind of thing, with a gold-colored dome on the top, looks like a dumpy kind of version of the U.S.A. Capitol in Washington, D. C.—"

"Let me go."

"I'll let your hand go, baby, if you going to walk along with me and cut the shit."

"I'll walk with you."

"Yeah?" He let her hand go; her arm slipped from his. He caught her wrist again as she began to run, and he jerked her towards him. "You're walking with me and you're listening to me, get me?" He yanked her arm down hard. "I said you get me?"

"I get you."

They climbed, his hand tight on her wrist. "Well now like I was saying, what this palace is for—" he paused. "Let me think—see, the business what goes on in here, Amarantha, isn't any different from any other cash business, but everybody stuck on it in a funny kind of way—they filling up their newspapers with it, sermonizing over it, even sending in money to it if you can believe it, and nobody could tell you why they doing it any more than they could tell you why

48

they want to build such a mausoleum of a palace in the first place—it's something they got to do, like some people got to throw salt over their shoulder when they spill it—you begin to get the picture?"

She said nothing. He twisted her wrist gently. "I said you get the picture?"

"I get it."

"Yeah well you might say the place is like a grand cathedral, the biggest thing in town you know, like the cathedrals and baptisseries they put up in Europe in the Middle Ages, you heard of them now?"

"What are you doing this for please?"

"Times you give me shit, you remind me of my bitch wife, and that's making this walk unpleasant, know that?"

"So now he has a wife."

"No, not now. So imagine for yourself some medieval town like the ones they got in France, and everybody's talking about what's going on in the cathedral, what the bishop's doing, what the monks, priests, and deacons doing—"

"You don't have to hold my wrist any more—"

He looked at her; he loosened his hold on her slack arm.

"No really, you don't—"

"Rest your hand on my arm like a chick meant to."

They climbed on. "What all these Christer cats in the cathedral are doing, see, what they deciding on, whether you can eat fish on Wednesday or Friday, or something like that, everybody thinking that's the biggest thing in town, and buzzing about which priest is on which side, and you see people altercating about it over their wine in the evenings and setting up the Wednesday party and the Friday party—while what's really happening in the place, nobody gives a god-damn. Dig it? Here we are now."

They stepped through doors to a long hall, turned

aside into a vast and silent room where their breathing seethed in a hush from the walls, and where their steps hammered out a reverberating doom. "What's this place, Gaylord?"—sssGaylord, the walls warned back to her—

"This here's the Reverence Room, and you've got to whisper when you talk in it. Ain't nothing here but stands of columns and bareboobed alabaster chicks called VICTORY and JUSTICE freaking out on the ceiling and statues of half-cats all around the walls in wigs and fobs and weird clothes frowning out at you, how you haven't done the beautiful things the plaques next to them say they done, serving the people, see—"

"Like what've they done," she whispered.

"Now baby, it ain't kind of you to ask such a question."

"Oh. Sorry."

"That's okay. Now you feel the proper kind of awe and dazzlement?"

They walked through a series of halls, each more reverberant than the former, each more aswim with footsteps, voices, jostlings, imprecations, altercations, stipulations, formulations—

"Pah," she said; "They all smoke cigars."

"They got to, see? Otherwise, you might be able to tell them apart. Besides, deciding on a price without a cigar, well, it simply ain't done."

They were on stairs again. Men in business suits brushed past them, depositing fragments of sentences in their ears. "Like we're beneath the dome, because where are the echoes?"

He looked at her. "That's right. Now above these stairs, see, there's this circular balcony and everybody's leaning on the railing all around it, watching who's coming up and going down, and hooking their thumbs in the pockets of their vests, they get the mode from the TV westerns, and all around here's where the deals are made. Now dig it—over there's the Senate Lobby, and over here's the House Lobby, now that isn't like a theater lobby, Amarantha, and we can't go in unless we're buying, but it's the place where—well now—how'll I put it—let's see, let's say the Senate's deciding on Wednesday or Friday? Now the business what deals in the marketing of fish, they send out a cat who comes roaring over here and up to the balcony and raps it to the Senators who run things, one by one see, puffing his cigar, Amarantha—Ahem. We cats at O'Leary Halibut and Cod Consolidated Enterprises Unlimited feel it's in the public interest to have the public interest consume fish, either halibut or cod we don't give a crap which, on Wednesday *and* Friday. We at O'Leary Halibut and Cod feel that the consumption of fish is good for the public interest's health, education, welfare, digestion, economy, sociology, ethnostructure, semantics, blood pressure, hemorrhoids, geriatrics, biophysics, that kind of bag, and we feel moreover that the general, nay the perfectly voracious, consumption of fish would promote civil docility, widespread cop-lovin', the anti-Communist menace, and libidinal race relations all around. Now we at O'L. H. & C. C. E. UnLtd. feel all this rather strongly."

"How do you mean libidinal race relations, silly? Because the thing is—"

"Well race relations, Amarantha, that's a kind of fudge ripple. Now the Senator, remember, he leans over the railing a bit, looks at the ceiling a while to check out the left boob of VICTORY, pinches the sweet little right buttock of some stenographer twitching past, haw-haws a haw-haw or two with some friends of his, turns to the cat from the fish dealers, blows his cigar a piece, Wyatt-Earps his thumbs, and says, Now, Mr. Shaunessy, I have to tell you, in strictest confidence of course since it was under those conditions that the situation was put before me, that Rabbinowitz Beef and Lamb Associated Meatpackers Incorporated was speaking to me this very morning through their representative Mr. Sol Klein about this very bill No. XYZ-10-9-8-7-6-47-b, and a case was made, a watertight case, I can assure you, for the banning of fish-days altogether, calling it an outmoded institution no longer in the public interest's interest, and Mr. Klein suggested that his firm of R. B. & L. A. M. Inc. feels the way they do rather strongly also."

They strolled around the railing. Knots of men with wary eyes gesticulated discreetly at one another. Feminine heels clacked. "Now what you got to catch on to, baby, is the jargon. Feeling something rather strongly, see, means five hunnert bucks hard cash on the line if the Senator votes the way you tell him to—Representatives get less of course, heads of committee more. They got it all worked out. Quite strongly is seven-fifty, very strongly a grand—goes on like that. So frightfully fine heinous old Shaunessy from O'L. H. & C. C. E. Unltd. zips to his phone in the Senate Lobby—dials—President O'Leary please—Hiya Mr. O'Leary—Senator Antonio Salubrio Salacio Riolo tells me Rabbinowitz is offering rather strongly for neither Wednesday nor Friday—What! screams O'Leary, The dirty YIDS!—Yessir Mr. O'Leary, that's the kind of stab in the back you just come to expect from these people—Ain't it? Shaunessy?—I hear you boss—Offer Riolo very strongly and a whore free of charge for the limited period of six months! No wait! Shaunessy! For a year!—Yessir! He slams down the phone, hardly waiting to relight his cigar, zips back to the railing, collars Riolo, and starts in over again. Meanwhile, see baby, the Senators got it going to delay the vote while the prices get higher. And if nobody but a lot of people without much bread are bidding for the bill, why it wallows in committee, and they call for an investigation of the cat what put up such an unprofitable bill in the first place."

Cavernously echoing voices droned to her right. "This the Chamber? Hey, is that them debating?"

"That's an interesting use of a word you got there."

"No but listen, silly, are we allowed to go in and hear them?"

"Well, it's working hours you know, and there isn't likely to be much going on—anyway it turns me off to wear these guards's eyes on my neck—" They stopped and leaned over the railing. She rested slightly against him as patches of movement and deliberation stepped out to her, distinguished from the ranks of sound, and she ordered them in patterns that pleased her as they changed. She let them recede; they dissolved into the rush that rolled beneath the dome and mingled with the dark.

He said in her ear suddenly and in another voice: "Let's get out of here."

"But why though? I was just—we were just—"

He pulled away with her hand, jerking her from the railing; not speaking, he took her hand and led her down the stairs, along the reverberant rooms, into the hall, through the doors into the morning.

"Gaylord? Did I—"

"You didn't do nothing, baby, now don't you start beating your head again. It's my doing. I shouldn't've brought you here."

"Were people hate-staring, though, is that it?"—He made no answer, and she tugged his arm. "Were they, though?"

"Yeah, you're always going to get that, but—"

They walked down the stairway in silence. He said

at last: "I'm sorry, Amarantha, that I didn't take you round more, it might've been interesting for you—but"—he shrugged. "The whole business is shit." He sat down on a stair.

She crouched beside him, laying her arm along his back and her hand on his shoulder. "There's no point in thinking about these things, Gaylord." Grunting and briefly smiling, he reached across his chest to slap her hand on him gently; he let his arm fall. She said, "No look, really, because what if I had taken you around the stockyards back home and woooah, woooah, like whole acres of it, shut up! Shut up! Well they're never going to stop, I've tried it I can tell you and you just go crazy—"

They were silent; she rested her head on his arm. "Gaylord? I'm hungry?"

●●● "How does it feel today, Mrs. Wilson. A little better?"

Dark eyes opened in an obese face, smiling at John as they found him. "Yes"—Her head hinted at shaking. "But I don't feel it coming back, Doctor John, not like last time—"

He held her wrist. "Rest," he said. "All you need is rest and you'll be up again. You in much pain?"

"Not so bad—Preacher Henry said he'd come by this morning—You seen him yet?"

"If he said he'll come by, he'll come by. He'll be coming round to hurry you out of here."

"He's coming around to help me get ready"—her head turned aside, her eyes closed. "Bless you, brother."

He turned and walked between beds, muttering to a nurse, "Continue medication; rest. And for God's sake keep the lid on her preacher. No excitement." As he turned away, the nurse nodded with a deep frown, beneath which bright righteousness glowed. He halted. "Let them talk quietly as long as they wish, do you hear?"

He went out, head bent, pocketed hands, his white coat flaring behind. Black girls, Jamaicans, Barbadans fair, where are your numbers? Replace these papist bitches.

To help me get ready. That great Day. Sinnah! White man. Raining down fire. She'll be up, though, with that cardiogram. For what?

Watch out!

He evaded a bearing-down gingerale-tiered cart and a swift nurse pencilling check marks on her schedule. Why must they rustle so? Eleven o'clock the girl's psychiatrist said. I'm done now.

I will not feel guilty. I will not. I am not chairman now and even if I were I couldn't urge against a march date because it might fall on my wedding anniversary and if it weren't for that girl breaking in on us this morning   Keeping her around was Marian's idea not mine

It doesn't help, forget it   Forget it

Are you ready my brother?

A flashing box dinged above his head: "Dr. Morrison in B117, Dr. Morrison please?"

What's this about? He stopped; he pulled open a sliding door to a stairwell and walked down. Look we got somewhere didn't we? She didn't answer about adopting but at least she saw me attempt to reach her And she encouraged me   I might well have been able to

Doesn't that item from the back wards have the sense not to walk into other people's bedrooms? Hey *I'm* sorry, I thought this was the guestroom   Like

55

hell you did you little schiz   She stands there chatting   Will we have to tear ourselves apart all over again before we touch each other? She wore that halter for me, flesh our flesh   That time in the waves You remember   You do, John   I do   One remembers forgetting oneself more clearly than anything   She's perfectly right, but we need the movement as well   What other social place do we have? I know her feelings though   Politics raises to importance such trivia   We will sit around today neutralizing crises concocted to harrass us   The cops will try to change the route   The firemen will kick about the wiring on the stand and will we have enough armbands enough bullhorns enough placards enough traveling toilets

He smiled. *Yes, Lord.*

I did try, though

I did try to feel the love that used to live in her body

He stood aside for a patient being wheeled while he turned an unopened letter in his hand. What do you suppose Mother wants this time. Can't her lawyer write? PLEASE she writes on the envelope   No Mother I won't please   I'm not strong enough Thanks to you   Her Christian Science stationery   What is she trying to impress on me by that?

He stepped into the voices of a ward. "Dr. Morrison!"

Now what?

A nurse rushed toward him.

"Hello, Mary."

"Doctor, there's a teen-age boy come in this morning, just about five-thirty, with a pain in the right lower abdomen, and the student who was on worked him up, but he hasn't let anybody touch him since that time—"

"Yes? Why not?"

"Well he's—he's one of these color-struck kids, Dr. Morrison, and he said he—"

The woman paused. John said, "They aren't letting Brother into anything, eh? How about Dr. Miller?"

"They say it's his vacation, doctor, he's in Maine—"

"That intern then, what's his name?"

"He's off today."

"Wouldn't you know it." They walked beside bodies. "What's the boy's name?"

"Harris, Allan Harris, his father brought him in and—we've let him lie up to now but I thought you might know him, that's all, so I had you paged—"

"Let me see, may I?" She handed him a yellow page, biting her lip and watching as he read. "Yes, I think I've met the father. Let me talk to him."

"He's in two-twelve, doctor"—she retreated and he stepped between beds and stood above a boy's squinting stare. "I'm a friend of your father's, Allan. They've been trying to reach Dr. Miller, who is a black man. He's in Maine. They've sent for me."

The boy's eye slid up and down John's body; he turned his head away. John said, "I know myself of half a dozen Boston brothers who are medical students or premeds right now. Next time you come in they'll be here to treat you." He waited; he went on, "Do you know what you've got, probably?"

The boy's voice broke as he shouted, "I don't give a *shit* what I got—"

"You've probably got acute appendicitis, which requires a routine operation, but if you don't let us do it it's going to be very bad for you. You understand me?" The boy's legs twitched and he clutched the pillow and John said, "I can't, Allan."

"Your fucking hands *off* of me"—their hands flailed as John sought to pin the boy's wrists. A coughing man next to them yelled in hoarse whisper, "Boy you do like he says—" The boy kicked and writhed. "I'll kill you! I'll kill you!"

The ward was in shouts. John leapt back as the boy's body lurched and moaned. "Quiet all of you! Quiet!" He said against the murmurs, "All right, Allan. We'll leave you alone." He stepped into the aisle and walked down it, gesturing with his eyes to the nurse for her to follow him out of the ward.

"Has he been N. P. O.?"

"He won't eat, doctor."

"We'd best calm him down some. Give him two hundred milligrams of seconal I.M. stat. and when he's quiet, two hundred-fifty milligrams of penicillin. We'll have to operate this afternoon if I can persuade them to fit him in"—he smiled, his hand on her shoulder. "Thanks, and don't fight him. Page me if he won't cooperate. We'll have to call the father in any case. I'll be on the psychiatric pavillion with Dr. Epstein."

"Yes—"

"All right, Mary." He turned away and his smile died; "The other way"—he turned round again and stood before an elevator that pealed; it yawned, expelling a woman in purple who bumped him and snapped: "Will you watch where you're going?"

He grunted and stepped in, "Eleven please"; he fingered the letter that was becoming moist in his back pocket. What am I supposed to do with a boy like that   There's nothing   There's no way of telling him I'm not what he thinks   Beyond my whiteness is the realm of fine distinctions and you don't expect subtle shadings from a man in a fury

Nothing and nothing happens to support my contentions and everything happens to support his, what should I say to him, things will get better? He's tired of hearing it and I'm tired of saying it. I'm the liar he expects unless I tell him if he fights he'll get more fascism and if he doesn't fight he'll get more fascism, my brother-in-law Mandus and his guerilla war and glorious black nationalist apocalypse, what am I to argue, Gee I wish you wouldn't?

Organize   Educate to organize   Organize to educate   Yes excellent but years you need and some evidence for hope   A most Christian people but you can't love down a tank   I don't imagine it's possible to be Christian when you've power anyway   If only power to scare   That's why Our Lord did himself in? Wasn't that a fabulous performance?

The letter was in his hand. I suppose she could be dying. She's well on toward seventy and now that he's dead himself—I ought to open it   Make a last attempt at reknitting the family etc   Yes and unravelling things with your wife   Things are bad enough with Marian without bringing Mother into it

I suppose   Clandestinely   It's heartless really

My brother-in-law. What kind of law is that? Do you suppose we'll have to emigrate if things go on the way they're going   Jamaica maybe   God knows where Marian would have to lengthen her skirts.

The elevator sighed and his stomach queased. Entering white neighborhood. "Out please." He stood before a receptionist in a booth. A television barked from out a corridor. "Dr. Epstein? He said he'd see me at eleven"

The girl looked at the clock, at a book, suspiciously at John. "Dr. Morrison?"

"Yes." He watched her cluck, then dial with a pencil. You must realize sir that our patients are deeply disturbed here and we cannot allow anyone who isn't authorized to

She pointed. "Turn to your left, fourth door on your right."

59

He walked past blinking blue bulbs, nurses with knees, relatives bearing crosses, and the deeply disturbed. John dear   Yes Mother but I do not like to be berated and then told I'm forgiven. For what? I've got enough anxiety and regresion without hearing your appeals   You can pray to Mother Eddy for your comfort

William! John's brought his darky girl!

We're married, Mother.

What!

We're married.

Oh my God, listen to that. I forgot how a television *sounds*. He laughed. Armpit lullabyes tressing our house now. Mah feller Amurikins, Ah want you to join with me in creating The Anti-Perspirant Socahity.

Join us!—Yell the peace kids.

Are you clean? Are *you* without blemish?

Join us! Join us!

Maybe I'll write her

He stopped; he crumpled the letter in his fist and banged it through an iron flap that said PLEASE. That does not mean I have to read. Goodbye, Mother. He knocked on a door beside a common room that shuffled and coughed with docile madmen attacking magazines and being attacked by a woman on a screen in a bubble bath.

Don't you wish *everybody* did?

●●●   No wonder she maneuvered staying over at our place. What kind of filthy place they think they running here? She's got a broom there but what she going to do? Smell her way clean?

Marian sloshed a mop along the floor of Amarantha's room. Must be a heartwarming kind of thing for her to feel these bugs suddenly crawling over her toes while she's standing around humming to herself practicing her finger reading, doing whatever she does all day, Lord knows how she kills the time. A roach scudded before her mop and changed its shape beneath her reaching toe. Mm. She scraped the toe against the edge of a dustpan. I could put down them traps we bought of course—she left them on the table. Place like this though   You got to blow the whole block to kingdom come and further, the earth don't belong to man *no*how, it's for the bugs and the rats You better believe it   Ever seen them pouring in a river from a tenement on fire? They're coming toward your house   Enough to make you want to join your ancestors.

She churned the mop in the pail and leaned on it, looking out. First real summer day of the year and what am I doing? Cleaning house.

I could've gone on downtown with them I suppose

And this afternoon, for excitement, it's manning the phone. We need a well-modulated black female voice on account of how it hints at the liberal atmosphere.

I should've grit my teeth and gone with them That wasn't too fair to Gaylord   Poor man   She runs upstairs here ahead of us   He's looking at that sign down there about out-patient residence this-and-that pavillion   Well what kind of chicken did you pick up off the street this time, Mother Hen?

Under that dresser and I'm finished

I'm not the mother hen he's talking about though Thats's the funny thing   It's John

What's this she got under here   An old wig?

I don't know what I'm supposed to think about what he said this morning   Can't he understand I don't want no third party if it's going to cut between us   Props   Whatever you want to call them

61

Maybe I'm just being jealous   But as far as I can
see he doesn't dare to face me direct any more
That's why he wants to adopt a child now after all
this time   And that's why he doesn't want to go
down to the Cape   He doesn't want to be alone and
face to face with me—Feeling closer last night with the
girl there   Can you believe it? That's what he said
She makes us closer by busting in on us and ruining
the first chance we get to make love in months?

Don't make no difference anyways   He wasn't with
me   Don't he expect I'm going to know he wasn't
there   He was churning around in some crazy corner
of his head   Probably filing down his speech for
tomorrow   Running over some sweet piece of tail he
examined t'other day   Be quiet   I was feeling all
right   Be quiet

She dumped the pail of brown water down the sink.
Yeah   Unless you burning your fire in some other
bed   Some nurse on your lunch hours   Then John
your fire gone out.

I don't know, maybe I ought to, maybe I just ought

"Excuse me. I didn't know you were coming on
Saturdays now."

Marian whirled toward the voice; a carefully gray-
haired woman stood inside the door. Marian said:
"Yes?"

The woman said, studying Marian's face pleasantly,
"You must be new then. I'm the housekeeper; Mrs.
Linton. How do you do."

Marian grunted, nodding.

"And you are—?"

"Mrs. Marian Morrison." She leaned against the sink,
her hands on its edge behind her; she waited.

"Well then, Marian, it's all right for today, but I'll
have to tell the service that—"

Marian interrupted: "Mrs. Morrison is my name,

62

thank you, and you're mistaken if you think I'm your cleaning woman, and while you're about it you might tell your service they have something to learn about their business."

The woman straightened her dress at the shoulders. "Then you'll excuse my mistake, and—"

"I won't excuse mistakes without being asked, that all right with you?"

"What are you doing here, Madam?"

"I'm a friend of the girl who lives here, obviously, and maybe I'm the one to ask you what you're doing here?" She crossed her bare legs and tapped the sink with her fingers, not smiling.

"Madam, this is not an apartment house. It is a hospital. We were not pleased when Miss Jones called last evening to tell us she would not return for the night. She hung up before we could object. She is not at liberty to pick up just anyone off the street, is that clear to you?"

Marian pushed away from the sink, took a paper bag of roach traps they had bought and shook it at the woman: "Distribute these under the sink and in the corners. Refund the girl for them. Have her laundry done immediately. Paint the fire escape." The woman straightened her dress again. Marian collapsed the empty bag into a ball and presented it to the woman's hands as she walked by her. "Wastebasket's next to the dresser." She stepped down the stairs.

She halted. "Wait, my pocketbook"—She turned round and looked up the stairwell. "Father in Heaven do I have to go back there?"

"Oh, thank God." The pocketbook was on her arm. She breathed heavily and walked on downward. "You tell me what's she thinking I'm the cleaning woman for when I haven't even got the clothes on for it? I shouldn't even be on the streets with these shorts

Off the street she says   The girl is not at liberty to pick up just anyone off the street   That bag want to choose the people going to rescue her charge from certain going out of her mind? Just anyone? What in Jesus name she letting the kid out for in that kind of storm anyways I want to know?

She said aloud: "Forget it."

She looked down a hallway lined with shut doors. Up against that iceberg   No wonder Amarantha wanted to stay over at our place   That must be the one she was telling us about   What's she doing in charge of sick people?

Why though   I'm never going to understand why You never going to be able to explain it to me   It's just so out of the blue

Forget it, forget it, I was feeling all right

Amarantha and me we're going to hatch some way to make life harder for that woman   Make some more of those gray hairs real   Why we'd be saving her beauty-parlor bills. She wrenched the street door open, mincing and twittering: "Madam, this is not an apartment house. It is a hospital."

Where'll I go now

Too bad John wasn't here if she wanted to see what a real *foul* temper's like   His fire ain't gone out in that department   I'll give him that

Where'll I—

She stood at the curb, fumbling in her pocketbook for change. I'm going to buy cigarettes   I don't care what he says if he's going to spend every bit of our own day making work for himself down the hospital, *he* don't need to call on that headshrink

A tall teamster, with cartons on his bare shoulders, paused in his work a few feet from her. His black eyes traveled over her.

Sometimes I think I ought to phone up these places

he says he's going to and see what kind of lies he's been telling me   He's probably glad the girl broke in on us   Save his stuff for the real business he got planned for this afternoon—Her hand shook and a half-dollar flew from it, rung on the sidewalk, rolled toward the teamster. Brother says I'm crazy   How's *he* know what John is when I don't even know my own self—The coin rattled gently as it settled by the teamster's foot. He stepped back, saying, "Sorry baby, I'd help you but I got a handful"—She stooped. There was yellow mud on his shoes. Of course I have to be wearing the shorts and the halter   Might as well be wearing nothing   He hasn't got any right leaving me alone like this—With the coin in her hand she stood slowly, and met clear eyes that grinned as they leapt down her breast. He said, "There's a whole lot of sunshine left when I turn in this rig at four—" She turned round and walked; he called after her and she ran. I got nothing to do with you   Nothing to do with you

I didn't John   I ain't had a smoke in ever so long
You could've turned aside   You could've held your halter in   No I couldn't   It's his fault   I wore it for him   A whole lot he cared   I might as well have worn a shroud   So what   You wanted that man to say something to you   You begged for it   I didn't   She that looketh on a man   He was talking about you   No he wasn't I wasn't   No I wasn't

He deserves anything he gets if he doesn't stay with me today   He belongs with me   Today at least   Today at least

She looked round to see if she were followed; she slowed, turned in to the side street that led to her door. We're going to Cape Cod. We're going to the Cape or I'm going somewhere my own self

Sure Sure   We could get her to come with us and

Gaylord too maybe   And two take the motorcycle
so we can follow the back trails like we done that one
time   He isn't going to think of it so much as
face-to-face if it's a party   Maybe he'll go then and
of course once he's there I

The weather says another storm tonight, a bigger
one than yesterday, storm like that time ago

I'm going to do it   I don't know how yet but I'm
going to get him to go

Sun John sun and the sea dripping off you and

What'll I fix for lunch?

And him white against the moon

V

If you ain't serving one chick's
demons, you're asking blessing from the saints of some
other chick, and that's a natural law, man, *viz*: what
for is Gaylord motorcycling Route 3 southbound in
brutal traffic with a prickly white addleheaded blind
chick behind me clinging to my belt like it a rein?
Instead of watching time creep in a normal fashion?
Because Mrs. Marian's needs got dribbled on my
schedule. The motorcycle droned, trapped in a herd of
cars that milled lowing and stinking out of Boston. Why
we couldn't all four have gone down in their Ford is
fodder for the headshrink   Please Gaylord   Turning
her eyes on me   Then looking at the floor   It'd mean
an awful lot to John and me   Women got no shame in
the framing of their requests   I got an A in pussiology
and what good did it do me?

He grinned, braked, quacked his horn, tilted and
swerved, shot across lanes. Weaving, he impaired by a
second the progress of a mauve Cadillac, which roared
to swing out beside him. Aw-oh, I believe some of the
local orangutans are planning to exercise their freedom
of grunt. Yessir. Framed in Cadillac windows, a brace
of mouths hurtled out jeers that broke in fragments
on the slamming wind. Hey, Amarantha? Reach round
and slip me a feel, that'll give them apoplexy. The
Cadillac listed into his lane, crowding him toward the
central barrier. He slowed, and edging him further, the
car slowed also. This may prove to be an interesting

excursion. Horns chorused from braking cars behind them, and the Cadillac shrieked ahead, rocking and weaving. Sweet mother of Jesus.

Vietnam, hot damn.

The highway rose on stilts; beneath his eyes sun and soot met in a sulfurious gauze that dressed the city as a wound. Dig it man   You breathing that   I'm moving to Botswana.   Puffing tubes loomed and retreated as he throttled by. Might as well   What the hell for am I saving up for a new apartment here Now Lasciv's been burnt out I got no connection with this town anyhow   John or anyone   Pisses me off he wouldn't tell me what's going on with him and Marian   He never kept quiet about what he thought of Martha   What's he figure he's doing   You ask a cat to talk and he comes on like you asking for his wife   Or his wallet more like   I never seen him so tight   What's he think, I'm going to leak what he tells me to the *Globe*? Shit he's changed   Marian says he nearly dropped out of that committee of his too and Mandus completely fucked up with that terror squad of his

Panthers is one thing   But a group like Mandus got What's it for   I can't see the point in politics Seems the most unnecessarily complicated way of making money   People fall away every time you turn around   I haven't hardly talked to Mandus since we went down home together   What's it   Three years anyway—We're moving out. The road was clearing; untidy redundant suburbs tagged along beside him. He clenched the throttle and leaned into the passing lane. Remember that disrepair of a Studebaker Mandus and I stomped down home in, the hood black with insects and the floor full of underbrush of shredded maps and old food, those barren Florida roads, absolutely flat through the green swamp, ninety miles an hour the car's going to fly apart from around you, there, a snapping turtle standing on its toes in your path like a royal stool, a full tractor rig sunk to its eyebrows in the marsh, stop, psssh, that silence popping with birds, roaring on again in your capsule of nowhere — what kind of power do you suppose this motorcycle has?

He throttled once again. The finned backside of a fifties limousine leapt toward him. We're stepping from the herd; we're going to whale it; we're going to take a stomp. Amarantha shifted behind him and he glanced down at her forearm, which was appearing round his waist. Her skin jiggled with the engine. He chuckled. It's been a long time—He bawled: "Lean with me, Amarantha!"—He slalomed round the fifties fins. You out of grass? take speed. I ain't been on one of these things in ten years. He roared out, freeing his good arm for a moment and shaking it out as if to whip the machine on. I do believe some of these folk are rolling backwards instead of ahead—Going to shave that tail of yours, Bonneville. With enough of this shudder, before you know it you can't tell where your hands end and where this brute begins—you gaining a four cylinder organ between your knees— The white line snaked beneath the black wheel. He crouched, droned steeper, wove, leaned back straight-armed, shot down the lanes.

Here I am a prop in someone else's phantasies   He think's he's a fighter pilot   I'm tired of having to hold onto him like this anyway   A little comrade-liness all right   But this machine was built for people who've known each other for a bit more than four hours and it certainly wasn't built for paranoids He's not one so we'll never understand each other, Jesus! Hold on   Does he have to pass everybody? If he thinks he's softening me up for the kill he can go ahead and try   But a little more subtlely please

You've got to adjust the formula for my type of personality, like I'm not so stupid as to think it's you that's powerful and not just your crumby motorcycle—"Slow down, will you please?

"What's that you're saying, Amarantha?"

"I said what's the big rush!"

"Baby, when we get clear of this traffic, you'll think we've been walking." And if you don't like it little whitey-ass, you can step off any time.

"Damn you!"

He leaned into the next lane again, skirting a whirr of red steel. "What's that?"

"I said you know what I said!"

He glanced down as her hand strained white into a fist at his belt. Well—he slowed. "That okay then baby?"

"Oh, you're *very* nice."

"Aren't I now?"

He stayed in his lane, following.

You got to be careful with her I suppose, you don't know what she—a fine whale— By Christ I'm hopped up again. I remember John taking me through that mental illness hospital out in Waltham, this chick was in one of those places

He putted behind a spattered trailer, whose mudguards flapped at him. What am I supposed to do, crawl the whole way to Wellfleet?

I never been in such a blank place as those wards, though, nothing on the walls   No place to go   Lot of shuffling and mumbling   Everybody dressed like wino bums   And them faces-utterly freaked-out souls with their hands behind their necks leaning down with their heads between their legs and the cat in whites who took us around he's pointing: Hank Borglum there's been on the ward forty-nine years. He's forgotten how to speak. One cat with weird bald patches sitting on the radiator biting his lip in a screwy grin while he whacks off in his pants. And cats striding round with these prophet eyes   Yelling out destinies and looming up over me one was   Did he stink? and bearing down on me like some obiah fixing spells, and hissing: You shall be judged. Whips over a nurse: Now Willie. Come along. This chick was shacked up with those ghouls   She was one of them Dig it

Route 24   Yeah

Well she ain't one of them now, so—

He soared down an exit ramp and swerved onto an empty road. Isn't no weaving needed here. She'll be okay. Make that needle on the dial wiggle like the haunches on a cat set to spring. The motorcycle flew between high banks along whose crests wire fences rippled. Ahead in the distance, silos and fields slept against the summer sky. Rare cars that he swooped on seemed to stop, while he passed, as if in courtesy, and in his spot of rear-view mirror he watched them withdraw to a point in quick deference and disappear. Your job, Amarantha, is to keep an eye out for speed traps.

Hold on   I thought I told him? He hates women He doesn't care if I exist   He's decided what's one white girl more or less I know it   I know it Haven't we got to whatever stupid place we're going to yet? He must be going ninety   That's how fast I'm going to be flying when I hit the pavement if I remember my physics   Christ now look   My dress is really up   I'm not having everybody look up my legs   Does he expect me to let go and fix it?

All right handsome. "Gaylord!"

"What's that, Amarantha?" If she couldn't talk either, we'd be doing fine.

"Stop this stupid machine!"

"What for, baby?"

"Just stop it!"

"Can you wait for a gas station?"

"No!" She took a fold of skin at his belly and twisted it. "Stop or I'll tear it off!" She giggled. "No, I mean it!" She wrenched the skin; the wind ripped a pained shout of laughter from his mouth. "Ouch! Bitch!"

"Stop and I'll let go!"

"Let go and I'll stop!"

"No!" She yanked.

"Let go!" He throttled.

They struggled.

You can't put him in this position, stupid, it ruins his line. He'll never stop. All right then: "If you promise to stop, I'll let go—"

She wrenched, gently. He throttled, slightly. "Please stop, Gaylord."

He slowed.

He'd better not look around dammit   I feel absolutely naked   I'll have to sit on my dress tighter from now on

Well here we go for another set of games— He looked round as they glided on the shoulder. Ah, so that's the reason—not bad, not bad at all—

Damn him.

The motorcycle stopped, jerking her against him; she leapt off and swatted her dress down. Still vibrating with the shudder of the engine, she stood on the staid ground, and the darkness whirled above its solidity. Damn him damn him damn him. The drone stuttered, died, called in the hum of the highway and rural silence. His step exploded on the gravel beside her. "So? Enjoying yourself?"

"You are, anyway."

"Well baby I admit it's kind of selfish of me not to let you drive."

"Big laugh."

"But—"

"Ha ha. I don't mind it so much really, Gaylord, but you're going too fast, that's all. I *know* I'm going to fall off before we get there."

"Naw, you won't."

"Want to bet?"

"You really don't like it?"

"Well—I don't want to ruin it for you but really can't we go a little slower? I mean the Cape doesn't go up in a tree for the night or something, does it?"

"Now baby if we chugged along at forty miles an hour like a pair of old bats, it just wouldn't be a stomp."

"Oh yes, because what's a stomp, please?"

"If you didn't beat your head about falling off all the time, you might find out, dig?"

"*You've* got the handlebars and *you* know when you're going to swerve, but I don't have any warning, dig dig dig?"

"Yeah. Now look, Amarantha, the real thing is that you aren't sitting right. Sitting sidesaddle is fine, see, and ladylike and all for a little city spin, but for a stomp, you've got to sit frontways."

"Frontways. What's frontways?"

"Sure. Frontways. Put your legs on either side of mine. That's the way all the chicks do it, believe me."

"So what do they do with their dresses in their faces?"

"Naw. I sit on it, see?"

"Motorcycles weren't built for nuns I can see that."

"So? You a nun?"

"No, but I have weak defenses."

"You got nothing to worry about."

"I don't? So where do I hold on?"

"Any place your hands feel comfortable, baby—"

"Mm." She crooked out her arm. "Lead the blind."

"Yaz'm." He took a pinch of skin above her elbow. "Forgot my pliers."

"Ha ha."

They walked thus to the cycle.

"So?"

"So what," she said.

"So what've you decided?"

"Listen to him? Just tell me who sits first."

"The lady. You."

Her hand set the seat firmly in space; she sat, legs on either side; she spread her dress out before her.

"Feet back on the rests," he said, "Here." He bent and took her ankle, placing it. "Got the other one?"

"Yes, thanks a bunch."

"It'll be different; you'll see. Just move with it. You ready?"

"I can't wait."

He jerked the motorcycle forward off its stand, straddled it, kicked the roar open while her hands laced over his ribs; the machine swung into the road, flinging her back, flinging her forward again as the gears changed. They yelled:

"I knew you were a bastard the moment I met you!"

"Thing is I'm legitimate. I believe that's my problem."

"Brothers? Sisters?"

"Guess?"

"Four sisters, all older!"

"More insults, more insults—"

"What then?"

"Five."

I'm not so stupid, you see? I'm not so stupid

That's not the funny thing about him though

Six mothers, he's spoiled, that's what. He gets every little thing he wants, or forget it. Meanwhile I'm going to get sucked off the back of this thing and get deposited in an automatic toll basket

It's something inside his talk though   I mean he'll say things in front of you like he didn't care where you've been   I ought to get off this machine right now   Dr. Schleppstein's going to grind me up for skipping out this morning   I can feel his chest muscles under my hands, did you notice? Because he's got his way of talking and you aren't going to control it by any kind of acting up   I bet he's going ninety, a hundred, a hundred and ten   I bet it's at least seventy though   And the way he made me go with him on the statehouse stairs   I mean he saw right through   Most people would have just washed their hands of me right there   He's right   You don't fall off   Listen, if he tenses in his right leg and right behind, then he's going left   That's easy enough   You never know what he'll say   That's the thing   I really could use a little less leg spread thank you   Shouldn't we go back   When he passes though I love the way it swings   Do you think he has plans   Mm   He said anyplace your hands feel comfortable   He could have said put them on the strap behind you which is what it's for you know   Well you can hold on to his shoulders just as well as anywhere else since did you notice how this muscle kind of lines down from his neck because sometimes I think we aren't on the ground at all A hundred and ten, a hundred and twelve, a hundred and twenty-five I always did want to see what the upper part of the darkness was like   If you just hold on   If you just hold on   Who are you   Who are you   Who are you

The wind

You don't get this kind of wind on the floor you know   It takes you up and slams you apart and rapes

right up your clothes   Makes you feel like you don't
have any on at all   And you can't hear anything
with this drone   What I mean to say about male legs
is   Get off this machine   Tight and hard   Tight
and hard   I was right   I always thought the
darkness was a sphere   A person's stuck in the center
of it most of the times and it's all cluttered up with
people to stop you and things to bump into   Eyes
get out   So the thing you have to do is get out of
the center and fly around the sphere where there
aren't any things   We're flying right under the top of
the dome   In and around the vaults   There's
nothing to bump into   Eyes get out   Eyes get out
Tight and hard   A hundred and ten   A hundred
and fifty   That Parsons girl   *You* know the one,
her father owns some elevators? Well they caught her
with a nigraboy this afternoon   Her own brother
found them   Can you imagine the shock to the boy?
No I can't   Shit on you   It served him right for
snooping and I bet he got his rocks off watching them
first   Blah   Well they're going to send the girl away,
oh yes, her father won't hear of anything else   Just
thrown her life away for nothing   Think of it   For
nothing hell   At least she got some screwing in
That's better than you did   Think of it   As for the
nigraboy   The men have already taken care of him
My father always said that's what comes from making
concessions to the   Shit on you   You're not taking
me over   You're not me   You've always been the
craziest one of us   If I can get something out of this
I'm not going to let you ruin it   You've already
ruined the sphere

"Gaylord! Faster!"

"What's that, baby?"

"Go faster! Go faster!"

The roar rose, slamming her backwards, wrenching

her arms, forcing her to jam her thumbs inside his belt
at his stomach and to clench his thighs with her knees.
A hundred and ten, a hundred and fifty, a hundred
and seventy-five— The wind raped, smacked her with
flat-handed air, mapped her with blatant fingers. She
grinned. Because I've got the body and see what you
can do about it

"We're almost on the Cape, Amarantha—"

The machine rattled at her thoughts and shook her
bones. Up the steep bridge over the Canal, stretching
her, rapping her head back; down the hill to Cape
Cod, hurtling her forward onto his back, her head on
his neck, her arms belted round him in embrace.
Anything! Anything! She hid in him, she collapsed
into herself; they rammed through the blackness of
the dark. There isn't anything here   There's nothing
to bump into   Nothing to bump into and you'd float
if you'd fall and you'd dissolve into the dark, and
float all down like a bushel of leaves, like someone
took you and slammed you apart and there was
nothing to stop you any more

God damn chick's getting me hotter than a cooking
spit with them hands of hers

Fine road   FINE road   Trouble is though I don't
seem to get one spot warmer with all this getting
hotter, like I felt on the stairs on the Common there
Like I want to smash her one or buck her off the
machine   Jesus   You better turn her off someways
You know she's expecting a gentlemanly hog all at
attention for gallant penal servitude   Take a dip in
the gutter and bounce on home having titillated her
democracies.

A sheet of sun dazzled on distant water beyond
pine-green hills. Curving, leaping over a rise, he swung
the sun over his shoulder, and the light skittered off
from a blue bay. Surf lined its shallows in ranks of

white hems. That's the lady I'm going to bury in today— Below him, a thin road writhed down valleys to her shore. His eyes chased the road back from the sea till the road dove, on the hill just approaching him, into a copse of scrub pine, whose russet trunks contorted as if in prayer. He slowed. Go down, bathe my various turpitudes off of me—send them over to Senegal on the next out-current and drift up man onto that strange shore— At the road junction he squinted at a sign listing Yankee destinations: Falmouth, Mashpee, Cotuit. Better keep going. If we stop off alone now it's going to give the chick ideas   Not to speak of myself   I got principles   But I ain't a pillar of restraint.

He droned on, chuckling. Yeah I never did mind stepping on the white chicks just a little

I suppose if it was clear we were doing it just to ease our minds a bit and let our private poisons

I ain't had a white chick in six seven years and more Since that journalist in Queens. What'd she say? Looking at her browridge and yelping as she comes, Gaylord! I just love your blackness! Something like that   Jesus Christ   These broads   Perfectly disgusting   She moved like a paraplegic   I yanked it out then and there and split. That was the last of them.

He glided round a rotary, and throttled on to rattle over tracks; he putted behind a length of cars. Trouble is though   You hustle this one on her ass   She going to freak out sure as shit   While you slamming it in she'll be whimpering and writhing around in hellvisions— He glanced down where her arms gripped him, one hand clutching at his breast and the other at his belt, fingers dangling toward his groin. Beside his denim pants her bare thighs caught the sun. He laughed uncomfortably. I don't suppose she knows what she's doing but—.

78

Oh yeah bullshit   She figures all she got to do is call attention to herself and a room full of black men gon queue up for her pootytoot. I'm not interested, understand? Get the hell off my back there! He shook his shoulders; she tightened her hold. I said unpeel yourself the fuck off me bitch

I'm half ready to reach around and tear her off the seat   Keep quiet will you   You're letting her hang you up with no reason   She's nothing but a chick that's horny   She hasn't given one sign of thinking color   Christ the poison anyhow   Will you pour it out on the frightfully fine heinous old Route 6 here You could've passed these dink-shits long ago

Topping a rise, he crouched and swung left, pitched up the drone, leapt past the stilled trucks and the dead-standing cars. What the hell   If she's asking for it   No strings attached   Why not, so long as she don't start talking politics— He bulleted down the cleared lane. She took that statehouse story fine   If your wife refuses to listen to stories you might as well try strangers— That's it! You make the yellow dashes blur— The wayside world whirred into a shimmering green. White sand raced on the shoulders. Hills rose and dipped like gulls. Against the slap of the wind he bored through the miles feeling nothing, hearing nothing but the vibrations of the machine that was himself; into a high with a fist, owning nothing and everything, he shivered down the godliness of the open road.

● ● ●   "Amarantha? You still there now?" He shook the girl on his shoulders. What's she sleeping? "Hey there, you still alive?"

"Gaylord?"

"We're here, little thing—"

The drone roared down, shut its wings; the wind drooped, the shudder died; she landed on a humming silence.

"So," he said.

"We're here? Where?"

"Wellfleet, Massachusetts. The"—he read a buzzing sign—" 'Quiet Nook Motel. Under New Management. Recommended. Vacancy.' It's where the Morrisons go."

They swung their legs off. "So where's the ocean?"

"Couple miles over the dunes. Come on; we've got to walk. I don't like this thing on the gravel."

They crunched up a rise. She said: "Doesn't it feel funny now though? Everything sort of buzzes."

He smiled down at her quizzically; looked ahead again. "You liked it then huh?"

"Well didn't you know?"

They were silent, walking. He said then: "Here we are now. Stairs." He swung open a door that dangled a chain of bells; they stepped through. "Hello? Dingaling?" A small man in a brown suit rustled behind his counter; Gaylord said: "Ah. Well we got another couple coming so we need"—he hesitated—

The man filled his silence. "I'm sorry, sir, but we're all booked up for tonight."

"What's that?"

He blinked behind his eyeglasses. "We have no vacancy."

"Say that again? That isn't what your sign says out there."

Amarantha said: "Didn't Marian call ahead?"

"Yeah I guess she did. Got a reservation from Morrison there?"

The man lowered his eyes and turned a page, pausing in the stillness. "I'm afraid we have no record of it here, sir."

"Yeah? Let me see that." He walked to the counter, his arm forward.

The man shut the book and slid it beneath. "Our records are confidential, sir. You understand." He smiled. "I'm sorry." He folded his hands.

Gaylord stared at them, his mouth working; the arm that was forward went up, flat-handed. With fright in his eyes, the man said:

"I'll call the police—"

"Yeah? You just go ahead and do that"—his hand hovered, shaking; it fell, it took her elbow, fingers nailing in. "Come on, Amarantha." They walked out and down the stairs in silence.

"Gaylord, maybe we should call the police up ourselves, I mean isn't there a law about—"

He yanked her arm quiet, muttering, "Shut up."

The door behind them jingled and closed.

"Gaylord, do you think if I went in alone? To another place I mean? And anyway I don't think every place around here could be like that, since the sign said that man was new here—"

She stopped talking; he said nothing. Suddenly he shook her off and walked down the rise; ran.

"Hey Gaylord?" She heard him jolt the motorcycle off its stand. "Hey what's the big idea?" She ran down, swinging her cane and stumbling.

"I'm going back, Amarantha. You can wait here for the Morrisons. They'll be along soon." He kicked and the motorcycle roared and sputtered out; he cursed. Catching the curb of the driveway with her foot, and pitching forward, Amarantha was next to him on the grass. She found his arm. "I'm going with you." He dismounted from his motorcycle and looked at her as her blank eyes gazed up; he took a fist of hair at the nape of her neck. "Be careful back there, Gaylord, I mean it's all right but—"

He yanked the hair down, jerking her chin up. "Just what do you want from me, little girl?"

She reached back for his hand; he eluded her. "Gaylord, really you've got to watch out back there, I've—"

He yanked; she cried out. He muttered: "Answer me."

"I will, well I don't know, but stop it, that's where my scar is Gaylord, stop it—"

"Answer me!"

"Nothing! Nothing!"

He let her go; her hands went behind, cradling the back of her skull awkwardly, starting her bosom out to his eyes in a pin-up pose of offering. "You've hurt me, Gaylord, and you shouldn't have pulled, I told you not to—"

He slapped her. "Cut the whimpering." She did not. "God damn you, you listening to me? I'll show you what you want, little girl." He wrenched her hands from the back of her head, and stumbling her forward so that her head knocked on his chest, he thrust her hands down. "Isn't that what you want little girl?" He shouted: "That's what you were fumbling around for on the motorcycle? Nice piece of black hog to write home about?"

"No it isn't, it isn't!" She tugged at his hold; she gripped him. "Yes! Yes! Leave me alone! Leave me alone!"

He let her go; she embraced him. "Gaylord, I don't care, don't you understand it doesn't matter to me—"

"You don't care." He hissed: "Don't I understand, it doesn't matter. Well kiss my ass." He threw her arms away; they came back; infuriated, he flung her aside and shouted, "Will you fuck off, white girl?" He slammed his foot down and the motorcycle roared.

She staggered from his shove. "White girl? You don't—" She gasped and backed away. "White?"

"You got it straight then?" He mounted the motorcycle once again, "You finally got it straight then, I'm not for sale?" He shouted a laugh. "Big switch, big surprise." He looked at her as her face clenched. "And go ahead and freak out, see if I give a shit."

"Gaylord, it's not a question of sale, who said it was anything but—"she heard him shift into gear, and as he moved slowly forward she ran at the front wheel and embraced the handlebars. "You aren't going to leave me here—"

The motorcycle dragged her while his feet danced to keep balance. "Get off of here!"

"White yourself! White yourself!"

He cut the motor and tore at her arms, kicked her out of the motorcycle's path as it teetered and crashed jingling on the grass. She fell on her shoulder at the curb. He stared at her, then kicked her twice more in the back.

He stopped; he sat down beside her, took in breath and held it; she was silent. "Amarantha?—Listen, I—" He paused and looked at her as she lay face down; he put his hand on her hair. He watched a small blue forked pennant on the prostrate handlebars flutter in the breeze. "I'm sorry I hurt you there, Amarantha, I didn't mean to hurt you at all really, only what you stand for, you got to understand that—" She made no answer; he stroked her hair. "Now, Amarantha, you got to forgive me for hurting you like this, I just started seeing nothing but your skin, because of that scumbag up there—Amarantha? Hey now, baby, you all right there?" He turned her over gently, pulled her onto his lap; "Hey, Amarantha?" she lay still and stiff; "Amarantha?" Her mouth gaped and her rolled eyeballs stared white.

vi

"Marian?"

John's hands shifted packages, dug for pocketed keys. "Marian?" His knees opened the front door. "You home?" Closing it: "Ah"; steps sounded in the upper hall, and above the stairs her eyes and palms and a yellow dress shone in the shadow among invisible limbs. "Don't you look splendid."

Sideways descending, dark thighs glimpsed from beneath the hem. "Had to get out them shorts and halter thing. Got stared at so much I had to take the back way home—"

"I'm not surprised." Her arms hooped his neck. "Wait"; his eyes lunged over the dress as the packages met the floor; "Anyone here?"

"Mm. *Mm*-mm." Her arms pressed down his moist shirted back. Grunting after a moment, he said, "Props. You're quite right."

"Well if you want to know, they went—" Marian faced beyond him, gazing past his shoulder at the closed door.

"She had to see her doctor, I know, he told me. But unfortunately"— he read his watch beyond her hair— "unfortunately it's well past one and we're due downtown at two." They embraced; her hand passed over his cheek. He grinned, bent for the packages, offered his arm as she said, "What'd you get, hey—". She took a paper bag and rummaged as they walked together into the living room.

"What's for lunch, eh?" His arm crept around her its full length and fingered her breast as she ripped at the box he had brought. She smiled, "Cut it out," and stamped her foot on his, said, "Hey, what's this, a ray gun?" She swung out from his hold, pointed a gray muzzle to the window, her back to him, knees apart: "Zap! Zap!" Turning round to him slowly, "Bzzzzzzzzzzap!"

"You won't shut off *my* advertisement I assure you—"

She looked at the thing as it drooped from her finger. "What are you talking about?"

"It's for television commercials. You shoot them. They shut up."

"You kidding me?— Oh yeah, I heard of them. I thought they'd been made illegal though?" She stepped to him and embraced him again, saying: "This here is Marlboro country." The muzzle snubbed his spine. "Blam."

"That's correct. They weren't made illegal though, they were pressured out of business. Found it in a junk shop."

She turned and said to no one, nodding, "Ain't he really clever now?"

"I had your same idea and bought the following." He split the other bag behind her back. "What'd you say was for lunch?"

"Steak tartar." She pushed away, but he held her to him with one arm; with the other he dangled the second bag's contents beyond her reach. "It's a steak tar*tare*, you know."

"Oh look! Waterguns!"—he kept them from her. "Hey!"

He said, "Steak tartare? Shield your peasant origins? Move with ease in middle-class circles? Steak tar-tare?"—

She struggled, reaching. "You can't have both, hey—" she dropped her shoulder, ducked from his hold, wrenched a dripping toy from a fist that he relaxed, and they swiveled out each on a heel to face each other in stance. He squirted her throat; "Steak tartare?" She squirted his eyes: "Steak tartar."— "Hah!" he squirted her bosom: "Tartare; tartare." She fled and squat down behind the curled arm of a sofa. Her gun gasped; streams glinted in silent lanes of sun. "Tartar!" A lampshade that hid him splat softly and drooled. He shot at her: "Ah!" her cheek dripping, she leapt onto the sofa and bounded over to him, yanked aside the lamp, rained on his face, "Tartar! Tartar! Tartar!" They fell back together on the sofa and his gun spat spurts of water in her laughing mouth.

The gun was empty; his hand fell. Her eyes blinked and widened and her face streamed. "John? John John John? Steak tartare, my baby steak tartare—"

His mouth worked; she touched her fingers to his face in the stillness. "What, John?"

"Marian I've been thinking and—"

"I know you have, baby—"

"About what happened this morning"—Grunting, he sent back his hand to his hip pocket for a folded handkerchief; he shook it out and touched it on her skin. "Hey then—hey now what's the matter?"—He swung his legs off and crouched on the floor near her head. "What?"

"No, it's nothing really it's nothing"—She smiled and turned toward him on her side; two fingers reached out to spread apart his frown. "It was just—you know—"

"I know, Marian, and we will begin again, we already have begun, you mustn't lose hope because—

come on then"—He lay down beside her. "Tell me what is it—"

"Well"—her teeth labored her lower lip as she gazed. "Marian"—

"Well it's just, John, it's just I though maybe how what you were thinking about a new start was a whole lot different than what I was thinking, and maybe—"

She was still, and he said, "What then, Marian? If we talk about it?"

Her fingers worked at a button at his chest. "The thing is, John, well the thing is I can't help feeling how you want to go on like before, only doing it better, like being together really together I mean once every three or four weekends instead of once every eight or nine weekends, I don't *know* how many weeks it's been since—"

"Don't, Marian, we're going to change that."

"I know, John, but I just can't help thinking about starting over again, I mean really all all over again and being each other's again and I keep jumping back to that night together in the waves—"

"We can't wind everything back like in a dream, Marian, we've got to live with what's gone before— Look, how long has it been since we talked like this morning?"

"We were just destroying each other."

"No, that's not true, now don't—look at me now—I want to tell you, I was thinking on the trolley, watching a baby girl—she reminded me of Trudy, and—"

"You don't want to remember her—"

"But I did, Marian, and I was thinking since we have this trouble now we ought to adopt an infant right away, it'd be easy to find a light-skinned one and they never see their real mother and we'd feel it was ours in a matter of weeks, and besides it's very common that adoption stimulates a natural family, well it is, it's true, and that isn't going on as before now is it? Don't you remember those weeks when Trudy was here? We felt like king and queen?"

"I know, John, but don't say it, don't tell me"—she shifted and rose on her elbow, smiling for a quick moment, looking down on him; sun through the window lit his hair. "You think of her often?"

"Not so much nowadays—when I fall back on the past though, I usually think of then"— He shrugged. "Children like her die and meanwhile we keep people alive who are finished with living. Like a woman I saw today. She wants nothing better than to join her sweet Jesus and there I am feeding her digitalis. Sometimes I wonder if dear old sentimental Mary Eddy of my childhood wasn't right all the while." Marian snorted and he added, smiling, "No it's Puritanism runs the hospital, you know, a love of decrepitude. Hate the flesh, the flesh is evil. Whereas Christian Science teaches the flesh as innocent and the mind as evil." He twisted and sat up. "And they're right, it is."

She sat up also. "A lot of good that does us."

"Well—" He frowned and looked at his watch. "Did you find that girl's cane? How'd you leave things with her?"

"Don't worry yourself about the girl. Gaylord found it. He's with her."

"Oh is he?"

"Yeah, well I was feeling crampy, and he said he'd take her and drop her off at the hospital, so—"she plucked her watergun from between the cushions and studied it— "They went."

"Yes."

She waited a moment, staring up close at the muzzle. He said nothing more. A distant trolley's clang touched on the still room. She stared at her stretched-out calves and squirted them glumly. "John"—she looked up, squirted at the ceiling, let the gun fall. "John, I don't know about the flesh or the mind or any those things but I know one thing, and that's there's something evil flying around here and nesting in the eaves, and it isn't the atom bomb either or the war in Vietnam or any of your white man peeves, and whatever it is it's sitting right there right now baby, and there, and there, and there"—she squirted in succession her temple, his temple, her lap, his. "And I'd like to know how that college-educated mind-evil of yours might go and define it, I'd really like to know."

He swatted the drops from his trousers. "Listen, Marian. I don't know what's wrong with us any better than you do. I've presented my case for a solution as best I can. I think things might get better if we keep on talking. Meanwhile we've got to eat and get down to headquarters." He turned to her and smiled slightly as he sat forward to stand. "Okay?"

She squirted him. "Don't you move an inch."

"Cut the nonsense."

"I said don't move, John."

"I'm sorry, Marian. We haven't the time now."

"John, don't move!" She clamped her shaking lip between her teeth as he looked at her quizzically; she leveled the gun at his heart. "Now don't move."

"All right, what then?" He leaned back, crossing his legs and arms. "Come on, what then?"

"Putting up with your childish little wife, John? Patience of a Job?"

"Get cracking."

"All right? I will. And we're going to be very calm, John, we're not going to *pick* at each other, or do any shouting or destroying of each other, we're just going to discuss our little problems ever so nicely—I'm trusting you, see?" She lay the gun gently on her lap's yellow field. She paused.

"You've got something to say, Marian?"

"Yes I do, baby." She went on quietly, "Since you're talking about headquarters, you know what we do at headquarters, John? We try to believe in the power of the people and militant nonviolence and interracial brotherhood and a whole lot of other nice phrases?" She smoothed her lap with her gun. "Aren't they ever so much nicer than the phrases my brother Mandus and his friends use when they talk together, like you know better than me what they are so we won't go into them? But they got one fine thing over there, baby, that we don't have in our place, and that little thing is they don't meet to whip themselves up to believe in their phrases, like we do, they meet to shout their phrases, John, because they already believe them in their black flesh and their evil minds"— She let the gun rest and turned to his frowning eyes as he said,

"Your brother's a racist, Marian. He's the worst kind of self-indulgent revolutionary. He's a fascist."

"You don't understand him, John—"

"I love him and fear him, isn't that enough? Do you understand him?"

"I don't know, but we aren't talking about him, we're talking about you, and whatever he believes, he belives it, but you—time was, baby, it isn't so long ago either, I knew a white man who really believed in brotherhood between his kind and the black man, who really believed in it I mean, he didn't have to work to pretend to himself he believed like all them professors and clergymen did, there never was a question of him not keeping the faith, because there wasn't one cell in his head that told him not to, and I married that man,

John, I married him not only because I loved him with all my heart like I still love you, John, but because I thought I might be able to help you just a bit to keep that faith burning inside you when the going got hard, but I failed to, didn't I, John? I did, didn't I?" She shifted toward him; the gun fell. "And I remember thinking when Gaylord was here one time with Martha and we were talking about the ghetto and he says, 'The dream's gone sour now hasn't it?' and I thought to myself, funny, he thinks it like it was a sweet dream, while I always thought it like it was a light, and you carried it, John, and I remembered that time this morning because Gaylord was telling the girl about you when the three of us were out together, and I thought while we were walking, how come I went and chose a light to think of it all, and I thought maybe because he's white, or maybe because I was raised a Christian and all those hymns talking about lighting the way, though you're the real Christian, John, though you say you aren't, and though they raised you a cannibal—and I said to myself, however it come about I thought of it this way, the shine of the light is dying in him now, and I said as much to Gaylord when the girl wasn't listening, and he said if you still follow it, don't matter how bright it is, and I told him that he's your friend and could say that, but I'm your wife, John, and I can see it flickering there in your eyes, flickering bad, and I don't like seeing it at all, I'm afraid it's going to go out, and if you think that girl is blind, John, just wait till how we stumble when it dies."

She was still. He said, "Surely you must know now what a glorified romantic picture that is"—

"That don't matter, John, didn't you—"

He interrupted her, "Anything I did I did out of

personal necessity and not out of anything that makes me a Christian or an honest man either and—"

"John, you didn't listen to me, it's all in the faith you have, everything's in that, and I wouldn't be talking to you like this now nor telling you straight this way, I'd have tried to help you in quieter ways like I tried to do other times, except I feel this time like I'm all tied up in it, like it's me you don't believe in any more, like when the light goes out for a second in its flickering there's a voice that's saying in you, 'I don't want my wife, I don't want my wife'—then the light goes on and another voice says: 'You mean Marian? Of course I want my Marian, she's my wife, isn't she? Of course I want my wife.' And the light goes off and the other voice says in the dark, 'You don't want your wife, you don't love her any more, and you don't love your black brothers either. They won't move and they won't get together and they keep making mistakes and they bug you and you hate them.' And then you hate your own self, John, and I can't help feeling that that's what it is going on in that churning head of yours, when you stand around and frown so like you're doing all the time now, and I don't know how to help you, I sit there and watch you and think sometimes that you were wrong to love me and marry me, because you mixed all your feelings about brotherhood all in with your feelings about me till it became the same emotion, and then when your love started dying for me, because I was pushing thirty-five, because I didn't give you children, because I wasn't educated maybe, or just because I was just another woman who isn't any different from any other woman, and a man's love always dies down for his woman, though every bride belives that her man's won't—"

"It hasn't died down, Marian."

"It has, John, and now that it has, your faith is going down with it."

"That's not true—"

"Took me a lot of coaxing to get that light to burn this morning, John, and you don't really want me anymore. I know you don't."

"No you don't know it and it's you that make the connection, dammit the sex is not the problem, it's not the problem."

"I didn't say it was, John, it just shows it up but if you do want me, John, if you say you do—"

"I say it now, I do!"

"Then, John—well I'm sorry for asking this, baby, I'm not a crude woman you know that, but you're saying you want me, then why haven't you made love to me more than once or twice in the last six months?" She reached to lay her hand on his groin. "John, why won't you? Why won't you have me?"

"I've wanted to, you know that—"

"I know you want to want me, John, but I can feel you, I can feel you here, and I know you don't want to have me."

"That's not true, I will, you're not being fair, you can't tell me how I've failed your idea of me and then expect me to leap on you—don't now, Marian, we're talking, we're talking things—"

She stood. "We're always talking, John."

"We *aren't* always talking, how can you say that? We haven't talked in months."

"Yes we have, John. We talked this morning and we're always talking to each other in our heads and we never do anything, loving or going any place or—"

"Talking's doing something when it's like this. Don't you think you've just done something?"

"Talk's nothing, John. Kids talk and politicans talk and hip cats talk. We're man and wife, John"—she crouched before him. "Time was, John, you'd have wanted me now, you'd have cut through the talk and we'd have made love and shrugged this all off our backs and laughed it could have bothered us—John, don't you know you aren't acting like yourself, you acting like that Man, talking about doing everything but never doing anything, don't you remember how we used to laugh at my friends dropping hints at me: 'Well, Marian, it sure is nice to have a white man, fine living and all,' and they wouldn't say the rest which was, 'But isn't he a *lump*?' " She looked up to him, half-smiling, gripping his thighs. "You weren't one, John, you were real as any black man then, I don't know what you charmed into now—"

"I'm obviously charmed into someone who can't compete with this black man you've got parked in your head."

"It ain't a question of that, John. It's a question of what you were and what you are—"

"You want an idea not a man. You want your myth of the gallant black sexual warrior."

"I want you! I want my husband!"

"You want me as long as I'm your myth and now I've failed to be it. So why don't you go on out and see if you can't find it somewhere else? and if you can't then come back and maybe we can make some progress. Go on now"— He shoved her upwards, his hands beneath her shoulders. "Go on!"

She embraced his legs. "I won't, John."

"Go on I tell you!"

"Stop it! Stop it! You talk like I was the one who's gone away."

"Haven't you?"

"No!"

"Then what is the problem, Marian?"

"I'm asking you! John, I'm asking you! What's happened to us John, what did we lose—"

94

He stood and stepped around her, walked to the window, gazed out to the afternoon. She said to his back, "I'll give you lunch now, baby—"

"No, I'm not hungry. Besides I think you deserve some kind of answer—we can be a little late I guess." He was still.

"John—"

"Will you let me think a minute?" She sat back on her heels before the sofa and watched him, biting her lip; for a long minute he looked out across the street, studying a poplar that paled to the light of the high sun. He turned to her at last, saying quietly, "Shall I tell you"—he paused as sudden fire engines screamed; he went on: "Shall I tell you what took me so long to get back today? Not that it's the first time this has happened—a boy was admitted near dawn this morning with a pain in his belly, I presume it's appendicitis—I couldn't find out for sure. He wouldn't let me touch him. You don't know him I think—Dudley Street boy, not well off, has a good reputation—I argued with him; no dice. He wants a black doctor. Well, there isn't one. I asked a black nurse to give him an injection. No dice. She's working for the honky. I had to call the father and then simmer *him* down because he wants to beat the boy for this—We ended up using straps, of course; a handsome scene." He shrugged and turned to look out the window, again as she answered,

"Baby, I'm sorry and you should have told me that's what's bothering you—"

"No, Marian, I just—"

He paused and she went on, "You always had these kids, John, and you always going to have them and they haven't got their knife in you but once in all this time—"

"It isn't a question of knives any more. This boy doesn't go on rumbles, he goes on strikes, and this strike was against myself and white-run hospitals and the whole concept of a Doctor John in the first place and how do you think I—"

"You calling what he done today a strike? Listen to me, John. I'm not going sit here watching you get rocked back on your heels by some two-bit rioter who the only satisfaction he's ever going get is making it hard for people like you who are trying to do something for him, that an burning down decent folks' houses and giving the police an excuse for calling in the tanks—"

"All right, Marian. Number one, you have no information whatever except your own extrapolation that this boy is or was a rioter, or arsonist, and number two if he were it wouldn't alter his significance one iota. You talk about my belief, well that boy proves for the thousandth time that what I believe doesn't matter for a damn down there any more. Do you understand?" He walked past her, rubbing the back of his neck with his hand. "Look, remember the last School Committee meeting we went to? Eh? Can you think of anything more absurd than a white politician preaching against Pantherism to a black audience? This racist man, this corporative tank-deploying man telling *blacks* about brotherhood and nonviolent methods and urban harmony?"

She said sharply, "What's this man got to do with you, John?"

"This man has to do with me, Marian, because the whole thrust of political and cultural nationalism in the ghetto now says he has to do with me. It says I am of this man because he and I are white Americans and it says the black man will do best to go it alone without the help of white Americans, no matter what they believe, and you tell me where am I when I agree with a point of view that excludes me?"

"I'll tell you where you are, you're wrong, because

it isn't your kind they're trying to exclude, you're different and people down there know it and that boy's just a kid, he doesn't know who you are—"

"Is that a fact? I'm not different, Marian. We feel I'm different; that's all. How much do you think I count for down at headquarters where once upon a time I was chairman?"

"Baby, don't you understand how everybody's caught in the phase things are going through, I don't know why you just don't leave the politics alone in the meantime, you always done your most good as a doctor anyways—"

"That may be so but I find it difficult to steer between an ambition to bring the races together and a clear sense that there's nothing much I can do, which contradict each other, and you urge both on me." He stopped pacing and stood before the shelves of bound journals that lined one wall. "Take my role as Doctor John. I'm a missionary. I'm part of the rich-white-man-is-trying-to-help-the-poor-black-man swindle, and there's nothing I can do about it. It doesn't help that I understand the swindle and know perfectly well that the poor are taking care of me and not vice versa, because I in fact do the same things the philanthropists do; and when a man gets wise to a swindle, as the poor are now to this one, you can't expect him to make exceptions for the one or two men who did the same things but felt differently. The law doesn't excuse a criminal just because he's tried to transcend his role. And furthermore the philanthropists take courses in the right things to feel, so how am I to be distinguished, when trust is shattered, as one of the few who aren't lying? How do *you* know I'm not? How am I to know?"

He turned round to her and they gazed at each other; there was a short stillness. Her eyes fell. She said in a low voice, "You make up theories and phrases. The poor got plenty of theories and phrases. They don't have enough doctors."

"That's true, but I don't enjoy going down there as a mechanical body-fixer who's unfortunately necessary but who merits every dirty look there's leisure to give him."

"It isn't as bad as that, John. It's just a phase we have to weather like any other."

"It *is* as bad as that for someone who considers himself a guest down there and whose feelings of worth vary with how he is received there—"

She said loudly, "You're a fool to feel that way and I'm telling you it's just a phase—"

"You keep saying that. Just how do you know it may I ask? If this were the eighteen seventies, would you have called the end to that reconstruction a phase? The history of man counts freedom in years and suppression in centuries and you talk about the light of faith shining on brotherhood when all I see it shining on is continuing white-majority PR-fascism and occupied urban provinces and terrorist retaliation and detention camps and increasingly blatant soldier rule and rebellion and Guernica all over again."

Jerking at a thread in her hem, she said almost inaudibly, "That war ain't going on any place except in your mind."

"You think so. I don't think so. Listen, Marian, what I do in my mind is be afraid. I'm afraid of the white man because his civilization is insane and I'm afraid of the black man because he opposes the white man who unfortunately happens—" standing above her, he leaned down and tugged the skin of his cheek at her—"who unfortunately happens to include me. Do you understand that? It's not a detail. I'm white. I am barred from becoming militant and despised for remaining moderate. My country is splitting apart and I'm falling down the middle. I'm nowhere. I'm obsolete. I'm scared. I wish I were dead." He tugged his cheek once more at her and stood up and turned away.

He said to the shelves of journals, "Half the time I wish I was black, and the other half"—he shrugged. "I got another letter from my mother today. It took me two hours to throw it out. I think I may write to her, Marian. I didn't let the thoughts surface but I felt drawn toward her in a way I haven't been in twenty years."

"In what way, John, in the way she felt about color? That what you been trying to tell me with your phrases?" Her high voice cut off. She watched him look down and clench his eyes. He muttered after a pause, "No it's just regression but I—"

His voice failed. She stood, slapping her dress. "I'm not going to listen to this. We've had our say. We're going to eat now." She walked down the room.

"Marian!"

"What."

"Help me."

He caught up with her and embraced her from behind. She looked aside and down, her hands in fists by her thighs. "I can't, John."

"*Why* not?"

"If you've lost your hope and you're drawn back to her, then you're against me because I'm black, and there's nothing I can say to you."

"No that's not it, don't you understand, I've always loved you that you're black but now I'm afraid because you're black, I'm afraid of you and that's why I can't make love to you."

Her hand moved; she forced it down. "Why, John?"

"Because I'm afraid you'll turn against me because

your people are turning against me, and it's only a matter of time till you have to choose between them and me—"

"No, John. That isn't going to happen."

"I'm afraid it will!"

"And what do you choose when that war goes on in your mind, John, you choose your people? Your white mother?"

"Marian, no, don't you see I couldn't go back but you could and maybe you will?"

"I can go back. You can't, but you think I can."

"Our life is the ghetto and the ghetto is black—"

"My life is this house, John, and sometimes I think I've gotten whiter than you are in it"—She pushed him away from her; he did not look at her as she spoke. "I've got no retreat that you're talking about, John. I take the train down to Roxbury to see my friends if that's what they are and I come like a foreigner, I'm not the same as them, John, they don't talk to me like they do to one another or even like they do to you, far as they're concerned I've either outdone them, or I've betrayed them, and you telling me there isn't any hope of brotherhood and there isn't any Doctor John except his husk, then I'm telling you there isn't any Mrs. Marian either, because Marian is Doctor John's wife and that's all she is baby, and here you're announcing how your belly's full of moths because your wife's a black woman, well I'm telling you, man, she isn't, she isn't black except in name, and she isn't white either, she's nothing." She smiled at him without friendliness. "So where you think *I'm* going to go when your war comes? Listen to me, John, you afraid I might go home, well I'm afraid you might go home, and sometimes I'm afraid you've already gone home and already found yourself some lilywhite bed to console yourself with."

"What kind of nonsense are you bringing up out of the blue?"

She shouted: "And maybe that's why you ain't going to touch me and you talking this political horror show to prepare me for my being abandoned."

"That's completely out of kilter do you hear? I've never once considered anything like that. It has nothing to do with us and you know it."

"I don't know it, John—I don't believe you haven't considered it, I don't believe you haven't done it, I don't believe anything you're telling me these days—"

They stared at each other; the room rung faintly with the after-stillness of their shouts. He began to speak and she turned her back on him. He said to her, "Marian, this doesn't make any sense, I told you my problem is a lack of confidence which has nothing to do with infidelity real or imagined"—he paused; she said nothing and he went on, "Nothing is pulling me away from you, something is holding me back from you, and I told you what it was."

"I don't believe you, John."

"You must. You have nothing to support any doubts."

"You told me you tempted to go back home and set up a lilywhite house with a lilywhite wife in it—"

He said quietly, still to her back, "I didn't say or even hint one word of that. Did I. I said something else but you understood it according to your fears. Didn't you."

"I understood you aren't going to act like a husband to me and you got nerve asking me about adoption when you every bit as impotent as I'm barren."

"You won't help me, Marian—"

"You won't help me either. I'm sitting here day in and day out thinking how you hounddogging on me and you won't show me one bit of loving to disprove it, and how long you think I'm going to rot in this house before I start getting tempted my own self?"

His voice rose: "Don't expect to entice me by threats, didn't I tell you it's the fear of just that that paralyzes me as a lover?"

"That's your fancy excuse and I'm supposed to sit here like a piece of taxidermy while you out there drilling one hussy after the other, well I ain't going to, I ain't going to—"

"Marian, that's crazy, listen to me, you aren't sitting here like that, you're my wife and I have nothing to do with other women—"

"I don't believe you. I don't believe anything you say. I don't even know who you are any more. I feel like you already left me." Sobs coughed out into the room with her words. "I might as well go whoring like Martha since far as I can see you don't care what I do."

"I care enough to be made helpless if that's what you're after"—There was silence. Saying her name then, he stepped up behind her and lay his hands on her shoulders; she shuddered and ripped away. She stood against the wall, her face hidden in her raised arm. "Marian, don't"—again he approached her, and before he touched her she reeled aside as if shoved. He caught her upper arm tightly and she turned toward him perforce, her body bent and cringing, her black irises glinting from a face drawn and puckered with hatred. He shook her and his voice trembled. "Listen I'm not like that. I don't deserve this." Her stare continued and his fingers tightened on her arm. "I've been a good husband to you, I've tried to be—if I've had some failures, any man would have—"

Her eyes fell; then his. The afternoon stepped in stillness across the floor. He let go her arm. With a small clearing of the throat, but saying nothing, she walked round him and down the room. She slowed her step slightly as he said, "Come to headquarters with me?" She went on toward the stairs. He followed her. "Look, it'll be better if we go, it'll take our minds off this for a while"—he paused at the front door, looking up the stairwell as she climbed. "Marian?" She stopped, her limbs invisible in shadow. "Talk to me? Marian?" She climbed on. The yellow hem disappeared into the upper hall. "I'll be back in an hour or so, maybe you'll come with me then"—He opened the door and he walked out.

His steps thocked faintly. A trolley shrieked and flapped its doors. In the bedroom, she heaved the television set he had given her out the window and did not watch it shatter on the ground.

vii

"It don't hurt you to walk, Amarantha? You sure?"

"Nope, I told you. Only a bit. Just as long as you aren't leading me off to some out-of-the-way hollow where you can pulverize me in private so I never get up again."

He laughed quietly. "I'm real sorry, baby."

"You don't get the luxury of apology. Just tell me where are we? I can't hear the highway even."

He said nothing. She butted him with a swipe of her hip as they walked. "Feeling guilty? Great. So speak."

"Yeah."

"Because this path is through a pine forest? Miles from anywhere? Bluebeard's Castle? I thought Cape Cod was beaches?"

He stopped, suddenly smiling. There was the smell of soddenness and rot. "I always liked this place. Guess what's here."

She stood still in a resinous coolness. "It is a pine grove."

"Oh, yeah. I was going to tell you. Whole Lower Cape is sort of a mountain range of sand dunes, running north and south, covered over with a brown heather-bush—the valleys in between them full of pines. Right now we're climbing out of a valley and toward the sea. Guess though. Besides that."

She studied a silence pocked with infintesimal thuds of fallen needles landing. Small animals scrabbled and conversed. "Wait, a chickadee. Not that."

"Go on."

"Rust, and moss—Hey, some sort of a spring?—an old watering trough."

"Goddamn good." There was a wheeze; knocking; a screek.

"An old hand pump."

"Yes ma'am. I'm trying to see if it still works. Wait. It's a brother of mine; listen." She stood by as he heaved at the handle of the pump. Deep glugs groaned. He labored; the pump raced its coital pantings up the scale which Gaylord joined: "Ee, ee, ee, ee-ee-ee-eeee—ahh." A splurge of cold water exploded on the ground and blew its metallic clean scent through the grove.

They laughed. "Can I pump?"

"I don't know, baby; got to ask him." He brought the handle to his chin and muttered to it as to a radio. She said, "Well he's going to have to let me." Stepping forward, "Uff," she walked into Gaylord and stood against him while her hands ran up his chest to find the handle. She tugged it. Gaylord looked up; "He say if—" he was silent, and shoving the handle and their hands down between their bellies, he leapt his face at hers. One kiss was ground into her mouth. She stepped away.

His eyes went after her: she was frowning and biting her index finger. "Baby?"

"I'm afraid of your shoes ending up in my ribs again that's the only thing—well it isn't the only thing but it's enough."

He kicked the pump, which shuddered. They walked on hand-in-hand up a dark path which was tigered with stripes of light from the hidden sun. In the stillness he looked up the rusted columns of pines, whiskered with dead stumps of fallen boughs. Above, a lane of blue sky flowed quietly. He said at last: "I lost my head, Amarantha. You know that."

105

"Of course I know it, but I also know about patterns, don't you see?"

"Things have been breaking down today, Amarantha. I usually just talk."

"That's usually enough."

He waited, then went on, "You said it's not the only thing. What are the other things?"

"Oh it's just—" a dead branch whipped her. "Ouch" —he reached across her to rip it with a crack from its trunk, which shook down on them an answer of needles in a shower. She pawed the back of her neck. "The needles get down and itch under your clothes."

He stopped to strip twigs from the branch. "Make you some eyes so you don't get stung—You were saying. The other thing."

"I know, well the thing is I've got this sort of person in me who's very hostile to all this."

"To all what, baby?"

"Being with you, obviously."

"Because of what?—Here you go now."

"Don't give me that because of what—Thanks"—she took the branch, switched it before her. "What if I asked you because of what did you attack me on the driveway, I mean what makes you think I'm allied with that greaseball?"

"Don't go on, okay?"

"That's all right with me, except how am I to know when it's time for the shoes again? So they'd better stay off of your feet if you expect—" she did not finish, and shrugged. They said nothing as they worked up a steepening rise.

They stopped for a moment, perspiring. "Look, Amarantha, I'd try to explain to you the whole thing what I done, except the trouble is, in my experience, talking color with white people is retrograde motion every step. The more each side sees what the other side means, the more they both understand they don't even have the points in common they been pretending they had."

"You think so? We're not talking about color though. We're talking about being threatened—because listen, remember how I was when we were fighting on the stairs to the statehouse? You'd found out I've been a mental patient, and wham, Amarantha was invisible and you were walking with some kind of weird species you had to humor and kid-glove until you got rid of it."

They climbed on. "It isn't the same, Amarantha."

"Not being treated seriously as a person because of your category, that isn't the same?"

"Sure but you actually were in a hospital, baby, weren't you?"

"You mean people are shitty and unfair to you, but as for me I really *ought* to be locked up?"

"No, baby. I'm merely saying you making a comparison when there isn't one. That category of madman you're talking about, you don't want to be classed in it because of something in your past; what you want is to get clear of it, and you figure people screwing you by keeping you into it. But I'm not interested in getting clear of my category, as you call it. I'm interested in seeing *it* get clear of things and planting its foot on top of a few places." Frowning, he looked down at her; she was biting her lip. "See what I mean about talking color?"

She made a claw at him. "I never said I was as good as you, I only meant I thought I was human—"

"I never said you weren't, Amarantha."

"*All* I said was I thought I understood why you got angry on the driveway and wham you're telling me I think you're like a maniac—because you know why? Because you're convinced I'm against you, and if I don't show it, that makes you nervous because how will you set up your defenses? So you're going to force my supposed hostility out of me even if it means attacking me." She smiled suddenly. "Hey that was pretty good, haven't I been shrunk?"

"Were you in one of those hospitals though?"

"One of those hospitals? Yes that's my status. I'm sort of like an ex-con only weird and without the glamour." He laughed nervously and she added, "Real funny isn't it? Once a freak, always a freak, they get you in a hospital, they make sure you stay in. When do we get to the top of this hill? Because the purpose of a public mental hospital is to put away strays and annoying relatives and political freaks, so if these people got cured, what would be the use of the hospital? You'd have to drive them nuts all over again. Because I'm tired of climbing, hey—"

Laughing, he swung her against him. "Couple minutes now, you're going to see. You coming swimming with me?"

"Yes but now listen, you ever been inside a state mental hospital?"

"Yes baby."

"As a patient?"

"No, of cour—no, as a visitor."

"Okay, so you know then. The way they manage it so they don't cure anyone, is listen, the lives that the patients went crazy to escape couldn't possibly be worse than a state mental hospital, and so the only sane thing for a person to do if he's living in one is to stay crazy, so as not to notice his surroundings too much—and like to make sure of this, do you know who supposedly takes care of you? Doctors? Nurses? Nope, orderlies who used to be other patients, or ex-cons, that way you don't have to pay them. I bet if you put any person in the world in a state mental hospital he'd be crazy as the rest in two weeks if not two days, that's all it would take, I'm absolutely sure of it. That's why doctors won't go near the place, they have to watch out for their sanity like anybody else—Okay so people know this, and they run into the exception like me who gets out and says she can function, well they don't know what to do with her. I mean I must be sick, wasn't I in a hospital?" She turned her face up to him, grinning. "It's lucky I'm blind, otherwise I might never get a job."

Heat suddenly belted them; "Hey the beach!" Their feet sunk in sand. "We going swimming? Are there people? Is the surf high? It isn't too early in the year still is it?"—She stopped walking to listen; heard only a rush of stillness. "No people." She crooked back her arms and grabbed for her dress clasp; paused and frowned. "No ocean?"

He watched her, his mouth drying. He cleared his throat and reached. "Baby."

"All right."

There was an elaborate kiss. "Um." She jumped on his feet and pounded his chest. "This isn't even Cape Cod, it's the Gobi Desert"—

He caressed her. "It's the dunes."

"Hey!"

"I took my shoes off."

"That was just a symbol."

"How does this dress work here."

"No, there're people—"

"There aren't."

"I'll get sunburn—"

"I thought we were swimming?"

"Then where's the ocean?" Their embrace discon-nected. Laughing, he struggled with his shirt, she flung sand into the air. "What's here!"

"This is the last of the ridges I told you about,

Amarantha, and we're near to the top, we're coming to a place called High Dune—there's a bird-hunter's shack in a hollow down there, that's where we're going to stay tonight. John and I used to trespass on it in the old days'" He emerged from his shirt and plunged its tails into a pocket. "You can see from miles around from where we standing."

"I know," she said.

They trudged up the sand, carrying shoes. "Yeah?" The pines receded; the sun trumpeted down.

"Mm, because nothing to stop the sound, it's not like in the woods, there's sort of a whishsh, you know, a silence—"

"The wind—"

"In the sand—"

"In the heather bush too, Amarantha, which covers the dunes, you can see them rolling out brown behind us, inland, with strips of green pines in the valleys in between, and blue bits of fresh-water ponds, round like irises staring at the sun."

"Where's the sea?"

"Over the rise we're climbing up now, you'll see, we're on the back of High Dune and it hides us from the sound of the waves."

"You can hear it though, Gaylord, grumbling down there."

"Can you now?"

"Sure."

"Well you got a pair of ears, and where we are, there's too much salt for the heather and so there's nothing around here except white bare sand, little washboard kind of wind-waves in it, and beach-grass clumps on the crowns of the dunes, and lone blades growing up the sides like belly-wisps, shshsh they going, gouging circles all around them from the tips bending down and revolving around in the wind, and you can't live here, can't even build a house here, and there ain't a sign of man in miles, Amarantha, there's never been a tribe of man messing around here, and rubbing it up, and leaving their spoor, not the black man, nor the white man, nor the yellow man neither, nor the red man before them all."

Among cubic-tufted hillocks they wove upwards, arm in arm. The gathering wind tossed them with sand that stung their skin, which ached with the sun. Floating in faintness to their ears, a shout turned his head toward the far hills; specks of a pair of boys chased along the sky. Her dress snapped and rippled in the air. Her hand fell on his skin, settled on his spine, cool, dry, he looked: white legs appearing as she stepped, tensing along the white sand, hips of hidden shape, breast undefined against her handing arm; clear neck rising into a sudden reddening wrinkledness beneath her billowed hair: he peered at it, they rounded a hillock, her hair fell. "Amarantha?"—"Hmm?"—Blankness veiled her eyes, which changed only with what they reflected, and which rested in sharp bones as the ponds in smooth dunes.

"You must be able to hear it now though, Gaylord, can't you? Like a subway train coming, way down the tunnel?"

Climbing as they climbed, pouring in their ears a more and more pounding warning, flicking out the grate of their steps, the snap of their clothes, the scribblings of their thoughts, the rustling revolution of the dry grass, a rolling tide of rising roaring whelmed their silence till they stood wind-slapped on High Dune's brow in the pouncing thunder of the sea.

He shouted in her ears, "Shield your eyes, Amarantha! The wind'll fill them with sand if you don't!" He looked out along the curing shore. "It's a two-hundred-foot drop steep sheer from our feet down

111

to the beach, Amarantha, the ocean you can see it screaming in for miles along, both ways right and left and way out, way out till the earth bends over to cut beneath the sky, and waves riding in stretching up and flopping over, churning in a boil of milk, all the way down, all the way up, land's end, the end of America—"

"Where's the path to the beach, okay? Because I've finally found a wind I don't like—"

"Ain't no path to the beach."

"Oh. We're going to fly."

"We're going down right now."

"*You* are. I'm not."

"There's enough slope, see, and your feet make your own stairs in the sand. Ain't no rock anywhere. You sort of glide, understand? Only problem is right here at the top, since there's grass-clumps that stick out over the face of the dune like a frown, and you got to jump over them. Ready?" He picked her up beneath the arms and began to swing her over the edge. She screamed and pummeled his head. He let her down quickly. She said, half-choking and half-laughing, "Christ, I thought you'd decided to eliminate me."

"Naw, you kidding?"

"Yes, but the bottom fell out of everything—"

He leaned over the edge, eyes clenched shut: a chasm of thunder. "Yeah, I guess so. Sorry, baby."

She smiled up at him, wincing slightly. "Pure paranoia?"

"Sure, you're going to see."

"Okay but be careful with me for a while because that just got the watcher going—"

"No problem." He leapt over the frown of clumps. His feet dug into the sloping sand and he slid some yards down, standing up, until his heels had ploughed hills enough to stop him.

Her voice wandered down: "You still alive?"

He yelled, "There's nothing but sand down here, I told you—only trouble, I can't climb up again to hand you over the edge—you going to have to ju—" She interrupted by appearing midair over the frown. "What you holding your nose for?"

She landed and glided, her straight-out arms pumping in quick circles for balance. She halted, shivering. "If I had more sense I wouldn't be blind in the first place."

He crooked his arm around her neck. "You're a good chick, dig?"

"Oh good."

"Lay hold of my hand and lean backwards as you go. We're going down."

They floated toward the sea in long leaping silent strides.

"Your feet don't hit till two seconds after they're supposed to—hey your heels go in deep, we won't make an avalanche? Did you notice how cold the underneath sand is? You sure we aren't going to pitch forward?"

"Yeah, now hold it back and stay leisurely. You're always rushing things."

"What did you think of me, first off?"

"Yeah." They soared. "Well let's see, I figured you had quite a decent backside on you, and an interesting vocabulary. I already learned one word from you, and a pack of nifty usages."

"Which?"

"Skoptophile, remember? Always wanted to shrink down to six inches and roll up like a pangolin, and sit there invisibly digging pairs of friends of mine balling."

"Hey, you know about pangolins? Those animals who look the same at both ends?"

"I saw one in the Amsterdam zoo."

"Amsterdam New York? I didn't know they—"

"Yeah, now lean back and keep it slow, will you?"

"I was going to be a zoologist when I grew up."

"Will you? Because you can get loping too fast and abdicate being able to stop—"

"Yes I'm beginning to learn about that."

"There's a little ridge coming up now, we're going to slow down."

"Who are you kidding?" Her racing feet found air where they had been counting on sand; her shoulders overtook her legs, her hand ripped from his; she splat on her side and skittered with limbs flailing down the face of the dune toward the throat of the sea. "Gaylord, what's ahead of me!"

"Nothing!" Lunging, he caught her by the ankle and braked with gouged sand. He laughed.

Panting and spitting: "Puh. Puh."

He crouched down. "You all right there?"

"No, I'm a wreck."

"I'll give you a ride."

"We aren't on the beach yet?"

"We aren't but halfway down."

She sat up, blinking. Her dress lay bunched round her hips. "The sea's not so loud here."

He brushed sand from her thighs. "Wait till tonight when the tide's moved in, you haven't heard nothing yet." His hands rivered up her belly. "Sounds like a squadron of jets." He ran his tongue up her neck.

"The ride! The ride!" Her teeth swiped at his nose, found it without sharpness enough to bite; she turned away nervously. "The ride?"

"Up."

"I'm weak."

"Fine." He stood and stepped below her, twirled her round so that she faced him and the sea; he dug his fingers beneath her buttocks through the sand.

114

"This is a ride?"

"Dune's so steep I don't even have to lift you up, just tug you onto me"—

"Aw-oh I think I've had it."

"Nice young dabchick full of beans, nothing like it." He bounced her once and she was against him, facing him, sitting on his hands, her bare legs around his waist. He swung round and began to carry her down what remained of the dune. "This is like the position you ball in standing up."

Her fingers laced behind his neck as she leaned back with the slope; she crossed her ankles behind him, stabbed the back of his thighs with her heels. "I don't know about that expression 'ball.' I mean isn't it sort of one-sided?"

"Naw. Ofay chicks who go astray with the field hands get black-balled, right? It's a derivation."

"It is? Oh. Ha. No that's pretty clever actually."

He padded carefully down the sand. "Got to stay next to me, baby, or we'll lose our balance"—she heaved forward against him, inching down his body as he jogged. His fingers spread wider and longer beneath her. Her head fell back, aiming her chin at him. He heard her teeth grate. "You got to take it easy, Amarantha, lay into it easy—"

"I know I'm trying but"—

"Ain't nothing to worry yourself." He ground his belly into the bottom of hers.

"I know, I know, I'm perfectly happy but the other one's absolutely screaming at me, Gaylord and I *told* you she would and I'm trying not to hear her but—"

"Now, baby, you just tell her to go back up the dune and lay an egg or something and leave us in peace, okay?"

"She doesn't appreciate that, Gaylord." As he walked, he dropped her hips once more—"No don't"— and caught her finally against him, announcing his lust to hers. "No stop it, I'm telling you we can't—"

"No problem, baby. We can."

"Gaylord, you're splitting me, please, I can't keep her quiet—"

"Why, I haven't split you yet—"

"You will I know you will and you've got to let me go—"

"You can't hold back now. You'd be killing me, baby." They were on the beach; he lowered her onto her back and lay beside her. "Come on now; it's all right."

"Gaylord, you've got to—"

"Lie still, Amarantha."

"No! We can't get rid of her!"

"Lie still now."

"We can't make her!"

"I'll make her."

"No!" She bucked him off of her and leapt at him and flailed her fists at his belly and groin. Shouting, he sat up and yanked her shoulder back, wrenched the hair at her neck's nape and she yelped and let go, and he flung her aside against the dune. "*You* did it, Gaylord! *You* did it!"

"What the hell kind of crazy thing you think you doing? You're goddamn lucky I'm not lying there screaming, hear me?"

"She wanted to, Gaylord, and you've got us to thank that she didn't and we told you, Gaylord, we told you we told you we told you—"

"Amarantha?"

"Don't come at us, Gaylord, don't come at us!"

"Why what you doing, Amarantha?"

"Beating her, beating her, shouldn't have done that, shouldn't have done that—"

"Stop it will you?"

She banged her temple with the heel of her hand: "She *needs* it, she *knows* it"—she pushed off the dune

116

and ran by him; she stopped, listening. "Gaylord? Gaylord?"

"Amarantha?"

"Oh good but don't touch us, don't touch us"—she knelt before him and embraced his hips; she turned her head aside and said over her shoulder, "It's all right, it's all right"—she turned to him and kissed briefly where she had punched him. She lay her palms against him; her face gazed up. "You see? You see? She's sorry."

"Amarantha—"

"Mm."

"Who's 'she'?"

"No don't touch us"—she turned—"Go away bitch!"—she lay her cheek against his belly.

"Tell me who the bitch is, won't you, baby?"

"Oh you don't know? Oh—well we *told* you, she's the watcher, Gaylord, she's always fighting us and she hates us and she says it's our fault but it—well never mind, she's shut up now, she's beaten because she's ashamed at what she tried to do isn't she—Aren't you? Aren't you? You'd better be"—kissing him, she said, "She is, Gaylord—"

"Don't now, baby—"

"Oh."

"I know you're sorry, baby."

"Okay. Well"—she stood up. "Come on then, we going swimming? Forgot our bathing suit but—"

"Amarantha? *Our* bathing suit? Two of them?"

"Oh—I never did get a bikini but—"

"Who didn't?"

"Well—what? Gaylord? What'd you say?"

"Who's this 'us', Amarantha?"

"Well *we're* us Gaylord—we're all of us us, don't you see—Gaylord?" She patted his hands, which were resting on her shoulders. "You? You there?"

"Who's us, Amarantha?"

"Oh there's a whole bunch of us and—Gaylord?"

"What, Amarantha?"

"I haven't done that in a whole year—"

They walked down the beach toward the waves. "Jump down now"—they landed from the sand stair abandoned by the tide's last reach; they shuffled slowly, shoving their toes into the sodden sands down toward the flaps of hissing wash. She started as an attack of water shot coolly round her ankles. It gasped away, padding her feet with wet sand. Letting go his hand, she turned to trudge along the shore, while the surf heaved and exploded down the emptiness.

Feet splashed beside hers then, and hands fell on her shoulders from the dark.

"Amarantha, what happened?"

"No—let me walk—"

"We can walk all you want, but answer me?"

"You'll tell my doctor, Gaylord."

"Why should I do that, now?"

"Well—you're supposed to tell them what happens, and I bet you will."

"You going to call the cops since I told you they were looking for me?"

"Well no of course not why should I?—Oh."

"What's happened to you, baby? You should've told me you're so scared of me—I thought you were asking for a shove to push off with, I didn't know, I hadn't any idea of all this."

"I did tell you, Gaylord."

"You didn't hardly but hint."

"Well—I guess I didn't"—she stopped walking and turned her back to him. "My dress."

"What?"

"*I* can't help it if I don't own a bathing suit—the ankle water makes me cold and we're not really on the beach if we're dressed for the city, and—well we're sunbathing, okay?"

"Will you make up your mind?"

"We can talk while we're sunbathing! And you're not my doctor so you shouldn't want to hear. You saw me anyway."

"I don't know what I saw."

"You don't?"

"I'm supposed to?"

"You really don't?"

"I don't got any idea what you were doing."

"Well"—the small clatter of her dress's zipper scraped along the sigh at their feet of broken waves. "Help me?"

"All right baby but I must say—"

"Come on!"

He reached beneath her raised arms, unzipped her dress, drew it off her shoulders. She took it from his hands, and gathering it at her bosom, as he watched quietly, she walked, waddling slightly, up the wet rise to dry sand.

"Up further, Amarantha, the tide's coming in."

She stepped twice more. When the dress dropped along her legs, she lay down on her belly, elbows out, her cheek on her hands. Beside her, she heard his clothes rustle in the silence.

"The sun, Gaylord—I don't usually like it, but—"

He watched it resound from the white back, white waist, white spot of buttock blinking blindly from a tear in white cotton; thighs, calves, white sand. He bent and reached to twist and spread apart the strap across her back. She stirred. "Those boys shouting?"

"No, baby."

The strap swung out to either side; he flung his black body on the sand.

"*You've* got one of her, Gaylord—you've got one just like her and at least his shoes are off—and what if the part of you that likes me if there is one and the one with the shoes started fighting with each other both screaming at the same time and neither would give up and there was no way to compromise, then you'd split apart too."

"It doesn't work that way with me, Amarantha. I feel one way then the other. And I can't understand what you mean by splitting, or this idea of calling my feelings 'him', or myself 'we.' "

With a driftwood stick she gouged holes in the embracing heat of the sand. "*That's* because you're sane, Gaylord, but it's just a lie you tell yourself. Because really you're a whole bunch of Gaylords existing all the time, and your self that holds them together is nothing but a habit you learn when you're little, it's something you invent and it's something you can lose—"

"I ain't been in these realms, Amarantha. You saying you free of consciousness right now? Then who is it that's talking to me?"

"No, silly, not now"—she tossed the stick and turned her head to him; yellow points of sun shone in her eyes. "Listen, Gaylord, there is an Amarantha like your Gaylord, an 'I' Amarantha, but she's not very strong, I guess I've found *that* out—I was blind from an accident, listen, and I had amnesia, and then I started remembering in dreams, and finally one night I woke up far enough to know that I didn't want to be the Amarantha who'd lost what I'd lost and done what I'd done, and who people could hurt and for things to bump into, I wanted to be nothing and not remember anything, and I pushed myself away from myself, trying to strangle the I-myself in me, and listen, it worked, it only took two hours for it to be destroyed. After that I never said 'I', Gaylord, 'I want this', 'I'm doing that', it was always, when I started talking again that is, 'She wants this', 'They're doing that,'—and when I got better, 'we're doing this', and 'we did that,'—but never 'I'm doing this' Gaylord, because for two years 'I' didn't exist, there was nothing but a lot of voices swirling around my brain and screaming down the darkness at me, and I hadn't one bit of control over them, because there wasn't any 'I' *to* control them, and I'd never know where they were coming from, except there wasn't any 'I' *not* to know, and I wasn't even really unconscious, like you said, it was worse, I had nine different people being conscious in the same head, and they didn't get along any better than any other group of people, and sometimes they'd shout and yell and rattle and tumble at each other, fighting and tearing at each other, and I'd jump around and break things and kick the other patients and scream and rip my clothes and bash my head against the walls. Then they'd quiet me with drugs. And other times, this'll show you—Gaylord, are you listening?—other times I'd wander around bleating like a stupid sheep and asking everybody 'Where's Amarantha? Where's Amarantha? Of course the other patients they'd either mumble or screech at me, or sometimes they'd tell their own stories back to me with this kind of haywire comradeliness, but the nurses, and the doctors when they were there, around once every six months, they'd come up and say, 'You're Amarantha. Amarantha, you're Amarantha.' That was my therapy and it was a lie, because I wasn't Amarantha, I was nothing but a fat sheaf of she's and a fat sheaf of shattered-up she's doesn't add up to a person you can name. Except one day this volunteer, this college girl comes up to me while I'm in a quiet mood and wandering around where's-Amaranthaing and she says 'I don't know, did you lose her?' and wham for the first time in about a year I answer somebody's question and I say 'Yes we did and we can't remember where we left her, do you have her?'

121

And the girl says 'No, but I'll help you look, can I?'—'Would you?' So we spend a whole afternoon looking under chairs and pillows and mattresses and tables and behind radiators and all through the courtyard and it started to rain and we're calling, she thought of this, we're calling, 'Amarantha? Amarantha?'—turning over rocks and digging in the flower beds—'Where'd you go and hide yourself, Amarantha?'—crawling under bushes and she's looking up trees 'Amarantha?'—and finally we'd looked all around and it stopped raining and I flew into this rage because we'd failed and I though she'd been tricking me she'd been hoarding Amarantha all the while and I butted her against the building and got my hands on her throat and I nearly strangled her."

A sudden hiss whispered below them; their toes were sucked by the climbing tide. Smiling, she took his hand that was bunched by her shoulder and squeezed his wrist as if to strangle it. The sun sat on their necks. "How'd you get out, Amarantha?"

"That college person—they tried to put me in a prison for the criminally insane? Those places are the bottom, but the girl refused to press charges, and she told her shrink about it, they all have them you know, and he got a lawyer, and my brother was in on it but he wasn't twenty-one, so *her* shrink who's now *my* shrink got custody of me and off I went from the shitheads to the lunkheads. And well he helped me by getting me into a private hospital, but I've never really got to like him because he hates my phantasies, for me to have them I mean, he loves them to play with, and I know damn well it was all because I was a stupid interesting case—"

"You sure of that now?"

"Well—I guess I don't know but—anyway Gaylord I've been pulling out of it slowly ever since, and I've been living out of the hospital for five months now, and Amarantha well I haven't completely found her yet but she's seeping into me more and more and—"

She shrugged and wagged his hand that she held by the wrist; she lay his fingers on her mouth then, counting them. Their legs, furred with sand, rubbed and swung over and back. When she rose on her elbows, her breasts loosed from their cover. Their perspiration mingled while his mouth moved over her ear. She said, "It's hot, we ought to go in."

He rolled over and sat up. "Yeah."

"Don't, Gaylord, it's happening—"

He rubbed his brow, which was heated to a heavy prickled weakness. "How long you planning to stand on the edge?"

She reached; held his foot. "Try? Help me over?"

"Tell me what this watcher is."

She thumped her fist on the mound of sand before her: "*No! No! No!*" She turned up smiling at his startled face. "That's her, all the time—"

He chuckled, swiped at a scouting hermit crab whose witch's claw of legs was gulped by a pock in the sand. "What's she doing, how'd she get in, why's she there?"

"She's the last of the she's." They said nothing for a while. He threw small smooth stones into the waves. Their baked thoughts slowed. Below their feet the war-waging sea rose in endless ranks to attack them at a run and to fall gasping just short of them and crash in a white roil. Their ears thudded with the thousand deaths. He gazed beyond across the barren fields, tufted here and there with white as with the smoke of far engagements, to where, at the round horizon, there watched a pale general's lens of moon.

She sat up next to him then, hugging her freed breasts; her back stung. He lay his arm along her

123

shoulders. She said, "I was telling you, remember? About the accident? It was a hit and run truck, no one knows exactly how it happened except the person who did it, because I can't remember it, or anything else a couple of months before and after, and then there was a third person—he was going to marry me, he said he was anyway, and I came to Boston to be with him, he was studying engineering at Boston University."—the length of her body shivered. "I have this dream, and there's no way of proving it's about the accident, but what happens is he and I are walking up this road in the middle of the night and we've been having this argument—he'd just put off the marriage for a second time and he's being shitty, apologizing and accusing me at the same time—he always did that—so I run into the road to get away from him and he chases me and we start running up this hill and I've shut my eyes and ears to keep his claptrap out; we're running and he's yelling, and we reach the top of the hill and suddenly there's a truck and he's there, he grabs me by the neck and slam he knocks me clear and there's a thud and it's him hit, and the truck goes by, and he's falling flying across the road and there's blood on his head and I see his eyes, Gaylord, looking at me—those eyes, listen, I wake up and they're there, ripped out of his head and hovering just out of reach in the dark like a pair of plums, and they're looking at me, holding it over me how they'd be alive in his head if it weren't for what I'd done—and this drill of a voice is with them, it's an old biddy gossip who used to blah at me back home when I was a kid and tell me what not to do because this child without a mother needed curbing, and the voice and the eyes are the watcher, making sure I don't forget, drilling and staring whenever anything begins."

He shook her by the arms. "Baby. If you saw this

124

cat of yours, and the truck had already gone by, how come you're blind then?"

"You mean how come I'm not dead? Because *some*thing smashed the back of my head in afterward, don't you see? Maybe another car coming over the hill, I don't know—but the watcher won't let the dream finish, and let me find out, because then it might turn out it wasn't my fault that I'm blind— that's the point, Gaylord, because the she's are supposed to be protections that keep you from risking too much while you're rebuildiing, and they sup- posedly leave when you don't need them any more, and they all have left but her, and I don't even think she's one of them, I think she's some kind of demon trying to take over my body and live off me."

His hands on her clenched in warning. "There's a couple of kids just turning the headland, baby. Think we'd better hit the waves for a while. You want to go in?"

"Sure, yes, I'm broiling—you think they'll bother us?"

"Naw. We'd best get you decent though. Sit up straight now."

"Well—"

He caressed her. "You look real fine, Amarantha— well, they're coming."

"Oh—"

"How the hell does this clasp—?"

"Here," she said.

"You got it?"

"Yes—shit, I was just getting used to this." They stood and walked; their feet splattered in thin rushing tongues. "So listen, it's not you I'm hedging against, it's her."

"She ain't too interested in having me around, I imagine. She vote for George C. Wallace?"

"She certainly did because just one slip and you could take over from her"—They shoved their shins through the heavy cold of the surf. "The people? They coming?"

He looked round: the specks had swelled into boys. A spotted dog searched in their wake. "Yeah. They'll go by." He watched her crouch into the spent surf. "Your demon won't go by, though. Far as I can see she going to dump you off the deep end and land you in the bin again before she letting me into you."

"*No* because the shoes and your picking me up at the top of High Dune got her going, I told you, but if we can get far enough along before she gets out of her mouse hole, then it'll be too late for her." She grinned up to him. "That's my strategy."

"Yeah? When?"

"You've got to have patience—"

He laughed loudly. "What is this thing, some kind of shit allegory?"

"No! God damn you—"

"When."

Barreling water collapsed on their shoulders; she sat back on the smooth nape of the wave. "Come on, Gaylord." She churned quietly into the cool dark. Her hair led her out, writhingly lazing, and her wet belly glinted with a crowd of suns. Chuckling and shouting: "Your time running out!" He splashed the ocean on his skin. Drops scampered down his chest as if in fright. He followed with his eyes the curled athletic brow of a wave as it sprinted down the sideways lanes of surf to finish on a sandbar and fling out its arms in triumphal exhaustion. The chattering contaminated rippling elves that had been his cat's bearers splashed into his memory, and he felt, hoping not to perceive by what association, his chilled loins licked by a warm fear. "Pale chestnut and blue eyes, My handsome brown."

126

"Hey, you coming in?"

He dove into a wave. Rising in a wilderness of blue hills: "Amarantha?" Her answer drew his glance as the concealing water abandoned her in a trough, revealing cloth-clung skin. She called: "We going to make a bargain?"

His wounded shoulder ached as he ploughed toward her. "What then?"

"*I* promise not to ask anything of you, I mean really not—"

She disappeared as a wave humped between them. "You will though, Amarantha."

He hovered on a crest and looked down on her as she yelled, "Well maybe I will but you can refuse me, don't you see? You'll have this over me, like what I'm promising you? So if you bother with me afterwards it's your choice and your fault what happens—" He tobogganed down the wave. Their bodies bobbed together, flailing intimately at random. "And you promise—well you promise not to whomp me absolutely like a steamroller, and to wait just a little, like till I tell you?"

"Such as when?"

"Such as till the sun goes down and everything's like you, the whole world's like you and it won't be so hard to let you be it? Gaylord?"

He patted her sodden head. "That little vigilant loves a good symbol, doesn't she?"

"No you don't, because we aren't going to talk about her any more, instead we're going to finish her, because that's my other promise, that I'm going to make this worth your while, you'll see, and that brings me to the other thing?"

"What then, baby?"

The surf hurled them under; rising and clearing her brow, she said, "Like you have to promise, listen, you have to promise it isn't any allegory and promise to lie

127

and pretend and not see and to say I'm not white, I'm not one of these white chicks, or one of these nonblack chicks or however you think of it, Gaylord? Gaylord, where are you? Gaylord give me your hands—I'm just a girl, Gaylord—promise I'm just a girl, just a girl—"

viii

On opaque windows, black letters shone:

ROXBURY COMMITTEE FOR THE JOBLESS
Richard Whitney, Chairman.

John stepped through the door into a long room filled with the voices of thirty men and women, who were seated in haphazard groups of wooden folding chairs. By the window at the end of the room stood the chairman, a small mustachioed man whom John greeted with a wave and who raised his eyes to meet John's briefly and, it seemed, without recognition. A weak snubbed smile remained on John's face while he stood in the doorway and stared round the room.

"Would someone shut that door?"

The voices receded. Teetering paper-white cliffs caught and mystified his eye; after a moment they resolved into reams of printed leaflets stacked along the walls. Shanks of shadow from the ceiling fan strutted over them. He heard then:

"Hey, would you shut that door?"

Shutting it, he sat down sullenly on the nearest chair. A woman was next to him. He watched her brown hands fret on her knees. He wondered if it were to him that she was saying, "*Yes* I'm telling you, just like it was a signal. Them union men start in with the fists and it ain't five seconds but there's ten, twenty, thirty cops slamming in everywhere and they're fighting alongside of the union, ain't one of those white men got busted, not one, while I'm sitting in the station in need of ten stiches and they got the nerve to book me for assault on an officer."

Another woman was answering her, "I know it, I know it—"

"Concussed heads and broken arms besides, I mean everybody caught it—"

John looked up to the speaker: a fortyish woman he did not know. Her head was bandaged with a turban of wrapped white gauze. He said to her, "When"—he cleared his throat, "Where was this, sister?"

"At the picket-line this morning, at the plant, didn't you hear? They say we lost our permit and there ain't going to be any march now—"

He frowned and for a long minute nodded abstractedly, though thinking nothing; when he looked up to speak to her again, she had gone. Over the mix one voice came clearly now: "Look, you're out to fight a union, you're into politics at a goon level. None of this is any surprise. Yes." The speaker was the chairman; he was leaning against the window and answering questions John could not hear. "That they worked it out beforehand with the cops, you can be certain. How much higher up it went, you don't know. Maybe besides stopping our picket there were certain people waiting for an excuse to get the soldiers out; that's the idea I think." Silence moved down the room as he went on, "Brothers and sisters, I guess you all know what went on this morning. It seems two dozen unarmed black men and women used dangerous weapons and superior numbers to assault four dozen armed police." He stood up on a chair and looked round, "I believe some of you were attacking those officers' boots with your bare heads. Show the folks what you used on your victims, Mrs. Henderson." Across the room, the woman John had spoken to rose.

130

"Sister, I understand the men in blue suffered serious injuries to the arm muscle besides, from too much swinging of the billy club. That true now?"

People laughed; the woman gazed at the floor and smiled beneath her bandage, murmuring as she sat down, "I guess they did, Mr. Whitney."

"It seems the Committee has sacrificed its privileges of speech and assembly because of this"—The chairman looked down from his stance on the chair, hands on knees in a half-crouch. "Didn't they teach you in school those were rights? not privileges? Somebody must've lied—well, brothers and sisters, there won't be any mass demonstration tomorrow, at least as far as they've got it planned."

A man interrupted, shouting: "That's one plan we ain't going to follow—"

The chairman whipped his body round. "They've called up the troops to guard that plant, Tom. They're letting fifty of us picket, with soldiers watching over us. They'll close off the streets to the rest. That's what they say."

"They going to leave one street open for the union to pass through and that's wide enough for us."

Someone said, "That's right, brother."

The man called Tom went on: "You listening to me, Whit? I say no union man gets through that line tomorrow until they agree on hearing our demands."

Whit said, "Wait a minute, baby. The union men got the army to escort them. If we get in their way they've got orders to send us to the emergency room."

"Don't tell me their orders, I don't care squat for their orders."

"You're telling me you're still willing to stop that one o'clock shift. You going to tell me how?"

Voices contended in answer; John, in the back of the room, half-listening, half-smiling at nothing, stalked with his hand a fly that wandered down his calf. He thought: The Socratic method today. That means he's got something up his sleeve. Wait. In whisper: "*Now!*" as his hand pounced on the fly. It fled in whining swirls. "Shit." People turned round. He looked aside and saw a telephone. Wait, do you think? She might have cooled off a bit— Her face, clenched in hatred by the bookshelves, leapt against his eyes and leapt away again. Why should he say hello. I'm no use here. Why did I come, did I think they'll bungle it if left by themselves? He nodded at a rufous handsome face whose voice competed down the ·room. *He* thinks so, loudmouth, what's he doing up front? I'm the only white man who belongs here. He shrugged, I don't know, she probably wouldn't answer the phone anyway, *she* doesn't want me, didn't she make that clear enough? What are you debating? If I were black, it'd be all right. Nobody'd notice. There he is. Get him. He lifted his hand and slapped at the fly while Whit shouted for attention, "People are saying—people are saying that—"

With humming complacence the fly touched here and there on John's body, rubbing its forelegs briskly together at each stop as if to say, like a safecracker, "Now then!" John laughed and said, "Shh." The fly departed to scale a ream of leaflets. In the room, arguments stuttered into murmurs, and Whit went on, "People are suggesting there are two objectives, one to get out a large enough crowd to clog all the accesses to the plant and try to stop the shift that way, and the second to try to force the crowd's entrance into the picket area. The first objective will require fifteen hundred, more likely twenty-five hundred people, but I think we have a way to do that, that's what Mrs. Henderson is here to explain to you—now are these to be our objectives, shall we discuss that first?"

"May I say something, Whit."

"Yes, sure, professor."

The man with the rufous face stood. "If these are our objectives, then I wonder why we don't ask some of the brothers from the guerilla groups to come and give us a lecture on tactics." There was stillness in the room. "Perhaps that in fact appeals to some of you. In that case I gather you realize that you're asking tomorrow for a bloody Sunday of no mean proportions."

"Why do you think that would happen, professor?"

"Because we know what happens when black people defy the U.S. Army. There is slaughter. Now if I understand the ideals of this Committee—"

John watched him with a smirk as he talked on. He's crazy, what does he think he's lecturing them on, does he want them to give up without a fight? He doesn't know anything and they don't want him, Christ, can't he see their faces? If he doesn't dare put his body on the line what's he doing here?

"Look we already have five in the hospital, where's our picket line gone to if they put the rest of us there?"

The professor was gesturing with his arms; John covered his eyes. Oh Jesus   If they took his advice they'd never forgive him   It's always been that way It's just come to the surface   He's deaf if he can't see it   With her too   She's always hated herself for wanting my approval   Her clenched face flashed against his eyes. She says her friends think she's outdone them or betrayed them   That's a projection She's the one who thinks she's outdone them and at the same time betrayed herself   It's obvious   What profiteth it a man   Our marriage is based on the neuroses of Tomism   These people have left that behind   She follows   She doesn't want me   She

talks about my hounddogging   She's projecting
She's always projecting   She wants to go back
home and be untied from me and be herself   Finally
she realizes I've been no use to her   No wonder
Gaylord didn't show up   I can't amuse him   She
can have the house I guess   I'm on my way downhill
now

Into his thoughts and the professor's words a
near-falsetto shout broke: "What you talking about
the Committee escalating? It's the *pigs* escalating with
bringing their soldiers in, we're only going on with our
picket line—"

The professor shouted back, "You make those
distinctions to the dead."

The man called Tom stood up, "You tell me what
distinctions you planning for Whit to make to the
people at that rally tomorrow? He going to tell them
go home, the man is arrived and we going to have to
lie down? We're done with that stage I'm telling
you"—There was a murmur as people echoed: "With
that stage, brother"—"Yes"—and he went on, "We
aren't planning any dead, understand? We planning the
same kind of unarmed protest we always done, you
listening to me, Iannucci? You afraid of the guerrilla
brothers with the guns, well you want to give them a
golden chance to step forward by having us sit on our
ass tomorrow and leave the field to them."

The professor answered: "It isn't the same kind of
protest we've always done. Don't you think the
presence of five hundred troops alters the picture?
For us and for the brothers with the guns? All I'm
saying is that we justify the troops in the public mind
by this kind of confrontation and the wise tactic is to
petition in the courts against the unwarranted use of
the military."

"Got him." By its mica wing John dangled the

134

dying fly up to the light and studied its last course of spasms. He's living in the past   Doesn't he know when he says the public mind he means the white public mind? What's he think they care for that? This is ridiculous   I'm no use here   Call her   Go home If I weren't such a paranoid   He stood, seeing her laughing face as he had emptied the water pistol into her mouth. Paranoid   If I thought she wanted me, I'd approach her and she would want me   And did I go up to speak to Whit   No   He's probably wondering why I didn't say hello   I'm laughable People would laugh if this were aloud   For God's sake don't invent mind reading— He walked toward the telephone. Listen   He's still talking about court precedents   Isn't he from a law school? I don't think so   Their faces are stones— He said aloud as he dialed, "Iannucci, you're ridiculous. We've obviously got to keep the picket going. You're just afraid for your skin."

Over the phone a computer sang dodecatonically in the emptiness between rings. The professor turned round angrily. "Did you say something, Morrison? We're all afraid, I think."

"They're afraid, you're afraid. They're afraid of losing everything. You're afraid of losing your toupee."—Hurry up, will you, Marian? She could be in the yard I suppose. Will he hit me? No; it's not a toupee. Maybe she's got that televison on, did I get the wrong number?

The professor was saying, " . . . no need for this. We're trying to discuss the matter according to the democratic procedure of the Committee—"

"In that case you've been heard and you're a minority of one. Shut up." I might have dialed the wrong number though. He began to dial again. "Shut up I'm trying to concentrate—"

"I will not, you have no way of knowing if I'm in the minority—We haven't had a vote and we aren't ready for one and your comments are only making it more difficult to get to a consensus."

John interrupted. "Will you look around you, brother, and then sit down or get out and leave this meeting to the people it belongs to."—You'd have thought she'd cool off by now   She's gone out to see one of her friends I guess   She'll have left a note I'd better get home   Is he still shouting at me? He put the phone down. If I show her I'm willing to try, she'll help me   She doesn't mean those threats You can't expect her to understand by words   When trust is gone you have to act   That's what this fool doesn't see

Raised voices were contending in the air. He made a quick paper airplane out of a note that said: "Argument at home Will be back PICKET," sailed it at Whit, and weaved among chairs down the room. At the door he looked round. The professor was approaching, shaking his face at John and hissing: "You're perverse, do you understand me? You're perverse."

"I'm perverse."

At the window Whit was calling: "I think we're ready to vote on our objectives—"

John shouted: "Picket!"

"Right on!"

"The brothers going to picket!"

Among general shouting he walked out and down the hall, past the elevator, ran down the stairs. Why does it bother me to be just a follower now   Am I afraid where they'll go to, like what's-his-name? She as much as said that   She doesn't mean what she threatened   She just wants to be able to reach me I don't know what I said to upset her so much   You

never know what you say in these things   They
heal   Nothing will happen   It was just talk   It was
just talk's nothing John
    Up against the leaflet cliff, professor
    Tartare! Tartare!

● ● ●   Look at these streets. Look at
these people.
    Marian leaned on her elbow against a stoop on a
South End side street and tugged open a beer can,
which foamed stickily over her knuckles. A white man
I used to know, he told me this is where I'm longing
to return. She swung the can up to her mouth. Well
here's from me to you up there, sun—Her heavy
swallows erupted in coughing. Yes, Marian. The place
of your dreams. Crapped-up newspapers kissing at
your ankles. Coming out the nighttime windows at
you, piss and jazz. For example you see this pert bitch
cruising by here, well you watching her make the
momentous decision of the day, is she or isn't she
going to finish her ice cream? No, she isn't, and you
think she going to take two steps from her path to
drop it in a trash can, presuming some merchant ain't
stole the one assigned for this neighborhood, sure,
because that ice cream just kind of swoops real natural
from her sweet black fingers and plops on the
pavement for some mongrel dog to gobble if some
mongrel kid don't scoop it up and slurp it first, and
you think she looks back? Why she didn't even notice
what she done. She's too busy looking up and down
the length and breadth of men like that tall dealer in
the poker game over there on the car hood, and I ain't
going to blame her for that, because isn't he a pretty
man?
    "Haven't seen you around, baby—"

137

The speaker leaned smiling over the banister next to hers. She turned her back on him with a jerk of her shoulders. Her beer can was empty and she fumbled to free another from the packaging as the man strolled past her, looked round, lingered his glance over her, humorously laughed, turned, and disappeared. She felt blood in her face and ripped the can open, angrily muttering. "If that husband of mine ain't hounddogging on me, well he might as well be, what the hell's he think he's doing by letting me alone after what he said? Man who loves his wife going to lay claim to her, he ain't going to stand there and listen to her threaten other men at him, he's going to get her by the neck and shout some kind of sense at her and what does he tell me but to go on go out and look for it—You tell me what I'm supposed to do with such a bunch of preverse crazy talk? Dog or not, ain't a man going to have some pride? I yell at him how I will, I'm going to get even with him and he answers real polite how he'll be down to headquarters if I need him. I never heard of such a thing.

"He probably bored to shit I went on so long this afternoon. He got some white hussy waiting on him downtown and he afraid she going to get impatient and wonder where he gone to—I'm real sorry honey but I was having words with that dumb bitch nigger wife of mine. He probably wish I would call headquarters so I get the true picture through my thick head once and for all that he ain't got time for me. He got sweeter fields to plow."

She hurled the full beer can to the stairs. It buckled and the foam swelled. Stamping, clenching her jaws together, she watched the foam dribble and seep down the steps to spread muddied on the pavement in a flat pool. She muttered aloud again: "Faggot son of a bitch he going to tell himself *I* left him. That's how

138

he's going to think of it. I can hear him, 'Well I guess it was the best thing in the end.'—Oh yes baby you going to handle it beautifully, same way you handled being weary of your black brothers, weaving a lot of your university doilies around it and deciding that it's them that are weary of you"—Her face cleared suddenly and she shrugged, chuckling. Far as I can see he kicked away his rights when he walked out that door, my anchor been ripped from his belly, and I'm floating on a sea of anywhere.

She noticed a patch of silence and looked down the sidewalk: hot stares from the poker game were covering her. With a slightly drunken wryness she smiled as she surveyed the dealer, her gaze intersecting his for a swift instant before turning aside. He smiled also and looked down to his cards. He seemed twenty. Her hand tumbled toward the banisters. Where's that beer. I got a mouthful of ashes. She ripped a new can open: The time I spent weeping my face. All that wasted time. She drank and heard from the car hood: "Jake's deal." She watched the dealer's hips as he flowed past her and up the stairs of her stoop, his body pumping forward and back as he walked, his thumbs and third fingers swinging by his thighs with tips mated in a suggestion of snapping. His throat whispered faintly: "*I turned my back on Jack and he ain't coming back*."

Above her on the stairs, he leaned on the banister and looked up the street as she looked down it, each now in silence. The poker game continued shoutingly. He said finally, not turning to her, "People watching you, know that?"

Smiling and gazing down: "No." She reached a beer up the banister. He took it but did not open it. He said: "Cats saying that's a foxy-looking chick to be out on a drunk, maybe on speed, I told them you ain't though." She smiled no again. He went on, "You got the smell of the honky on you; don't you? You one of Vincio's undercover?"

She stared at him. "You mean am I police?" He smiled at her, nodding slightly. She felt the beer gather weight in her stomach. Plucking the package of cans from the stair, she walked away.

His quick steps fell in beside hers. She watched her feet advance then as they ambled slowly. He offered his arm. She looked at it a moment, then taking it, she pointed, without looking up, to an abandoned tenement from which jagged windowpanes grinned.

"I was raised in that building." She touched her foot on his, "If I'm new here, then you haven't even got here yet."

"So where you been to since I got wise?"

"Springfield."

"Lots of chicks around here from Springfield."

"Are there?"

"Oh, yeah. Your folks here?"

"No, man."

"So where you making your bed?"

"Bus station." She added: "I come looking for work."

"What kind of work?"

"Could be domestic—thought it might be better here."

"If it is, that don't say much for Springfield." They laughed for a moment and stopped walking. With an amused smile he stepped aside to drawl his eyes carefully over her. Their stares met in pleasurable mocking. Then raising his eyebrows, he jerked his head sideways towards a brownstone. Stepping back, she squinted upwards: "I kind of like that sun, though—" He crooked his arm around her back, stretched his fingers, touched her breast: "We going to finish that beer." Her shoulders hunched with a shudder. "All right—"

He herded her up the steps and through doors. "What you call yourself, baby?"

"Hmm?"

"I said what's your name going to be?"

"It's Martha."

"Yeah? I got a kid sister named Martha—"

His heels thudded near her face as she followed him up stairways. She breathed with a sudden heavy exhaustion and did not listen to what he was saying. They stopped climbing; vaguely she watched him fuss with a key. "I'm Jimmy." He kneed the door open. "In you go."

She felt sober and old. "You said something."

"That's right, baby. Here's the place."

He stood in the doorway; dim furniture rested beyond.

"Yeah, all right."

"Come on, Martha." He led her in, his hand on her shoulders; he pointed to a bed. "Have a seat. I'm going to open us some cold."

She stood in the middle of the floor. "I don't want none."

"You don't? Thought you did." He took a can from her package.

"You say 'Jimmy'? You got a cigarette, Jimmy?"

"Yeah." He stood beside her, and descended his hand down her spine. "How old are you, Martha?"

She said after a moment: "Thirty—I'm thirty."

"Naw, you kidding?"

His hand reached the hem of her short skirt; she bit her lip, shivering. "Thirty-three—"

"Bullshit, I was thinking about twenty-seven or

something"—his hand left her frozen muscles and he walked away. "You keep yourself real nice for a domestic."

"Domestic? I ain't no domestic—oh." Her slow smile splayed into a chortle. "That what I told you?" Loud laughter gathered in her face and she turned completely round on her heel and fell back on the bed. "What else did I tell you?" Pressing her mouth shut, she laughed through her nose and watched her hands jump on her belly in its silent spasms.

"You told me you out looking for some time."

She saw his face above hers. Making a fist of her left hand, she shoved her wedding ring up to his eyes. Each stared at it. "That all he going to give you to take to bed with you, Martha?"

She turned away onto her belly. "Where's that cigarette."

He stood and walked across the room. Reaching into a drawer, he said, "Know what the trouble with you is, baby?" Walking toward her, he lit a cigarette and extended it to her in his hand. "You figure that wedding band is some kind of chain. Don't you? He could jugg ten honkie bitches under your nose and you'd still crawl and kiss his asshole any time he ask you."

She made a sound of disgust and said, "What do you know about it? Nothing."

He waved the coal before her eyes. "Smoke. I know about it."

"Then you just tell me, brother." She smoked. "You tell me."

"Okay, baby, here's to you." From the window he surveyed the alley below; he sat against the sill. "I'm a dealer, see? Going to make you a deal. You put out for me, I'll save a marriage before I'm old enough to vote. Get me? You think there's something Our Father Hallowed Be Thy Shitass Name about that cat of

142

yours. I'm telling you there's no husband ever lived that I ain't got a hog on me same as him. I prove that to you"—he drank and watched her from around the can as she smirked. "I prove it, that's what you going to do, you going to break into hysterics when you finally dig it that this cat you been moaning after all this time got no monopoly on what to do you with. You tell him that, he ain't going to treat you like furniture no more, that your opinion?" The empty can soared from his fingers and sang on the concrete below. "Meanwhile you got some catching up to do if I ain't mistaken."

She lay back, gazing at fly-walks on the ceiling. "You got it all worked out, don't you, Jimmy? Like my husband, he got it all worked out."

"That a fact, Martha?"

She smoked, grimaced, studied the ash. "Shit, he surrounded the business of loving so thick with his notions that he can't even get to it no more, and you telling me about your glorious piece of male organ so haloed around and about with your pride that you think I'm automatically going to worship it same as you do—" She shoved herself up onto her elbows and looked at him. "Nothing personal, man, but you telling me a mere pair of bodies slobbering over each other on the floor here's going to clean one inch of crap from our minds; well I'm telling you if we could look through that ceiling and far enough, we'd see a sky full of faces laughing at us. Bunch of weird contortions we propositioning each other with, we ain't got the faintest idea what for we doing them, you puffing your pistons ready to wiggle and drool and stink and slime yourself for nothing. *That's* my opinion." She paused, and began to chuckle again as he walked toward her from the window. "Got a hog on you same as my husband, do you?"

"That's right, Martha."

143

"Let's see it, then."

"You going to be first."

She sat up on the edge of the bed while he stood before her and against her, between her knees, and he reached round her shoulders for the zipper of her dress. She mocked: "You're going to drill me with it and you're shy about showing it to me?" Coughing spurts of small laughter, she reached out and rubbed him with her palms; she unsnapped his pants and tugged them down; she held his penis while it swelled. Her chest shook and the corners of her lips twitched as she studied it. Then she swatted it and lay back and broke into guffaws.

"Okay, baby." He stepped out of his pants and leaned over her. "Know what I'm going to do first?"

She looked at him with wide-open eyes. "You think I care squat what you do first or last or any time?"

"No, of course not." They stared at each other. Then he seized her wrist and twisted it; spidered his fingers down her hand to clutch her ring. Her hand bunched to a fist.

"Lay off that."

"There's the prisoner crying for her chains."

"That's right, now lay off."

"I never do a chick that's dressed, Martha."

Her free hand lunged to claw at his cheek. He caught the hand and bent her arm beneath her back. "No, baby." His naked knee rose onto her belly and his full weight clamped her to the mattress, and yanking back double the hand that wore the ring, he said: "Want me to break all your fingers, or just some of them." Her fist opened. He spit on her finger and wrenched the ring free. She shouted:

"Give it to me will you?"

"You don't need it, Martha." He held it up glinting to the window light and read: " 'J to M with all love.'

Aw, ain't that darling? 'June twenty-two, nineteen fif'—" His throat stung with her nails. Gripping the ring between two knuckles then, he slammed it to her cheek. "J to M." Blood bloomed. He kneeled up onto her, sunk his weight into her lungs, and smashed her breath out as he swung from her body, off the bed and to the window. The gold shimmered in lanes of sun. With a smile he watched her wheeze and double over, gagging, pawing for breath, till she heaved up at last; then he flicked the ring out the window and blinked while it leapt gently tinkling down the walls to be buried in a mound of old boards.

"Let me see where it went—please, Jimmy—"

"Time to see what's second, baby." He blocked her from the window, slapping her shoulders back playfully as she struggled.

"Jimmy please, I'm sorry, it was nothing personal—"

"That's all right. This ain't going to be either." He let her approach, then craned back her chin with the heel of his hand and shoved her stumbling backward onto the bed, her dress flying. He stood over her quickly with his fist raised. She cringed. "You going to get fucked while you senseless? Or while you still feel it."

Her hands leapt over her face while his fist shot down and batted her temple against the wall. "No don't, I'm telling you man you don't have to, I'll go along, don't you understand I ain't used to this, you went fast and I just got upset—" She reached to touch his thigh, smiling tentatively as he flinched. "I'd like to." Her hand slid to his buttock over naked skin. "Please, I would really—"

He lowered his fist slowly; laughed. "You're some kind of weird chick, ain't you?"

"You sure of that? You ever had someone old as me before?"

"No."

"So help me with my dress?" After a moment: "No hold on"—half-unzipped, she looked up and stayed his hand. "I forgot; is your john in the hall?" He nodded, frowning. "I'm going to go, okay? I'm still in my period." She looked aside to her pocketbook and his hand quickly fell upon it. She said, "Go ahead, I don't carry anything you're thinking about"—he scooped inside it with his fingers, saying then: "All right, Martha. I'll walk you down there."

He stepped back, kicked his pants up to his hands, began to put them on. Standing up, strolling toward the door, she watched him: "You some pretty man. Moment I set eyes on you." He looked down to place his second foot into a trouser leg; "Yeah." When the pants rose round both his ankles, she wrenched the door open and bolted down the hall toward the stairway. She heard him stumble and curse.

She ran down the stairs. Sudden laughter bellowed up from below, covering his shouts. Two men from the poker game stood in her way on the landing. "Well here's that nice friend of Jimmy's."

"Let me by—"

"Ain't you even going to say hello?" They grabbed her elbows.

"No let me go! Let me go!"

"Jake! Hold her!"

"We got her."

Jimmy said from the top of the stairs: "You got some unfinished work to do, Martha." He began to walk down, waving a pistol in his hand. The men on the landing turned their hips to her kicking knees. She screamed. "You best calm yourself, baby. Your man got a piece."

"He isn't my man and you let me go!"

"Sorry, baby."

A new voice said: "Don't a nigger move."

The new speaker was hidden on the hall below them. Jimmy stopped and called uncertainly: "Randy, don't you fuck with me, Randy—"

There was silence. Then: "That little Jimmy up there? Why boy you ain't two months out of the house and you playing with a piece?"

"Come out of there, Randy—"

"No, baby." He said to one of the men who held her: "Jake, let the woman go."

Jimmy yelled, "Unless you want her dead in your hallway? Or are you going to keep your faggot mouth out of this?"

"Who's the woman, Jake?"

"Don't know, Randy. She's Jimmy's woman."

"I ain't no kind of Jimmy's woman."

Randy said: "Baby, you maybe got a husband Jimmy don't want to meet?"

"He's in Springfield," Jimmy shouted, "and he don't care shit about her and you going to clear your ass out of here?"

"You got a brother then, baby?" She made no answer and he said, "Hear?" He paused. "I ain't getting shot for you. You got a brother now?"

"It's Mandus Williams."

The men who held her winced at her and shook their heads. Randy whistled and said: "I keep telling that boy he got to go to school and get some brains for his self—"

Jimmy was descending the stairs, saying mildly, "Her name's Martha. Mandus ain't got no sister named Martha. I know that."

"And how you know her name Martha?"

"Why she told me."

"She just told you she's Mandus's sister, and you figure you can tell which time a bitch is lying, you that dumb? Let the woman go, Jake."

"Randy Johnson, I am Marian, I swear it, get him off of me—"

"Baby, if this is Mandus's sister I hope you got your things packed—"

"Don't tell him!" Marian said.

"All right baby, you come down now."

They let her go; she rushed down to the hall below. She turned toward him, "Randy I—"

He hissed: "Get home."

She ran out, hesitated, and suddenly wrenched by cramps, she stumbled on towards the house where her brother lived.

ix

Gaylord?

Gaylord! Get the door over here   I know   Do
the latch first will you   Okay there   Gaylord?

Gaylord

Stupid car   Well it sounded like the motorcycle
You'd have thought he'd be back by—

Hurry up, will you please?

He said I won't be but twenty minutes baby   He's
as crazy as me   This is twenty minutes?   It's chilly
in here   Close the door then stupid   Well isn't it
night yet?

Underwear on the stove dry by now? Funny
woodstove   Funny bird-hunter's shack   We're staying here   He's gone to buy food   I wish that
crummy sun would hurry up and turn over and start
dreaming   Stove over here   Yes ouch

Dry I'll say   They're beginning to disintegrate
Wave them outside then   Window over the bed
I know   You'd better take his too before they
burn up   Okay   Some bathing suit   He was
wagging all over the place in the water   Fwap slap
along my leg   Lucky those boys were watching   I
think my hands have their own set of brains   It was
all I could do   And that one time   Grab   Well I
thought I'd done it   Don't tell me   Lucky those
boys were watching   I already said that   Because I
don't see how a person can get on with something
faster than this person does

On his way back by now, you think?

Well no wonder because the bed's in the other direction   All these bunks and he only puts down one mattress   Well I suppose I'll just have to, I don't know—bed? Okay

Oh, it's Saturday evening, there're always lines at the grocery store on Saturday evening.

Wind cool them

Hello out there! Hello dunes   Hello Cape Cod

Barren and clear he said, rolling out brown, miles, can you smell the wild roses, baby? Yes and the bayberry

The thing is I sort of have to now, I promised and he can always put his shoes on again   Well I know but   And the pines and salt and sand and heather flowers

Think about it

You are coming back, aren't you, Gaylord? I mean you are, aren't you? He said it'll be night when I get back, baby, and you know what he was referring to since after sunset you promised   Yes because aren't the pines rushing now?

Hey night hey you Afro-American, come on over to the Western Hemisphere will you please? Hey you frizzy-haired matron of the rain, handsome brown dunes to climb on?

Jesus—Jesus no one's here is there? No one's here no one's here is there? Quiet, wind! Breathing?—Come on there isn't anything, come on   You know where that can get you to and if somebody were prowling he wouldn't slam the door   Well, Gaylord, you might've thought twice before you went off and left me   Amarantha, you're not a child   Think about it   Underwear cool enough now   Put them on Okay   No what if someone's here   No one's here I know but if there is   So I'm not putting it on

He won't notice   And if he does   Mm-hm   Well
You don't suppose he's skipped out because I
Put him off I mean with that ridiculous scene on
the beach and telling him everything
Night night night
This shack he'll come back   This shack he'll come
back
I almost feel it's like the seeing-time with him
White is such a thing with him that schiz is just a
detail he hardly even notices   Though I suppose as
far as he's concerned I'm normal for a white person
Isn't that the nifty thing about being the wrong
color   If I were black he'd have seen me perfectly clear
as a nut and he'd have skittered off long ago   Good-
night gull   Go to sleep   Night's coming   Do
you think he likes me   How do I know   I'm a
white chick to him though and that's closer to a girl
than anybody's seen me for a long time and besides if
you were worried about fast it's no wonder he is fast
because it's my body that's white so that's what gets
attention, I've been a head full of voices and he says
I'm a body I'm a body I am though I am I'm afraid
Good night come here, good night yes you come
along old tender heart, old love-arranger
I've tried every schizotrick I know of to get him to
notice that I'm crazy so he won't be interested any
more   Nothing's worked   Isn't that something
Unless he's halfway to Boston by now   Don't tell
me   —That's the thing that scares me don't you see
he could make me into a girl and I'd have to be real if
you took the watcher out   I don't know what she'll
try on him next— More putting him off while leading
him on I guess   I don't know though   He maybe
won't let me   He's kind of forthright   What else
can she try though   I'm sort of being forced into
bed   I never would've believed it'd turn out so well

Do I think that though? What if I can't get ready for
him   He's coming back with the night   He is
There's no one around   You'll have to do what he says
You will   You'll have to and besides listen, it'll be
six months or something till I let myself know I'm as
angry at the watcher as today, I know it, and last
night letting me lose my cane and then in the shower
she has the effrontery   I could've killed her   That's
what I'm saying though, I really could kill her and if I
don't take the chance now, then in a couple of weeks
I'll have accepted her again   I need her though   I do
not   I do though   No,   don't you see you need her
for being the same   You don't need her for being free
Yes I know but if I were free I'd be to blame for
everything   So what, what difference does it make
because you'll already be to blame if you've flubbed it
and he's left   He hasn't   He's coming   Night's
coming   I want them   I want to give in to it   It'll
be like the seeing-time   Better than the seeing-time
Listen

Listen   An owl   A wonderer   It's already night
She's here   I knew that was her breath in the dry
grass and those are her bare feet walking on the dunes
and her knees are wrapping around the pines because I
think every one of those trees down there is standing
from the valley and waving for you night the way he
did for me, please come loving night, race him on
home with your shiningest moon, and if he comes
back, gentle night give me my if he comes

Gaylord!

It's just a stupid car and

Gaylord   Get the door over here   I know do the
latch first silly   Okay there   Gaylord?

Gaylord! Gaylord! Sputter motorcycle die   Pad
pad on the sand he's here squeak step   No Gaylord
don't speak   You're here   Your face Gaylord

152

Listen to his face   Will you listen to his face

Jesus, Amarantha, aren't I allowed to say hello even? Now ain't it like a chick   Can't touch her when you leave   Can't take a moment to put your luggage down when you come back   Yeah that's my eye We're going to be needing it

Nose Gaylord's nose   No stop   Don't say   Because I'm not going to listen   If we talk we'll never get there   She'll come out   Just drop your stupid packages and lend me your hands

Do you mind if I lay the dinner down before you squash it   That's if I've passed my phrenologicals Good now climb down will you? I got to get this bottle open   Pour some wine in you for will-weakening purposes

Okay   Packages out   Hurry up   Something's snapped because I want to but first I want to eat you I've got this funny feeling on the sides of my tongue

Quit jumping around, you got fleas? You're outrunning yourself baby, this business of losing our

Kiss please   I'm very thirsty   Kiss please

Little white virginities

Thank you

You got to cumulate these things in a deliberative fashion   Otherwise I'm going to be left standing and holding the bag (as it were) all over again   Yeah Well you finding any cavi—

Teeth   Gaylord's teeth   Something's absolutely snapped   May I chew on this large and delicious lip please   Will you bend down also-please because my toes are tired

Now baby, I ain't getting worked up so you can suddenly remember your proper upbringing   No thanks   We're going to adjourn the meeting, understand? before the black man in the front row gets up on his feet and starts presenting his demands.

All right Gaylord it's about those hands of yours since we've got to hurry up   Besides I'm beginning to feel rather blatant under my dress   Can we please get our clothes off please   Stupid buttons on his shirt   What? Hey listen where do you think you're going, aren't you interested? He obviously needs the blunt approach   Are you aware of the consequences of such an action Miss Jones   Yes I certainly am   The consequences are at last—Where'd he go? Hey, Gaylord? Hey, Mr. Limp?

She going to let me get this bottle open damn it?

Uff—Hello—Where are we—What's this—

Look Amarantha, I'm trying to   Well she ain't kidding with this is she   Okay baby I'm the last to turn down the request of a lady but I hope to Christ you know what you're doing since

Okay so where the hell?—where the hell?—for Christ's sake where the hell does he keep

Since two seconds from now I wouldn't give a nickel for that watcheress of yours.

Is *this*—? Pine tree   Big deal   More like an aging vegetable.

Yeah now hold on baby   Let me show you There's no need to squeeze   It ain't toothpaste.

Okay but will you please and for God's sake hurry and take off my dress before she gets here   Wait to see if it jumps when he finds out the dress is all I have on, mm-hm will you listen to Gaylord he's filling up   Gaylord's filling up

Just tell me how this dress clasp   Don't tug baby We got plenty of time   Christ you a funny chick

God damn this stupid belt of his   Get out   You'd think these men would make themselves more accessible

Oh yeah is this one of them hook-and-eye—Take it easy, baby, we got all the time in the

Get out   Get out   Gaylord hurry will you hurry

before she ruins things all over again   Tell him then
No I won't   I can't   If he knew he'd never be interested again   Just hurry and it'll be too late for her

One of the material realm's more satisfying little
shatters is the parting of the zipper on a woman's   Now
what? Where's she going?

Shut up   Shut up   Shut up   You've ruined it
You're always ruining everything   He's never going to
bother now

Baby? This ain't another—? Christ, I tried to get her
to move in easy—I hope she don't expect me to stop?

Gaylord, I'm frightened   You can't

You don't have to take this, brother. Once but not
twice. She started this proper, now we're going to
finish. This zipper's coming down.

I can't   It'll split me   Stop it

All right, keep your dress on then, see if I give a
shit. On your back, white girl. On the floor. You want
your arm broke? You sure?—that's better. Nope—
you're wasting your lungs. I already told you. There
ain't a soul in miles.

I am trying to stop him, you're the watcher, can't
you see? He's going to break my arm if I don't do
what he says and then he'll do it anyway and it's my
arm not yours   Shit on you   It's my body
You're not me   You're not taking me over

Dig this, will you? She don't have any pants on
her   I thought I saw them over on the bed   She
planned this whole thing, man, but she gets slow
reactions on my part   Well she figures, give him a
fight   A scenario   Splendid   Yessir   She's one
primitive chick, ain't she?   Fucking watch you going
to get your stones kicked—that's a beautiful scream,
my compliments—I still can break that arm, baby? Let
me in?

Ha ha because it's your fault   You weren't

watching were you when I got him going   You've
got the eyes but you didn't use them and I've got the
body   It's mine   I own it and I'm letting anyone in
it I please

Who's forcing who? Aha, the lady smiles, an odd
hot bitch, full of stories on your own, warm walls,
living walls, little one, little one, here's for you

Mine   That's mine   He gave it to me because it's
my body   It's mine   I'm here all together and I'm
giving in to him   I am   I'm a girl   I'm myself   I
am   I am   I am   I am   I'm Amarantha

● ● ●   Fingers do you know this face
Eyes and wide bones—Hello thoughts   Where'd you
go   It's summer   It's night

Wait, remember, it's the winds out there now calling
back and forth about maybe there'll be rain   Remember   Got that same rushing-around frenzy as the
first day of autumn like it was then   Sure   On the
fields near Rouen   Coming to on the bed of her and
Europe was ours

Oh it's just a man I met and stretched me out every
punctuation mark incredibly fast and isn't leaving

You know what reminded me   That smell they
have those rare times when you've taken their will
away comes crisp and eternal out of the animal
kingdom mad as a cat's eyes. Who the hell is this
chick anyways? Like did you dig how her body's near
the same as Martha's and something in the faces
besides   Yes, man   Perfectly frightening   Except
this one more at the breasts and different eyes, and I
never saw Martha smile like this, even that once

Gaylord   He's called Gaylord   Hey Mister Gaylord did you know you were lying on one of those

Cape Cod ponds of yours which I think would drain away if you weren't staking me down because listen Mister Gay Mister Lord did you hear her walk out   Did you hear her slam the door   Don't say it was the wind   I didn't want to mention it but have you seen her walk in again   No because you haven't Gaylord you haven't Gaylord you haven't

I poured a whole marriage-worth of poison inside of this bitch and she's lying there grinning and arguing with constellations, discussing the matter with celestial forces known only to females—woman who can smile the way you do baby don't need a shrink, needs to go out and teach bitches like my wife, teach them to revel in leaping to the top of being themselves and to make their man feel like he knew what he was doing, not like he'd failed her all the time like he had no power and she hops around from bed to bed trying to locate a man she said   She lied   It was her who wasn't the woman

Excuse me but if you don't mind my saying so, Gaylord, she's gone, she just stalked out   I can feel it   The same as when the others left   I don't know if she'll come back but   Free   You want to touch me? I'm a Buddhist   I'm empty   I'm floating off to the upper left portion of the air   If you want me again, I mean you do of course, you'll have to rope me in like Pecos Bill

Speaking of comparisons of breasts   Time to get that dress all the way off—kind of chick going to perform whatever you suggest just for the gusto of it and still be strenuous when you finished for the week—I expected the mildest pedestrian restrained kind of joust, believe me—no bra either, of course, an interesting combination: raunchy but with wit Come on, dress over the head

Gaylord, the thunder! Listen to the thunder!

White woman's breast, shallow on the top, heavy on the bottom, pretty little half-a-raindrop

Wham again thunder! Saw my Gaylord and tumbled off his chaise longue   Jumped down the sky to strut his clouds   If the man has the woman then the storm will have the night

Come on little chick   Listen to it smash out Sounds like a mind   It's time we battened down and

Leaping storm   Hurtling at her   Roar   Gnash Snap

Well here, this one is for you then, little one, I'll stoke if you'll shine

Gaylord, Gaylord, your stretching pulsing up inside me is the pouncing riding of the thunder in the night   Can you hear him   Pounding her Flinging out his lighting arms   Shattering out the rain, Gaylord, listen, the rain, the rain's come down, testing first, with funny pointed toes on the roof can you hear them, deciding should we rain here, raindrops?   Listen   listen   listen   listen   now they've come in troops, little elves of the night spatter-dancing on the dunes, beating little feet, thumping little stamps, scooting with a hooting on the tin shack roof, tramping through the heather up the sand to the steps, up the steps to the door, rap tap rap tap drum drum drum, knock knock   Gaylord, will you hurry get off, you log you truck, no all the way off because more more more scads of little raindrops joining in the revel, jiggling little bellies, hissing little chants, thwacking with whacking little knuckles on the panes, rain coming in, splat drum splat, drum splat drum, silly swilling spilling milling rain

Hey there, songbird   Bed's over here now Come down feather girl I'm going to preen you   Stop Gaylord   Wait Gaylord   Get the door   Gentle

158

strong handsome Gaylord please get the door   Take me out into the rain? Out into the rain!

No wait be careful   It's raining out there! Here I'll show you—Jesus H. Christ what a madness

Out the door down the steps   Out into the rain!

Hey, where you going to! Hey!

Rain! Ruffle up the heather bush   Frazzle up the pine trees   Rub down the dunes' backs   Swash away Cape Cod

Baby, will you come back out of there? Baby?

Gaylord? Didn't he come? Hasn't he got the sense to come out into the rain? Silly rain, roaring rain, rush swish drone such a rain? Hey you hammer rain, hey you fist, get on down there and punch in the dunes slap down the waves flood the tide drown the sea and flatten absolutely everything will you please?

Delicious, perfectly delicious, what she telling me she from Kansas? She's a goddamn bongo-pounding albino Congolese   That's a jungle in her guts No wonder she attacked me down the beach   That wasn't but a taste   She's going to carve me into steaks, broil my ass for dinner, and chomp my hog for a tea cake—   Screw it on tight   Give her a whupping with it   And ram it into Africa

Where's my satrap   Where's my stallion   Will he hurry please come mount his mare because it isn't polite to keep a person waiting

Shit this ain't no rain, it's the sea stood on its edge and collapsing into place again— Where's she gone to? Better yell   You kidding me, through this bellowing?

Roar ocean hiss   Where are we   Stupid spewing sea   Shiver I'm cold   Gaylord hurry take me back

Wait for one of those lightning claws   There.
To the shack   Take me back
Hey you shivering little witch dance, you going to get the rain kissed off of you?
No wait   The other way
Lie her down here, see, there's a hillock going to hide us from the wind, get some dry sand for her—I'm going to warm you everywhere.
Hey, he's warm—mm-hm not to speak of a certain hot ember next to my leg
You getting a rundown   A complete coverage A thorough inventory.
A blanket of Gaylord and besides I think every inch of the sphere is swooped down and crammed into this person washing over me   The vaults are on his shoulders   The deepest part is at his feet and the outside circumference is in his hands
You hear that sky-man shrieking his jazz up there, I think he's pounding about you, little strange cave-girl wandering in America, about your eyes, about the fall of your throat, about your breasts, which taught the dunes their neighborliness, thunder-man up there splitting his cheeks on his slide trombone, it's in envy of me grazing down your belly, soft hair, soft creases and folds, you hear them clatter-bone witch-men hordes how they clashing their cymbals and demoning and whooping about here, my cavern woman, where her black man sinks in now, all through warm-leafed waves, to drown in summer tides and silent glory.
Kiss me
Kiss these eyes first
Deeper, come in deeper—No stay away from there!
And on your neck, since I remember now little

one, and if you got any pain scrambled in with this scar

Gaylord, please   No I told you, stay away   not all that sadness

Rantha, my bones were cast in sadness, and its mansions stand in my heart, you walk on its lawns when you stroll on my skin, so this tiny plot of it hidden under your hair, let me suck it out and spit it to the thunder, he'll storm it away with his blues

Give me.

Rantha

Gaylord my   Rantha I'm   Gaylord my gay lord   Rantha, I'm inside of you   Gaylord you've brought the darkness inside me   In the middle of you Rantha I'm inside your body   Gaylord split me, pound me, wrench me, burst me, love me Christ you're beautiful Christ you're beautiful Christ you're beautiful

X

John swung off a bus. He walked quickly up steps into a dank vestibule and ran his eyes along printed names beneath mailboxes. He said after a moment, "What's this?—Do you suppose he's already moved again?

"Wait, maybe I've got the wrong building." He stepped back outside and looked above the door: "Yes, number seventy—I'm sure she's with him though, a brother's the natural person to run to—I don't know why I didn't try here in the first place." Through the window in the inner door he saw a form standing dimly in the hallway; he knocked on the glass. "This is probably just more of his mystification." The form approached and the door opened. A shaven head said: "Who?"

John coughed and made a smile. "I'm looking for Mandus Williams. Do you know if he's"—the door closed on his sentence. The shoulders retreated along the hall and leaned against a banister; the fingers plucked in a package for a cigarette. "Well for Christ's sake what kind of bullshit?" John punched the doorbells that stood in a row by the printed names, and he pounded on the glass. "Let me in, will you? I'm his brother-in-law." Smoke wandered from the open mouth, and eyes followed it quietly. "If this is more of Mandus's Apocalypse scenario—I'll bet you he's up there." He lined his forearm along the doorbells and leaned. "Separation he calls it while he apes every detail of his style from the boob-toob police dramas. I'm glad she smashed the stupid thing." The buzzers droned weakly and the shoulders lazily launched from the banister and sauntered toward him. "Oh Lord help us what volcanism. Wait, someone's coming." Another man climbed the steps to the building as the hall door opened. The shaven head reached and wrenched John's arm from the bells and crashed him against the wall.

"Where's Mandus Williams!"

"What's going on here?" A thin man with a dome of African hair ran into the vestibule; the guard drew the gun that had been nuzzling in his belt and stepped back into the darkness. The thin man said: "Oh. Morrison. All right, Walter." He walked past John into the hall.

John stood up, holding his shoulder. "Life is getting far too elaborate for me, I can see that. All I wanted was to talk to Mandus for a minute."

"Later. Dinnertime maybe." The thin man stood in the doorway. "He's not here now."

"He's not. Yes, all right." John scratched his hair, winced, ran his hand behind his neck. "Look, Sam, I came by because—I wonder if my wife's been here, I've been looking for her, she, I—she went off for the day and something's come up"— he was silent before the shaking head.

"Sorry."

"You haven't seen her?"

"In months."

"Yes. Look if she happens to come by will you tell her I was here?"

"Sure."

"No, this is quite important—shall I give you a note? That might remind you. Here." He reached for his wallet.

"Forget it, all right? She won't come by anyways."

"No, look"—He scribbled on prescription paper against the wall. "If you happen to go out, would you leave this with Mandus if he's here then or with your friend here?"

"The doorman. Sorry. We had a little—"

Sam paused and John finished: "Trouble; of course." He folded the note. "Here." He leaned round the half-open door and said to the guard: "You'll recognize her, she's a quite dark-skinned woman, hair short and waved, middle height, wearing a yellow dress today"—he leaned back and watched the thin man cram the note into a breast pocket. "Don't forget, will you, Sam?"

"No problem."

"Okay and thanks. Sorry to bother you—"

"Sure. Goodbye, Morrison."

"Yes well I'd like to come back later if"—the door closed. "Sam?" The forms receded into dimness. He turned and trudged out and down the stoop, kneading his shoulder. Well if she isn't there she isn't there I suppose. I really have called them all have I?

Goodbye, Morrison. Bleak little terrorist. I wonder if he's still an addict? He tugged Marian's address book from his back pocket and leafed; checks lay beside numbers and names. He lay it on the banister beside him. I have called them all

You think I should check the hospitals?

Her threats, I don't know, I suppose it's possible with that kind of anger   She couldn't even look at me   If it weren't for her leaving the front door wide open, I can see her dumping the television out, but the door, as if she didn't care a damn for our things any more   Well she might have stepped out for a moment and been distracted No, it still applies.

He looked up and down Massachussets Avenue. I don't know what to do now

Why couldn't she have stayed   I couldn't have been out for much more than an hour   She waits six months to tell me what she feels and then gives me no chance at all   She expects some kind of perfection— Fancy our case in a divorce court. My husband has submitted me to actionable mental cruelty by turning out not to be God. Don't I know I'm not allowed to tell her about things like Mother's letter or being afraid   The regressions She could have forgiven though   She could have and waited

One hour   One hour

I might as well go whoring like Martha since far as I can see you don't care what I do

Steps were behind him; a foot touched his back and stumbled him gently down the last stair. He staggered and whirled round and heard: "Suck off, pig." He stared at the guard's shoes, scratching his hair; he turned and forgetting the address book on the banister he crossed the sidewalk and stepped into the road. Crush him   Go home I guess

Wait, the address book

He looked back. Leave it.

He imagined the guard saying in concerned tones, 'I'm sorry, John, I'd like to be your friend, it's just things lately been'— He broke the thought with a snort of disgust. An actual voice rose insistingly then and came blurred to his ears from the building he had left; he halted in the avenue. He is

there, isn't he. Orating same as his father again
He's got his own hasty meeting on what to do about
the troops tomorrow   What will happen   You
don't suppose he'll get involved with that many
soldiers, with us in the streets   No it's probably
unconnected   Hey watch out!   Rusted fenders
screeched and snarled round him and he jerked back
among parked cars. Christ, enough to make you
paranoid   He turned round and saw a half-shaded
window close its eye. Maybe it's her up there   He's
sermonizing her on why she has to divorce me   I
could shout up, I suppose   That guard though
This is absurd really   He gazed round the scaling
ochre walls. I guess she isn't—I used to call him my
brother.

He walked away. You know, you should go see
him, Marian, if you think I'm imagining things   If
you think I've lost my courage or whatever your
idea is   My faith   Then you ought to breathe
his hot breath for an hour or two and you ought
to walk on these streets and look at them for
once

Perhaps if I walk around for a while I'll run into
her

Give it to me, baby, I ain't had it like this since
I got married   So you find you like the Negroid
anatomy after all do you, madam. Yes, John, you
finally digging me   Oh I am, well isn't that satisfying.

He crossed the street with nausea touching at his
bowels. Listen I'm wasting my time   If she really
wants to find some black buck to burble under
then there's nothing I can do about it. At least it's
out of anger not lust   She'll be revolted and she
won't feel a thing   She'll drag back as soon as
he's pumped his little package in her   The punish-

ment will be done with   And if she's pregnant, we'll have a new chance to isolate the generic deficiency. Bile was on his tongue and he spat. I'm making a fool of myself padding around after her   People are laughing.

What did I cross for? You need a Harvard bus from here. He stood in a crowd of shoppers at a corner; the light changed and he watched the shoppers flow into the roadway. No I'm not going home   There's nothing to do there   He turned and trudged down a hill. I loathe copulation for ruling my life   I loathe it   I don't even like it that much and I won't believe a few failures disqualifies my manhood   That's a sick notion and I won't be its victim

She can't want to, you hear? She can't want to.

Dammit, Marian, you've no faith yourself

Am I the one who talks against silence in politics? And was silent at home   I wanted things to heal in me without any treatment and instead there're these tumors of suspicion   I don't believe anything you say any more, John   I feel like you already left me   And so because of my tied tongue she leaves.

He turned down a side street to shuffle deeper into littered grayness. Find a pharmacy   Ring up the answering service   Maybe she's been calling me—

Shouts rapped at his thoughts. He looked up: police and children were tussling beside an unleashed hydrant that shrouded the combatants in spray. Black water raced around the curbs. Cursing, he stooped over a small boy who was squatting in the gutter and dipping a Seven—Up can into the stream. He stood the boy up and held him by the shoulders. "You don't want to drink that stuff, man, you'll get sick and have to stay inside for two whole weeks, you wouldn't want that, would you?" The boy squirmed and ran, splashing him, dropping the can, which John lunged for and missed as it tumbled with the water round the curb. He stood, shaking grit from his hand. "If he doesn't come down with typhus."

Poof. Another brother hit the dust. You could call it sleep.

Ah.

FOR THE SOFT WAVY HAIR YOU'VE ALWAYS WANTED

He stepped into the fanned air of a drugstore. These slum merchants, lovely persons. "Excuse me, do you have a phone?"

"In the back, sir."

Yes. That's where you give it to your customers. Sir. Do you call your local patrons sir, sir?

What, sir? Them black niggers, sir? Fuck, no, sir. Piss-stink in this booth.

Note the graffiti.

BURN

He stepped into the other booth and dialed. A scare. That's her way. She's throwing me a scare. She'll be home soon.

BuRN tHe HONkie.

Brother. In law.

"Answer will you for Christ's sake I thought you were an answering service?"

Marian *you've* no faith   *You've* no faith

"Heddo? What number are you calling pleeyuz?"

The voice disappeared. "Yes, hello! Operator!" He clattered the phone hook; there were clicks and dim buzzes. "Operator!"

"Dr. Morrison's office."

"Yes, this is Morrison. Any calls?"

168

"I think so, sir. Just a minute."

Just a minute   What's the minute   Why don't you have your

It probably isn't her but

I should have stayed home   Do you think she'll stay where she is   She will   She does want me She does I—

"It's from the hospital, sir."

"Is she all right!"

"No, sir, it's—" the woman paused.

"Answer me!"

"Yes, sir—well I can't seem to make out the first name but the last is Wilson—Sir? Are you there?"

"Yes. Yes, Amalia Wilson."

"She's had another coronary, sir. She's entered comatosis. Dr. Murphy is in charge."

"No other messages?"

"Two requests for appointments. I made—"

"Never mind. Nothing else."

"No."

"Thank   you—No   wait.   Did   they   get   the daughter?"

"Sir?"

"Did the hospital notify the daughter of the woman who's in a coma?"

"Oh yes. Just a minute. Yes. They say they can't reach her."

"No, she hasn't a phone. All right then. Thank you very much." He hung up and turned.

Marian!

A yellow dress stepped in and stood at the counter.

Marian—His eyes flitted over a young woman's body, not Marian's. Dammit I really thought Mrs. Wilson might pull through   She can't be much more than fifty   Obesity   Well she might still after all   Do you suppose he gave her digitalis

Are you ready my sister?

Oh well why push it, she's gone out of style.

He pulled his eyes from the young woman and settled into the booth again. I don't suppose she's home but it's easy enough to—his thumb struggled with a coin, which stuck in its slot. Young breasts yes certainly Marian certainly certainly. I'm sure you've found some titillating musculature.

Get in there will you   Get in there!

The dime popped out with his pounding and slid over his palm to the floor. He cursed and rapped his skull on the steel jamb as he plunged after to search among the mashed wrappers and butts and dried urine. He grit his teeth and heaved with exasperation. Stop this   Stop   Just get another dime and write yourself a tranquilizer and for God's sake go home

He walked to the counter, shoving sweat from his forehead. He stood beside the young woman and wrote. Tearing from his pad, he looked up; he squinted at the label on a brown bottle that was dipping from the pharmacist's hand into a paper bag. From the clinic, what's it, for lupus erythematosis? He looked for the first time at the woman's face: her cheeks and temples were crimson with scales. He heard: "Three-ninety-three." What? He touched her arm: "Wait." He leaned over the counter toward the pharmacist. "What'd you say that was?"

"Sir?"

"What's the price on that drug you're selling the lady?"

The pharmacist smiled gently at his customer. "Three-ninety-three."

John closed his hand on the paper bag and said to her, "Ma'am, the price of this drug is fixed by law at nearly a dollar less than that. He's trying to cheat you." He smiled at her and handed her the pills; she did not take them and he snatched them from the druggist's reach. "Believe me, I'm a doctor in the community and I've prescribed these pills more than once, and I work for a local group that looks into these things. Do you have change? Pay him three-ten."

The druggist said: "Give me the bag and get out of here." Staring at John, he said, "He's a trouble-maker, ma'am. The price is three-ninety-three."

"Will you call the police?" John said. "Go ahead, you'll save me a dime."

"Get out."

The young woman's frightened eyes gazed at John, her head shaking no.

"No change? I've got it then—wait a second. Here, take this, won't you?" She held the pills and he walked to the phone booth, crouched and searched again. "I dropped my last change down here somewhere—you'd think the state would make more of an effort to stop these people, since a lot of their profit is fraud and they don't pay taxes on it"—he smiled over his shoulder at the druggist. "Right? Mounts up?" He looked down again. "Why don't you clean your place up once in a while"— he heard sudden running steps and he shouted, "No wait!" He rushed out, halted, stood in the doorway, watched the young woman's handbag flail in the air as she ran weaving among bodies, as she hopped to rehinge a flopping shoe to her heel, as she looked back once and turned a corner and was gone. He stared for a moment down the sidewalk; leaning back into the store then, his hands on either doorjamb and trembling slightly, he said, "I don't suppose she took the pills?"

"You're goddamn right she didn't." The druggist walked out into the aisle. "What do you think you're doing by busting in here?" He said, "You people come into this neighborhood where you don't belong and cause nothing but—"

"Splendid," John interrupted, "Splendid, but how long do you think you can go on defrauding your customers before they turn around again and burn you flat? This summer? Next summer? Next week? No really, will nothing warn you? Do you actually think they don't know you cheat them?"

The man shook a paper. "I got the prescription you wrote and believe me I'm getting the police after you for intimidation."

"Bravo!" John called—he pushed from the door and walked. "Bravo!" He laughed and his limbs suddenly shook and he sat down on a stoop, his stomach roiling.

Why do you do this   When will you learn it's useless

If fifty sworn statements and a thousand signatures can't even get them to investigate in Roxbury   what good is an isolated bluff in the South End   You can't stop him   He'll stop when he's dead   You frightened her not him   He has her prescription and she won't get her pills now   She's probably collapsed with that running

You haven't the strength for this. Will you forget it?

There's no excuse for such an advanced state of lupus   The girl's had it is my guess   You can assume that half the pills he sells are dummies   These bland little servants of Satan never cease to amaze me

I have no doubt that he thinks he was completely in the right in our fatuous little interchange   In fact I'd better be on my way before I find myself wasting time in a police station. He's convinced enough to call them   They're convinced enough

to try to jail me   He stood up and walked quickly
toward a bus stop. Maybe I'm growing a persecution
mania but I can see him dialing with the same bland
blink that he'll give when he chooses the trash he'll vote
for in November   With a satisfying shove of the lever
he'll will the disease and the hunger he lives off— A bus
wheezed, flapped its doors open. He hefted himself
in. For the sake of the down payment on a
cottage in Hyannis. A squad car squealed through a
light and brayed down the street he had left; it
halted by the pharmacy. He shrugged and handed a
bill to the bus driver. Cops don't come that fast.
Probably a coincidence.

Go ahead, pharmacist. You and the cop both.
Sail the city on like a paper airplane into the
furnace.

He swung down the aisle. You know the more I
go on, the more I have difficulty in defeating
Mandus in my mind. Much less the Panthers. How
else can you change such a man as that pharmacist
except by terror? or wholesale revolution? Do you
understand, he saw those scales, he knows the
disease, he's a criminal totally at liberty among a
nation of criminals.

I'm afraid of tomorrow

Wait— He stooped and peered through a window.
Wait, I've overshot. I've got to see the Wilson girl.

Doors slapped open and he ducked out; he walked
on. I don't know what makes me think she'll come
back. I don't know what makes me trust that things
aren't really going where they're obviously really
going. I don't know what makes me hope my
nightmares will wake one soul, and furthermore I
don't know why I imagine my petition to Roxbury to
let me in has one pin's weight of validity on the scales
of that young woman's life and her death and her

173

orphans. That shaven guard has a perfect right   I have no passport here   Jesus said peacemakers he didn't say peace-suers   One stretched-out hand among a thousand fists is only in the way, in the way of the fight

He stood at a crosswalk, gazing at sodden paper in the gutter. I've had such a hope for my country   It was nothing but phantasy

He turned down an avenue of gleaming emporia whose windows were spangled with scarlet stars and moons that screamed usury. He curved round an arc of men pitching coins and clutching bills. She'll fall back into the life again easily enough. She thinks I don't want her   Marriage is all misunderstanding and evasion   An op-art composition that changes with each step you take and has no one truth   She could have stood over here and seen what's behind my impotence   She doesn't want to   She chose to stand over there and perceive that I don't love her since that pleases her suspicions and it frees her to go home   She thinks she's freeing me   From where she's standing she can't see I've nowhere to go if she leaves   I told her that   But I also told her I was drawn back to my mother and how is she to know when the man is talking and when the infant?

Soul-music oldies shouted from a record shop and he sat down on the curb, his ears thudding. Turning, he watched the march of passers-by step on to the sidewalk carpet of beat and ripple to the changes of the song. *Yes I want to testify*—He alone was still, staring at patterns of rust on a car door. *What your love, is doin', for me*— He rose and walked again— *everybody sing now*—and the music failed into silence.

I know, and she would sing

Her voice would go dark, I'd sneak under the sound of the kitchen radio and watch her by the stove

Reaching up for something   Her dress hitching
Seeing me and revving up a hip: hello   She was
that music   And her skin   It'd blend with the night
I remember one time   We woke   She was there and
I sunk into her half-awake   Down shades and no
light   No hands before my eyes and she was the
darkness   All silence and she was the earth, I
thought I was Atlas and held her in my arms, then
fear   Where was she   I switched on the lamp   She
was there   Her eyes winced   Don't need that my
baby   Her breasts fallen to either side   She was
there   I shut the lamp and leapt to kiss her neck and
in the last fade of light I saw her smile

If only she'd

Surely she'll call once more   If only to tell me
she's decided to

To leave and I can tell her I

One hour   One hour

Marian

What will I tell her though, I am white, I can't
move, I don't act, and I have no music

She had to leave before I could see, I didn't take
her when she asked me, all I had to do was make one
gesture but I threw away my chance and told her to
wait, it's as if we were playing out the story of
America

Our following my program for reconciliation seemed
so much more important than our being reconciled,
and now I can't even remember what the silly program
was, it seems so

"Hiya, Dr. Morrison!"

So long ago

Hearing, he stopped and looked down at turned-up
small faces, whose tight-drawn pigtails jounced ribbons
beside his hands.

"Hi, Debby, who're your friends?"

Her hand bunched at his knee; sent out a pointing finger. "That's my doctor!"

"That's right, and I'm pleased to meet you. May I shake your hands?"

One child's jumpered shoulder hung out a brown arm; he stooped and held her flesh, which seemed to him edible, in his. She said: "You funny looking."

"You aren't, though."

"No he ain't, Doreen."

He crouched and popped his eyes at her. "Yes I am." Swinging his stance then, he peered at the third ·girl, whose shoulders swiveled forward and back, her hands behind her. "Haven't I seen you somewhere before?" The head shook.

"That's Destiny. She kinda shy."

"Shake hands with me, Destiny?"

The shoulders swiveled; the head shook. The first girl said: "Know what we doing, Dr. Morrison?"

"No I don't Debby—I bet I could guess, though."

"Uh-uh, no you couldn't."

"Think she should tell me, Destiny?"

The head shook; nodded; everted wet lips and said almost imperceptibly: "We picking a *bou*quet."

"In the park?"

"You kidding me?" Debby said, "Ain't no bouquet in the park. In the *lot*."

"Oh. That's good."

Doreen said: "Aint no lot, dummy, it's a church-yard."

"Yeah."

"Where's that, Doreen?"

"You don't know the *church*yard?"

"Nope."

"Well it down the street. Come on, Destiny."

"Goodbye everybody."

"Bye!"

"Bye!"

"Bye!"

Ouch

He watched the dresses bob as they skipped, watched heels, peeking underwear, thighs, winging arms, hands, jouncing hair. He stood up and strode after. Like a child swooping down and off a slide, a tune plummeted from memory and plopped onto his consciousness:

Only you—you are my Destinee-ee-ee

He smiled. *Frankie Laine*. The fifties. Buddy Holly. Jerry Lee Lewis. Those names.

All my love, all my kissin', you don't know what you been missin' oh boy

1961: The most ingenuous of twists: a dance. Standing in front of me, her back to me, hips chugging, leaning to left then to right, I to right then to left like two pendulums in opposite phase, I lunging over her shoulder for her breasts and her buttock grinding into my obvious cock as she swiped by, others at the party digging us, we all innocent, lascivious, parochial, dated, safe in a parenthesis of history whose not yet burst brackets, by their very imprisoning, kept us undivided as a brood, and in whose thousand-roomed palace of brown faces I lost myself and gained a world.

The three girls swirled and whipped round a corner like a cat's tail. "Come on, Doctor Morrison!" He followed after them still, walking briskly. To be as the—"I'm coming"—Worn lives leaned on elbows from windows above him, craning at light and motion and city air. As the little children, isn't that what I think? I accuse her of tossing a net of myth over me but what about mine thrown all over of them—Can one love a people, can one love anyone or anything without that net? Perception is distortion. What if I said aloud I loved them   Immediate derision   What if I said they were innocent   Not in what they'd suffered but in what they'd not done   They were not guilty and they had not loathed, was it true? I believed it, didn't they forgive me for who I was? I'd walk down the street and want to embrace every one of them—man woman and child, for what? For taking in a penitent conqueror as one of their own? I was happy; but what if they weren't conquered, would I have loved them? No. You want them to be conquered so they can forgive you and you can be absolved, or why else does this black power give you separation anxiety? You need your pool of innocent sufferers. Doesn't Vietnam make clear once and for all that the humanitarian and the conquerer, read murderer, are two faces of the same guilty and incomplete soul, seeing all that is different from itself as intolerably accusing, needing to stamp out the accuser and at the same time to earn his forgiveness so that the accusation ceases? I am that pharmacist, save for a quirk of style.

Breathlessly: "Come on, doctor," the children turned once more; he waved behind him at the usurous avenue as it disappeared. Burn, raze every one of them for taking my wife from me yes but that's only an exemplum, a mere tactic, the main thing is what Malcolm insisted on, get out from under the Christian myth of innocence   Abandon the victim's stance   Release the rage   Don't forgive the white man   And that will unman him.

His downcast gaze warned suddenly of the slim feet of a pubescent boy standing directly in his path. He stopped just short of collision. His eyes rose over sleek unbelted trousers, a tight white T-shirt, black elbows raised and hands to the mouth: "Hey, Susie-Q, you going to send that key down?" A huge voice; the hands fell; it was not a boy but a small bearded man. John bit his tongue against an urge to touch his shoulder and to kiss him on the high cheekbone. As the brown-tinted whites-of-eyes, unaware of John, gazed up the building, something struck John's shoulder and rung on the pavement. The man turned, started at John's apparition, waved his hand in front of John's staring eyes, shrugged, smiled, stooped for his key.

"Hey, doctor, you coming?" His eyes focused and he walked on. He followed the girls into an alley; he stumbled on a page of newspaper trapped by his ankles and a wind. Small heels slapped on cobblestones and sent echoes bounding in zigzags up the alley's walls. If we could shed the myths   If we both could with time   As a people they themselves have only just begun to abandon the role of victim   It's a role with some consolations especially for the woman And there's a kind of riskless moral ease in despair— Our problem together is that our marriage is the myth itself   White man and black woman sneaking illicit love from the cookie jar of caste and neither of us sure we want the jar smashed   Her image of me carrying the light, she may say, be just a doctor, but she wants the crusader, she wants the old holy Christian nonviolent crusade not the new what they call the nitty-gritty confrontation and the war, armed or unarmed, I hope the latter, of independence. This afternoon was the fruitless kind of   Why aren't you my phantasy!—Well what do you mean, why aren't I your phantasy? why aren't *you my* phantasy! Marriage Should Signify a Union of Myths

Huh I mean Marriage Should Signify a

Good Christ how did *she* get in here. Oh the Mother Church is around here I think

Yes and by the Father-Mother-God-in-Heaven will you

look where we've got to?

"See, Dr. Morrison? *Lots* of bouquets."

A child clutched roses at his thighs. "White ones and red ones and yellow ones"—he crouched down and drew her between his knees and embraced her. "Want one?" He nodded and a brown hand shoved petals to his nose. "Ain't they smelling *fine*?"

John, dear, don't pick the flowers! You *must* learn to think of other people

Holding her, he looked past her hair; they had walked through the sightless walls of the ghetto into green. He heard her murmur to herself by his ear, "Giving my doctor one," as he watched her mates cavort in the gardens of a park, faces gliding, ducking, disappearing behind branches that shouldered flowers.

He held the rose. "Thank you, Debby"—he felt her limbs struggling for movement, and he released her. "You welcome"—she ran to join her friends, who were shaking down petals in a rain from a spent wisteria bower. Standing, hearing her musical shouts, he made a step after her; he halted. Wait. They've a pay phone in there. It's nearly half-an-hour since I called in.

He turned round toward an enormous Neo-Neo-Renaissance church whose gray dome squat against the sky. Yes why don't I go in. A gas.

Oh I doubt she'll have called yet, she'll probably wait till later in the evening

He took his eyes from the children and crossed an asphalt driveway. We've still got ten years to get us one of those.

I think she'll come back. She'll stay out tonight most likely. To make her point, that's how she thinks. She'll appear at some chosen moment Maybe at the rally— She'll come back. She'll come back.

Ain't dis da joint what don't believe in doctiss?

Yas. He stood grinning at the monument's entrance

with one foot on the first granite stair. Middle-class mystics of the world unite!

John dear, do hurry up! We'll miss the first hymn!
The Spiiiiirit that enfoh-oh-olds us
I think I'm going to enjoy this

He trod the steps into a box of a vestibule, on the other side of whose glass walls a woman sat. Oh my God yes, I'd forgot about this business—Conceal your rose.—Smiling, the woman tugged a tasseled rope that descended beside her, the pinched skin beneath her triceps jiggling; a door emerged from the glass and glided wide. He ducked in, the flower cupped in his palm.

"Good afternoon, sir. Is this your first visit to the Mother Church of Christian Science? If you'll follow the carpet across the foyer and up the stairs?"

He pointed to rubber matting that flowed down a quiet hall into the dimness. "Stick to the line, eh?"

She sang: "That's right, sir"—she frowned; she peered through the glass. "Oh those darky children they're at the roses again." She clucked. "Really, they have no respect."

"They certainly don't." He shook his head in time with hers; she slapped her lap and stood and clacked down a hall. "Oh George? Geo-orge?"

God is *he* still here? He gazed after her; he turned and bent and jerked the tasseled rope; the door swung in silently beside him and oscillated as he tugged up and down.

I always wanted to do that.
"George!"
He flipped the rope into a knot round a slat in her chair and let go; the chair shot into the air and dangled on a single leg, rotating, hanged. Morrison, you're regressing. As he followed the mat up twisting marble stairs, grinning, he heard:

"Oh George *there* you are. I want you to go out to the garden and . . . "

Yaz'm.

"You know I'm really very fond of them, poor things, but I simply . . . "

Yaz'm.

He stepped through a small door into a vast arena of velveteen pews. And lo, before mine eyes doth bloom great tracts of The First Church of Christ, Scientist, Boston, Massachusetts, U.S.A, Earth, Our Galaxy, Hoyle's Expanding Universe, and in ineffable eternity nuzzled. Hi Baby!—Hello dear. —How stillborn you've been keeping yourself!—Thank you dear, so nice to see you too. Why I remember you when you were just so . . . —I was knee-high to an organ stop.— My! so you were. My word. Oh do tell me how's your sheepish father, they say he's joined the fold in Worcester? Oh and *how's* your wolfish grandfather, he willed us simply zillions, *the* dear boy?

Croaked. The both of them. He laughed.

"Would you like to join our tour, sir? We've just begun."

Two female and one male smiles perused him pleasantly.

"No."

The lady visitor said: "Oh!"

The lady guide said, "As you wish, sir. We ask our guests to remain on the carpet during their visit."

He grunted and the three trod down the aisle as he flung up his vision past grand balconies to the high dome; light flew down from it in blades. Laid out precisely like an opera house without the gaud. Who but an American mystic would build a palace? He pointed. That's where we sat.

The balconies roofed him as he wandered behind the last row of pews, remembering the shuffling, the droning, the huge rustle of thousands standing, the hymns, the squirming, the prayers.

Our Father, which art in Heaven

(Our Father-Mother God, all harmonious)

Howardly Bee thy Name.

I pointed in her father's garden. Mom, is that Howardly Bee? What, dear? Buzz! Him! Silly boy whatever do you mean? I never know what you're saying

"The inscriptions you see on the walls are taken from Scripture and from *Science and Health with a Key to the Scriptures* by Mary Baker Eddy, our Founder. They were chosen by her expressly for the purpose."

"Oh yes!"

Every Sunday night we'd read it. I'd stumble. A peculiar exasperation would come over my father. None of us knew what it meant.

John watched the visiting pair crane and read, hands behind them at their smalls. He turned and strolled. Ah and here we have   By Christ yes   He read large letters knapped into the wall:

'The Science of Mind Denies the Error of Sensation. Only Spirit Exists.'

That one got me. The Physical World, man. Fuckin' unreal. The girl just thinks she has lupus. Run me out of business.

"Our main organ is one of the largest in the world and contains more than five thousand pipes. Many of the smaller are of fine silver."

"Oh yes, I see, how lovely! Isn't it, dear!"

"Yes it sure is, hell of a thing. Must have a hell of a sound."

"You can be sure it does, sir."

Mommy what's sensation?

It's what you feel, John.

Why is it wrong?

Well dear we think it's there, but it isn't. Voice nears. Now eat your cereal.

I can feel things though. Foot displayed. I can feel my shoes.

You think you can. Orange juice poured. But they aren't really there, you see.

Then how come they pinch?

Your mind tells you they pinch, dear. You're just making it up.

No I'm not   No I'm not!

You freaking out over nothing. Like you telling me this piss stink don't exist?

You invent it Gaylord   You're inventing me

Yeah? I inventing this prison   Every one of them chink cocksuckers? I'm inventing Korea? You telling me 'Yeah'? Well joy in the furlined shitmachine morning because it's time we faded right through that door, you listening to me? Come on, daddy, you lead—come on—I'm waiting—

I ran full at the steel and broke my nose.

Sheet, ain't you something?—Hey man you all right? Damn, John, you going to kill your fuckin' self someday

People think I must have boxed in college.

He shouted a sudden laugh. I really did that didn't I—I must say I was a little upset at the time but—well if matter doesn't exist—you don't suppose Uncle Mary didn't need to open doors? I must have got the whole thing wrong somewhere. He laughed again.

"Please be quiet, sir!"

Oh my yes excuse me

She'll come back. She will.

Out of that bag sonny and dig this one:

'The Belief in Sin is Punished So Long as the Belief Lasts.'

Oh, is that a fact.

He ambled lightly down the aisles beneath the dome. It is, though. Consider: if you don't believe there's such a thing as sin, you won't be guilty. Guilt is pain, pain is punishment. Very simple. Uncle Mary does the papists one better. Having no absolution, however, the Protestant has no serenity. He freaks, he distorts. Out damned spot! The Lady projects her own damnation onto the blood of the King; She believes that not she, but the blood is damned; the Protestant projects his own guilts of sloth and lust onto the lives of the blacks: he believes that not he, but the black, is lazy, big-dicked, wipe him out, be pure, cheat the girl with lupus put your dollar in the plate, praise God. He said aloud, his voice reverberating: "She was perfectly right. We need a new religion or forget it."

Hearing steps behind him, he walked down past the pulpit towards a door. The phone's down here.

She's making dinner. She's home making dinner waiting for me to call.

"Sir?"

He stopped at the entrance to a corridor. He said, not looking round, "Yes what is it?"

The lady guide stood beside him. "We don't allow our visitors down there, sir. It's not lighted."

"I'd like to use the phone."

"I'm sorry, but all our phones are private."

He turned round to her. "What?"

"They're private, sir."

"That's a lie." He stared at her; her eyes saw a stranger. She said, smiling, "I think it would be better if you left now." Her bracelets slid as she pointed. "The door you came in."

He gazed past her and round the empty pews. "Yes. All right. I made noise. I'm sorry."

"You're forgiven, sir. But we Scientists believe in silence."

"Yes, I know." He walked quickly up the rise

beneath the quiet dome, down the marble stairs, out past the woman with the rope who heard his echoing steps and fussed with her hands.

"I'm sure I remembered there was one—

"Go home I guess—"

He stepped down to the pavement among long and darkening shadows, and his shirt filled and ruffled with a climbing north wind. "No I can't, I've got to see the Wilson girl." Across the street and into the gardens: "Find another phone." Fallen roses were at his feet; the children were gone. Remembering the flower in his hand, its stem flopping with weakness from perspiration, he stooped and laid it down beside its fellows. He stood up; his life paused. Vents, sparrowed aerials, cisterns and round chimneys with Vietnamese hats, elevator housing, ladders and twists of laundry, the treetops of the urban woods lay across his eyes in black against a gray-white summer evening sky that hinted rain. Clouds of dirty milk with bellies of charcoal trundled above him, sowing chill. "Perhaps tomorrow's the one demonstration we want rain." He shook his vision and moved again down a green lane.

What if she called just after I did and has been waiting forty minutes   What in hell's a church for if not for everyone

He smiled   I still resent that do I   At this age The woman was perfectly right   Whether they have a phone or not I don't belong there   I don't know what made me think to go in there

How about this street

Fifteen year away is too long   There's no return

Try down here maybe

Fineboned houses of the comfortable nudged their faces beside him in close-leafed quietude. Preened cornices beetled without pigeons; ginkos offered green palms to discreet and shuttered eyes. All right so where's your corner pharmacy?— He trudged brick sidewalks along steep and crooked cobbled ways clogged with station wagons and sports cars. He passed no one. He looked up, grinning, and said aloud: "Fuck every one of you." He put a finger to his temple and shot himself.

John dear, do come along! Maggie has lunch waiting!

He turned without thinking to look down the silent hills, and smiling, remembering, he descended those same New World's old streets he had trotted down barekneed thirty years before, stepping on sidewalk cracks on Sunday noons. Fenders had shoulders of spare tires in those days: weeds had ants, and bricks had weeds; church was out; shadows were alive. Roof-tree, stepping out from the hymns, his shadow would shoot out from his feet along the sunned stones, to chug beside him as he ducked into the lanes. That his shadow was never to be seen in church, nor at Bible reading, nor at the dinner table, nor at bedtime, caused not envy but complicit triumph, in that deceit was proven possible and freedom not a madness to desire. The shadow would load him with amazement as it fluttered up walls, rippled up stairs, shot out down a hill like a chameleon's tongue; became two. It could also loom— John gruffed aloud: "What's that boy doing, Esther?"— It could thump his father with enormous shoes; it could pinch roofs. Disappeared, it would peek around the edge of black blocks when he peeked, show nothing but a thumbed nose when he thumbed, then burst from hiding to be chased, grabbed for, stamped on, lunged at in vain. He would laugh and toss his flat blue button-cap into the air and jump to catch the black cap his shadow had tossed—"Dear, don't dirty your cap! Don't you want to walk with Mommy and Daddy?"

Why did she do that!

Thumping the spare tires that passed, bending to rip a weed and slowing to dismember it, he would see his mother's form through the stalk's splayed fibers and would run to step his hand into hers. 'Mommy?' He would look up and tug; the faces were away. 'Hi, Mommy'—'Yes dear now shh, Daddy and I are discussing.' Taking in breath he would whisper, 'Hi Mommy Hi Mommy Hi Mommy'—He would try to hear his father's words but they would blur, and he would drag on her grasp, swing out and search up the walls and down the street for his shadow, only to find it eclipsed, like the small boy who cast it, by the longer darkness of authority.

"What am I doing in this place? There's no public phone here."

He turned and jogged down a hill. "Christ, it's nearly an hour since I called in and I never did call home—"

He muttered, "No wonder I have trouble trusting you, Marian. She never meant a damned thing she said. She kept her promises like a politician and she was no more real than that shadow or than Mrs. Eddy's matter. It pinches but it doesn't exist. She says, Come here dear But she means, Please disappear dear, you frighten me. I thought she hated me. It was not me she hated but feeling, perceiving, intimacy, existence. A child cannot make these distinctions."

He chuckled. "Will you consider what majority of the power-classes would be shrieking incurables if it weren't for the institution of the Maggies who have lunch waiting?"

The double bind—I never thought of it quite this way before but—An elevated train screeched; he walked on level ground into the slums.—Sure If I couldn't have her, I'd want to go free, but that might mean some criticism of her   Being constructed of guilt she couldn't withstand that   So I had to stay with her I was punished for wanting her   Shh dear Daddy and I are   And punished for not   Don't you want to walk with   Come along son be nice to your mother   Yes means no, no means yes   I thought it was inevitable   In a way it is   My emotions are as crabbed as his were   I will be a bad father   But it had never occurred to me that people existed in any other fashion   Then Gaylord   He was their opposite   He never made a syllable of comment on the matter but he loved me   I assumed all blacks were like the one I knew   They could feel   They existed My choice was obvious. Why go crazy? Switch worlds.

"Where are we?"

Dusk billowed gently from the pavement, sucking color from the buildings and draping their walls with a tangible light skin to the moon's. "Don't they have street signs?" Above the vaults of the elevated tracks, the moon's orange eye already rested on a water tower, descrying the city as if it were a male.

As he walked on beneath the steel arches, John suddenly waved and yelled, "Hey there's a phone booth!" He ran; a woman was inside. He paced, rubbing his forearms, cold.

Yes. Don't touch them. They're like animals. They're sensation. They feel. They exist. They love. They're not like us, thank God. Thank God indeed. Marian is certainly strange herself to have wanted all this garbage. My whole life's a perverse reaction to perversity.

The phone slapped down and the light extinguished in the booth. Ah here we go. A woman emerged. Madam you've been reading too many AT&T advertisements. He stepped in and dialed. And I bet you spend more than if you had your own phone Well the

deposits run up to a hundred dollars around here Why
should a poor black have a telephone Your colossal
monopoly might risk a penny   Oh cut it out

Waste. Waste of time. Talk's nothing.

He waited, hearing rings.

All right so she isn't home   You knew damned
well she wouldn't be and don't

He dialed again.   Sleeping alone   Love me or
leave me   Punishing everybody   Marian this isn't
television

No she pointed that out.

"Dr. Morrison's office."

"Yes, hello, this is Morrison. Any calls?"

"Yes, just a minute sir."

Bitch. Crush her.

"From the hospital I imagine?"

"Yes, sir. It's about that Mrs. Wilson."

"Oh? Yes?"

"She's dead, sir. At 7:43 P.M. She remained coma-
tose. It is hoped that you'll notify the family."

"Yes. All right. No other messages."

"No, sir."

"Thank you."

Damnit, Marian, you

Her daughter lives on Dudley Street. Get going.

He walked from the booth and down the avenue
beneath thundered rumble of trains. I tell you it
means nothing   It's irrelevant   She's a woman
whose life is finished   No one can cure auricular
failure

Oh my God look it's raining

Yes, Lord

Fine glinting dashes descended silently through the
streetlight and spread a delicate chill on his skin. You
make these connections Set up an environment to
meet what you need   Then things change and you

can't recover   You are left   You're like a divorced man

You approached them through charity   It seemed as good a way as any to get introduced   You settled in with a marriage and now they both
Both

He stopped walking. "Wait, the house numbers are increasing, I'm going in the wrong direction"—he turned round. Black night shone now on the pavement where his soles began to splatter faintly. Reflections, white from street lamps, blue and red from neon, were shimmering on his path in trembling wide bands like spectra. Traffic lights hummed to themselves as if to keep courage in a wilderness. Above him, merged with the hovering weight of lightless rain clouds, the invisible tracks uttered screams.

He clutched his ears, stopping again, looking round in the dark. "Look, according to my calculations this ought to be Dudley Street but I don't recognize anything—" The rain came harder, audible now, reaching his scalp through his hair. "Unfortunately I think this is more or less the Ranger gang territory—"

"Try down here I guess—"

The rain spat loudly round him while he trudged on, hatted with a newspaper he had snatched from a barrel. Down from the lighted doorway of a transient hotel three boys called as he passed: "Hey, we going to get the pig."—"Yes, man."—"Shit." Their running steps slapped lightly down the wet stairs. John ducked into the street between parked cars and sprinted on his toes. His shoes splashed in puddles and gathered weight. Hearing shouts, he looked back: the boys, beneath a street lamp, were throwing with wide swings of their arms. Broken bits of brick thumped and skidded at him; one struck his heel sharply. He cried out and in a limping run he reached the shelter of the

El; he walked on with heavy sloshing steps. "Wait."
He stopped short. "Isn't this the place? You didn't
have to go down there at all goddamn you"—Chipped
crimson letters wrote an arc across a store window:

EZEKIEL WHEEL PRAYER TEMPLE INCORPORATED

"All right, this proves this has to be Dudley Street
but I still don't recognize it, I think everything's been
moved"—He squinted into the murk, feeling an un-
canny falseness in the buildings. He pushed open a
door that yawned from its upper hinge beside the
window; he ducked into an acrid hall.

Ezekiel saw the wheel
Wheel way up in the middle of the air

A mass of stairway loomed down the darkness. He
bit his lip a moment and said with a quickly rising
voice: "Is irrelevant, do you understand that? Is
irrelevant?"

One wheel turned by faith
One wheel turned by the graaace of God

He climbed, unable to see, patting the wall. Curls of
flaking paint scratched between his fingers. "I suppose
once she's stayed out one night, the next will be
easier, then the next after that"—On the landing a dim
swaying bulb flung a gray arc over a rat that sat like a
kitten on the top stair, vibrating its nose. He kicked
out; it reared, bared its teeth, ducked and disappeared
with a scratching rustle out of the light's arc and
down the hall. He followed it and called out: "Miss
Wilson?" His voice echoed alone in stillness and in
pitch darkness. A larger rustle neared. The down
stirred on his forearms. He could not see his hands.
There was the smell of turds.

He called out again, "Miss Wilson? It's John Morrison, your mother's doctor?"

A child bawled faintly. Towards it he placed slow
steps, his throat working, his feet kicking out before

192

they fell, his fingertips sliding as his guides against the clammy grime of the wall. His hands found a door, behind which feet shuffled. The door opened.

A candle flung leaping shadows behind the young woman who stood in the doorway. A cotton dress hung from her. Points of gleam danced on the grease that flattened her short hair. She did not look at John's face, but at his feet. She said nothing.

"Miss Wilson? I'm John Morrison, your mother's doctor. We've met before, I—" he paused; she made no answer. "I saw your mother this morning, and she seemed on her way to recovery—"

She made no movement nor sound. He tried to see her face without bending down awkwardly; he could not. Behind her, the infant choked on its bawling. She did not look round. The child breathed, and John went on: "I got a call from the hospital this afternoon, Miss Wilson, and I'm afraid I have some unhappy news." Again he paused, and again she did not move or speak. He said, "I'm terribly sorry. We did everything we could. You knew it was heart failure?"

A train deafeningly screamed outside the window past her shoulder. The window's rattling and the infant's screech emerged to their ears when the train passed. The young woman still stared at his shoes. He raised his hand and she flinched very slightly. He said, beginning to speak hurriedly, "I don't want you to be too upset. She died in peace and she lived a good life. Perhaps if I could help in some way—I don't wish to intrude, but I think I—" he stopped short; he realized that the door, with the faintest apparent motion on her part, was closing slowly in his face. "Miss Wilson?" She disappeared; the door latched; he was in darkness.

An explosion of squeaks hurtled through the silence and soft paws scrubbed under his trouser cuff. He kicked and shouted with loathing. A sudden pain seared his shin, bringing tears. For a moment, silhouetted against the light on the landing, the animal hung by its teeth from his calf. Gagging, he batted its haunches with his hand. It twisted and dropped. He ran down the stairs. He walked through heavy rain, shuddering.

xi

"Gaylord."

"Yeah."

The rain lifted its skirts and was gone. On the shack floor, shoving aside his paper dinner-plate, on which a gnawed steak bone and a rim of white blubber lay crossed, Gaylord swiveled round in a crouch toward Amarantha, who was sitting on the bunk on her heels. She said, chewing: "How long since you've been away from your wife? Presuming you're not still with her?"

As she ate he rested his chin on his folded arms by her knees. "Eight months. Since November." He watched her wag her head downward in search for her raised fork, then bat her lip and teeth with an oleaginous square of meat.

"This is great, Gaylord."

"I blow all my bread on food; you going to see."

"Don't tell me. I haven't had a kitchen in three years."

"You come stay, we're going to liberate some beautiful spreads, believe me. Shame is I used to have this whole set of French pots? Copper ones? My wife took them. You going to see, though." Noticing a panic chase across her eyes, he added: "It'll be easy, Rantha. You'll figure out where everything is inside of two days."

The panic remained; she smiled under it. "Did you meet her in France, then?"

"Who, Martha? Naw.—I don't feel like a story now, baby."

"Just some basic facts, though. It doesn't have to be a story, silly."

He laughed, "That ain't possible," sitting back on his heels below her, watching the moon's shadowlines shake on her skin as she moved. "I'm not ready to get rid of it, see."

"I told you mine, didn't I?"

"Only because it got forced."

"Fuck you then."

"Thing is you got a body on you same as her, except a little bigger at the boob, ain't that frightening?"

"You're watching me and I'm putting on my clothes."

"No ma'am. Didn't I tell you the rule is you aren't allowed to put your clothes on again, I'm talking about ever again, Rantha?"

"I'm getting up."

"We going to keep the shades drawn at my place and we aren't going to study clothes no more."

Frowning, laying her plate aside: "Mm."

"I wonder how racism gets along in nudist camps."

"Why is it 'frightening' that I'm the same as her except a little bigger, please?"

His hands considered her. "Like in the nude, you figure you got the thing presented to you in toto all the time—"

"Cut it out because it doesn't explain frightening. Since if you're thinking about me for the same bad reasons you decided on her than I have a right to hear about it. Will you please pass the beer."

He watched her pour from her cup slightly askew into her mouth, causing dribbles. "I got to admit you got some not too usual talent, though, like you put real vivid into my head one of my first times with her, before she tightened up on me, on a field where we'd spent the night and the moment of first looking up came back to me just when you and me had finished, the first time tonight, though I can't recall a single other thing about that time with her, or about the place, except the name, it was Rouen."

"Oh that's nice to hear about."

"You asked."

She ate for a minute, then said: "Did you take up with her there, then?"

"Naw, I'd known her in high school, see. She was a friend of Marian's and I'd gone with Marian for a while and so when—"

"You went with Marian? Did you—"

"When I heard Martha was over there studying while I was there, I looked her up."

"Sleep with her? Does John know? Because what was Martha studying, does she have a career or something?"

"Wasn't nothing with Marian. Which one are we on, anyways?"

"Oh. Does Martha have a career or something."

"Something, yeah. She's been working for a cat. White cat. Commercial art. I don't know if she calls it a career or what."

"Mm, and how long ago was that when you started with her?"

He laughed. "Shit. Six years."

"And you were studying what?"

"Naw. Well I'd gone to night school in the service, that's when I met John, in Korea, and sure I was thinking of going on with the studying when we got out, he was pushing me, but then my mother died, see. I figured Europe'd be a good place to piss around for a while."

"Oh. Christ do I know nothing. Wait, did you get married over there?"

"Yeah, no, she came back later; then we did."

"How come you didn't stay, then."

"Lost the job I had, see—no particular reason. Place lost its interest. You're a foreigner there, so you're less of a threat than you are here, you know, being black, but it's the same. You tend to figure there's something in America made the white man lose a screw in his head when he got over here, like maybe it was us; it isn't true. White man over there is just the same."

"People bother you there, then?"

"Naw, bothering; ain't a question of bothering, Rantha. Question of realizing all over again double that whatever you do got nothing to do with it, since whatever happened to him happened so far back in time, question of seeing no rhyme and reason behind the thing, question of getting scared—Anyway it was time to go back. She wanted to make it here. She couldn't save a dollar, though."

Amarantha waited for a moment, then went on, "What was—"

He interrupted, "What finished it? She started making it on the side, see. Cat she worked for, another cat than now, he broke her in. After a while it got more blatant and more various, she didn't have no sense of her own value, she'd glut on the shame of it and having me slap her up and having the power to rip a thing down; ain't nothing new in that story. She used to do it at home, even, when I was out driving delivery, though I never did catch her at it. That don't mean I didn't try. Zip home during my route, that kind of thing. I could smell it sometimes."

"Bitch."

"Yeah, I suppose."

"So did you leave?"

He said nothing for a while as he stood and dumped the paper plates and the bones. He went on then:

"Yeah, thing is, I kept telling her it was for her to leave. We had a lot of shit in the place we'd collected from around, like the pots I told you, we'd built this and that into the walls, I told her it was mine, she'd forfeited her share in it." He paused in his cleaning up. "She wasn't going to leave, though, Rantha; whole proceedure we was going through suited her fine. One time, when she hadn't even had the manners to clean the recent bedreek off of her, and I'd bashed her up fine like I done to you today,—well what's she going to do but stagger on up again, blood winding out of her mouth, she's taking her dress off and coming across the room, and down she go onto her knees and grabs a hold of my hog in my pants, that's something she ain't offered to do for me in more than a year, see, and with her mouth full of gore. I told her okay, sure, why don't she take off the rest of her clothes, which she did, then I dragged her out the door through the hall onto the sidewalk and hawked her services to the public at the top of my lungs. It was the middle of the rush hour."

Amarantha had been laughing and abruptly stopped laughing as he stopped speaking; he went about collecting cups and cans, frowning, swiping bites from a border of raw fat he had stripped from the meat. He went on with mouth full: "She didn't fight; just bawled. Cops came, beat the shit out of me, sent me up for sixty days. Thing was, it had been the perfect scene for Martha. She had to do the slave bit, see; it was bursting up from under the flagstones of her arty businesswoman architecture. I'd just let it have its day. So she comes over to the shithouse once she's cleaned up and she tells me she's ready to begin again according to my specifications once I'm out of there, and I do believe she was. I told her my specifications were she go do herself using any and all ornate implements might be striking her fancy; because I ain't going to touch again. So I go home when I'm out, and she's gone, and all the furniture and junk from Europe and pots and china she bought even down to the shelves I put in, they gone with her, and my clothes besides, except for an old shirt and some underwear in need of laundering. I believe she must've found a man about my size."

"Since why the hell did you get involved with her please?"

"Fuck it."

"Did you see her afterward?"

"Not till yesterday."

"What?"

"In a liquor store. She was out with a cat; not my size."

"So what'd you say to her?"

"How much of this you got to know?"

She waited for him to go on, and when he did not she said: "I'm sorry to have laughed back there, Gaylord, but it's sometimes sort of hard to know what—"

"I told you it wasn't ready, Rantha."

"I don't know what you mean by ready though, like what happened last night with her, how's it ever going to get ready, since if you don't talk about a thing till you're over it then you never will be over it."

"Bullshit, you told me about what happened two years ago, you ain't told me a thing about what you doing now—"

"I have so and I will—"

"You do and it'll be a piece of mishmash, it ain't going to be no kind of a story I can understand."

"It doesn't have to be a story because that's one stupid idea if you want my opinion."

"Yeah, forget it." He turned and leaned out the

open doorway into the still night. Above him clouds raced on winds of high altitude past a small and stationary moon which, by staring, he made in a blinking shift to gallop past stationary clouds. They said nothing for a while. He turned round then: "Look will you, Rantha, I don't want us to get hung up on this, I'm merely saying I don't like going too much into things that bother me, I prefer to let them settle by themselves and then I can use them or not how I please, and I always done that, it's a method got some dignity to it, and it's got nothing to do with you."

"All right then but excuse me, Gaylord, because maybe that's why she cheated on you since you slipped out of her hands like you were greased every time she tried to get a hold of you, and maybe the only way she could get you to show her you loved her was by cheating and getting you to hit her and maybe that one time it worked and she really was grateful—"

"That what you planning? You asking me what's frightening?"

"Yes I am asking because you're not going to march me through her patterns, that's not what I'm here for, because I don't want this not being able to get to you, and I'm telling you right now that it's been eight months for this thing with Martha to settle and it's going to be eight years unless you talk to someone about it."

"Bullshit. I just have been talking about it and the—"

"And making it just as unreal as you can."

"I told you that's how I try to handle it."

"Because I don't even know if the story about your fight with her is true, Gaylord, and if this is how you handle things then how come just running into her in a store is enough to send you out bright and early the next morning to see if you can't get some ridiculous policeman to shoot you in the back—"

"All right, Rantha, but that was before this afternoon, and did you believe the part about France, baby; you did or it wouldn't have made you jealous, and like that part was ready, and the only reason it was was since you and me'd begun and we'd overlaid that time with our own, and don't ask me how I'm handling things, I asked you to come stay with me, I asked you, but you aren't going to answer; I'm the one who can't be got to, but you aren't going to answer."

She stood sucking steak fat from her fingers; "Oh, sure." She crossed the room and patted for the sink, washed her hands. "Because I know perfectly well what's going to happen and you haven't any right to pretend like it's anything else."

"That's the answer I get?"

"It's the truth, though. Isn't it."

"What's the truth, that I'm going to ditch you?" He laughed a single shout. "And that's the only kind of breakup you can imagine for yourself? Like you know when I'm going to do this, and where, and how, and who for?"

"I know when, which is soon, and I know why."

"Oh?" He walked from the doorway and stood behind her; said loudly: "Why?"

She turned to face him, crossed her arms over her breast, shrugged her shoulders. "Because of color."

He mocked: "Because of color. That's why I sat over there asking you to come stay, because I was going to ditch you because of your color. I'm the kind of person just says things for the sound. Since far as I can see you been trying your damnedest to get me to walk, because you way down mired in a dismal opinion of yourself, and you're afraid I'm going to try to drag you out of that, which might be painful, so you'd better drive me off fast, and then you can flagellate yourself something delicious." Some of the defiance left her face, and his voice quieted: "That's a little more like what you got planned, is it, Rantha?"

She said to the floor, "I could never live with you."

"Yeah?" He sat down on the bunk, ran his hand over his hair. "You going to tell me why not?"

She said after a moment: "Because you're black."

He stood up quickly: "What you mean because I'm black? I'm putting up with your being white—" A hotness jumped at his eyes and he shouted: "You were the one who went and said forget the color, like I was holding something against you that you didn't do, and I let my guard down and I let you in goddamn you, and now you've got your fill you the white bitch again."

She made no answer. He grabbed a fist of hair at her neck; she winced but said nothing, and after a minute he let her go and turned to stand up on the bunk, asking no one: "I'm supposed to feel guilty for what I think of women?"

He leaned out the window, rested his eyes on the still dunes. On a near crest a man and woman stood overlooking the sea, their silhouettes bridging, their wind-cast hair angling in a river of stars. He said to himself, "There's a couple out there"—suddenly, they ran. Their limbs shook out eels of shadows down a road of white light that led to the moon. At the brow of the dune, they stopped, leapt, disappeared over the edge while the sky tossed down falling lights that bathed them in its shower.

Amarantha was speaking, her words too faint to distinguish. Turning round to her, he said, coughing: "What'd you say?"—her voice remained at a murmur, and he muttered at her: "You can't even see me."

She raised her face toward him and said as he stepped down: "I can't stay with you because I've been committed to a mental hospital and I can't get out until they decide to let me out, and they won't if it's to live with a man even if I love him and I'm afraid of their putting me back into the stinko just to get back at me for the little time I've already spent with you—"

"This has got nothing to do with color, Rantha." He leaned his elbows on the stove, rested his forehead on his palms. "Anyways you out of that hospital and I don't see what place it got in what we do."

"It has everything, will you listen, because I haven't been released, I'm just in halfway house and any word from my doctor puts me back on the wards again, and he just might because he's strict and I skipped out this morning and today and now tonight and I'm not even supposed to take meals outside, so how could I cook—for you or sleep with you? I said that about color because I thought it would be easier, I didn't think it would hurt you coming from someone like me, you'd just think it was ridiculous, which was stupid but that's one of my problems, I'm not used to places where what I do makes any difference."

"Oh, yeah. I'm evasive but you been spending the last half hour furiously trying to kick the sand around to cover your pride. Except color is the reason, Rantha. Because if you had any respect for me you wouldn't have toyed around with color like that."

"Yes? Because did it ever occur to you that I feel just as crummy about my being in the hospital as maybe you feel about your being black—"

"I don't feel crummy about my color, understand? Right now I'm feeling crummy about your color, Rantha—"

She sat down on the bunk, pulled the sheet across

her breast and up to her mouth, bit on it. "It doesn't matter because they won't let me live with you, and I don't know what we're arguing about."

"You never asked to get out of there, Rantha. You never had any other place to go. Now you got a place to go and only reason you ain't taking it, that's because it's a black man offering it to you." He sat down on the bunk beside her. "Only thing you interested in this bag for anyways is stigmatizing yourself and degrading yourself with me, that and shaving off of some horns, and if your doctor isn't going to let you out, I believe that's going to be why."

"Because it's different for you, is it?"

"I don't know, maybe it isn't."

"There aren't any good reasons?"

"If there are why can't you tell this doctor about them, maybe he's going to take that into consideration? But you ain't about to do that."

She dropped the sheet and smirked a moment. "Because you made love to me like I was a person, he's going to take that into consideration? You've been finding people like that among people who like to run things?"

"There's such a thing as lawyers, Rantha."

"What we want to do is legal?"

"Sure."

"In the state of Massachusetts? Your honor, I submit for the court's inspection this signed affidavit attesting to seventeen fully accredited orgasms reached by the petitioner on five separate occasions—something along those lines you had in mind?"

He laughed. "You haven't ever ever looked into it, though, have you?"

"I know I can't stay with you tomorrow, Gaylord, or any time soon."

"They got police standing guard on you twenty-four hours?"

"What's that have to do with it?"

"Then there's plenty of time in a day; see?"

"Sure because a minute ago you wanted me to stay and already you're shying off so that a couple of hours a week is plenty of time for you."

"I didn't say anything of the kind; did I now."

"Because what good is it if I'm always sneaking in and out like a school girl from some ridiculous convent"—His steps receded across the room. Clanking china, he asked:

"You want some dessert? Store pie?"

"Yes, *I* don't know, fuck."

"Big or little."

She shouted, her anger troubled by amusement: "Even if you don't give a shit about it you might have the courtesy to pretend to be interested—"

"I'm interested in what your headshrink got to say. Until then we're wasting the time that you're complaining we're short of."

"All right, but shouldn't we decide what I should say to him?"

"Yeah? How about the truth?"

She paused a moment; said with disgust: "Oh, I don't know, I suppose so."

He laughed at her delightedly. "Thing about you is, you thorny but you equal to the task."

"You started this one, though."

"Here comes your pie."

"All right but it's blown over, hey?"

"That's up to you, baby."

"Phooey because do I have to dry my hands on the sheet? They're still all steaky, yecch."

"Ain't no napkins whatever."

"They're being wiped on you." Reaching out at

random with open palms, she landed her hands on his belly and plowed back and forth as he stood before her, holding the plates of pie.

"Rantha?"

"Yes."

"We having our pie or what."

"My hands are still greasy, though."

"That a fact." He looked down and watched her hands slip and slide about his groin.

She said, "The only thing is I'm sort of sore."

"Make up your mind?"

"I can't." Her hand passed beneath and behind.

"You just did."

She leaned forward, grasping. "Mm. This is what you didn't let Martha do."

"That's right since it's for making love, not for making amends."

She said indistinctly, "Did you just make that up? You going to hawk me on the public thoroughfare?"

"You wouldn't fetch such a price as her."

"I would so."

"You ain't as well muscled."

"That good or bad?"

"Can't say yet."

"Oh. Now listen I know this may sound sort of ridiculous but can we hurry up? Because this is very unsettling and I'm almost sort of practically already—"

"Yeah." He lifted her beneath her shoulders, dumped her on the bunk, and practiced archery. She cried out and thrashed. They ceased.

"Rantha."

"What? Yes?"

"Do you mind if I cook you for breakfast tomorrow?"

"No, that'd be okay—Christ. Christ, I'm embarrassed."

Pause. "Want a story?"

"Gaylord it stings, all right?"

"A ready story."

"Yes but could you—? Oh good." She landed on the floor and walked about awkwardly. "Ick."

He laughed. "Use the sheet."

"No, *oog*. We'd have to sleep on it."

He threw her his undershirt. "A story?"

"Yes."

"You sure."

"Of course I am. Come on, come on."

She sat down beside him and leaned over her plate of pie, forking at it. He waited, then lay back on the bunk along the wall: "See, baby, I once read a—"

"Mm. This is good, Gaylord. Sorry. Mm."

"I read an old book once which said that a long time ago men and women weren't apart from each other like now, they were joined"—He shifted up on to an elbow, and gestured on her body: "Joined belly-to-belly, chest-to-chest, shoulder-to-shoulder, groin-to-groin, lodged and stitched into each other and eight limbed, see, like a Hindu god—"

"And we got around by cartwheels and hand-springs?"

"You must've read the same book, Rantha."

"Uh-uh."

"No? You sure you want to hear this?"

"Shut up and how about our heads, where were they?"

"Our heads, yeah, they were turned right around and fixed together at the back of the skulls I think it was, and we had two faces, one facing back, the other facing front, except there wasn't any back nor front then of course, we were just in things; we were full, Rantha, and so there wasn't any money or desire, and people lay around in the diamond night feeling like you and me feeling now except a hundred times that, a hundred thousand times that, and we didn't die no kind of death either, nor any birth. That's according to the book I read, anyways—"

She put down her plate and lay back against him; through wisps of her hair he watched the still starred sky and black dunes. Ships of moonlight sailed slowly across the floor. "A thousand ages come and gone and one day, sitting up on his cloud, a huge perfectly enormous pink bird name of Thaddeus Rapacitus Blade, who is hog butcher to the Big House, unsurpassable maker of plans, and genuine gold-star god, he's having a daydream and cooking a plot in his hog pot."

"Okay, how did he get in here?"

"He isn't in here, he's up there in the realm of the thunderheads, in the Tanzanian diamond mine of the night, he's a god, baby, every one of them stars up there had a god living in it, those days anyhow. Mr. Blade, though, he's about the only one used to come down to earth regular, on account of a hog farm he had down here. Every day he used to swoop on down and pounce on a hog or two, stab them with his cunning beak and suck out their souls, spit the effervescence deep into his net and wing on home to boil the souls for lunch. Because gods don't care about the flesh part."

"Well I do."

"Yeah. Now Blade was a cook besides of unspeakable plots and plans. He used to fly up to the Big House and serve boiled hog soul to his Massa Lord God and to Mrs. Voracia God, who sit at the head and the foot of the table in the realm of the thunderheads and Tanzanian fields, and all the while he'd be dreaming up schemes to simmer in his pot when he got home. Because he's tired of hog; it isn't fine enough for gods like him. He wants human. He's been down here, spying on the humans, drooling, hearing them bringing out their flavor with their talk, thinking what tiers and strata of delectable soul they got for him to wrap his tongue around, if he could only idle up and snatch one in his stealthy claw—and that's what he never could think of how to do, until the day I'm telling you of.

"You can see what Blade was up against, baby. How's he going to clutch that sweet prey of us if we got eight limbs to whip around on and if we got two faces and eyes on the backs of our heads? But Blade, he's a clever bird. He got a scheme boiled to perfect in his pot. So he toss down his stirring stick, piss out the fire, revv up his wings, and flap-flop off his star and up the sky towards the Big House, clacking his heel-claws together at the thought of setting a delectable broiled human soul down before the gluttonous crimson eyes of his Massa, who he finds on the terrace, watching *As the World Turns*. 'Massa Lord God!' he yells—

"Miz Voracia screeches, 'Why ain't you in the kitchen!'

" 'Shut up, Missy,' Lord God grumbles. 'What you having, Mr. Blade?'

"Blade bawls, 'I'm talking about what you going to have, boss'—he starts out his chest feathers and drum-rolls his beak together—'Boss,' he say, 'I done tossed out the whole mess of hog soul I caught this week.'

"Miz V screeches, 'What you do that for, no-good?'

" 'Shut up, Missy. Bad batch, was it, Blade?'

" 'No, Boss, except'—he does a little turn, slapping his yolk-yellow claws gently on the flagstones, and he croons, 'Except, Boss, compared with what you going to have'—

" 'Out with it, Blade. I got a show to watch. You and your cussed chickenfooting around.'

" 'Boss'—Blade's chest inflating out and out till I think it going to burst right there all over the Lord God's TV's—Lord God wears two of them, see, like pince-nez, down to the end of his beak—

" 'I got a show, Blade'—

" 'Boss,' bombs Blade, 'I got a plan.'

" 'What kind of plan, I damn you?'

" 'A plan, Massa LG, to put human on your plate this very night.'

"Lord God thunders, 'I thought you told me you can't get to them because they got eyes on the backs of they heads?'

"Blade coos, cool as a preacher at a funeral, 'LG, you done stuck us with the point of my plan. We going to sneak up on the humans and split them in half down the middle of theirselves, and then they each going to have only two eyes like the rest of us, see, and—and then—and—'

"Blade sort of peters out, his beak hanging open just a bit, he in the dimmest ignorance as to why LG and Miz V they squawking and leaping swirling feathers all over the terrace, they so furious at him, *him,* till finally Miz V got the breath to gurgle out, 'If they got eyes on the backs of they heads, how you going to sneak up on them to split them in half down the middle of theirselves in the first place? clunk? meatball? come-to-nothing trash?'

"Blade, he hadn't thought of that one. He making a quick exit through the pink blizzard of feathers when he hears from Lord God in the most murderous kind of mutter: 'Blade, you bring us human soul tonight or we dining on yours.'

" 'Boss,' he sings out, 'Now you *know* they got eyes on the backs of their—'

" 'Out!' "

She struggled onto an elbow. "Hey, Gaylord, this is terrific, I mean did you really make it—"

"Like every kind of thinker and maker of plans," he said, "thing about Blade is he maybe can't see the noseholes on his beak but he got background, resources, resilience, a fat quiverfull of lusions, so soon as he gets home, he dresses himself up in his finest evening wear and he flaps on down to earth. Pretty soon he spies a human being cartwheeling along singing 'Old Black Joe'—in parts I think it was— 'Hrumph!' Blade say; he's putting on airs. In fact he so scared he think he going to show it to his linen.— 'Hrumph, human, how you doing?'

"Human stops stock still between the end of a cart and the beginning of a wheel, stares at this huge perfectly enormous pink bird all dressed up and dizened with fobs and boutonnieres and glittering festoons, and collapses all his eight limbs ashake with a shatter of laughter."

"Oh, poor Blade," she said.

"Yes, baby, Blade pissed off; he mortified. 'What you yuk-yukking at my image for?' he yells—'I happen to be Thaddeus Rapacitus Blade, hog butcher to the Big House, unsurpassable maker of plans, and genuine gold-star god, I'm tell you—'

" 'You? A god?'—They at the guffaws again, baby. Whole crowd of them now.

" 'Who says I ain't? Who says I ain't? Who says I ain't?' he's spluttering, turning around and around as more and more of the humans come handspringing up to get a load of him—after a while, the laughter's moving further off down the plain and getting softer, you know, like the echoes under a bridge do, and the first human pulls himselves together and gets up on his four feet and says, 'Mr. Blade, we real sorry to have laughed at y'all, but you done surprised us no end'—chuckles bubbling on his face—

" 'I don't see what's so surprising about myself.' Blade says, still sort of hurt—

" 'Thing is,' first human answers, 'We never could have imagined a god being so ugly as you is. Tell us now, all the Big House gods ugly as you?'

"Blade about to bawl, 'I'm the finest of the gods, what for you calling me ugly? Even Miz V never call me ugly'—but he don't yell it, baby, though he coming near to tears; because Blade, he's a clever bird. What he do come out and say is, after a blink and a swallow, and he smile: 'It's true. We gods are ugly. and you, humans, are gracious beautiful. And that's why I am here, my friends. Massa Lord God and Miz Voracia God, who are my boss man and woman and who sit at the head and foot of the table in the realm of the thunderheads and Tanzanian fields, done ask me to fly down'—he flaps his wings a bit, figuring he going to dazzle the humans and awe them, all he do is set them laughing all over again though— 'Hrumph!—to fly down and ask some of y'all to come visit. Massa LG and Miz V, they anxious to see how beautiful you are, and especially (Blade's planning how this'll start them snapping at each other) especially which one of y'all's the most beautiful there is.'

"*Damn.* Because the first human say, 'Why, Mr. Blade, we can't think of nothing so silly as that last part, because as you can see, we're all of us equally beautiful.'

" 'Yeah? Ain't there no difference between you?'

" 'Sure; but what that got to do with it?'

" 'Yeah.' He pace a bit, twiddling his primaries. He never heard of such damn-fool ideas. 'Ah!' He got it. 'Tell me though, friends,' (Yes, he figure this a brainstorm straight from Dar-es-Salaam and he hope he don't blow it) 'Tell me, ain't there no difference between one half of a human and t'other half?'

" 'No, man, not a hair—except the threadmole, of course.'

" 'Oh yeah; the threadmole.' "

"What's the threadmole, silly?"

"That's just what Blade want to know. He burning to know. He's afraid to ask, though; they might get suspicious. See, Rantha, what he don't understand is, if he were to say the word 'suspicious' to them, or 'hate' or 'death' or anything like that, he'd have to go through a year's worth of explanations to make them see what he was talking about, and next time he used the word, they'd have forgotten all over again. So while he's scratching his pileature and tugging his wattles trying to figure how to get this secret out of them, up pipes a human voice behind him: 'This is the threadmole.'

"Doesn't Blade whip around? A human is pointing to the chin on one of his two faces. Right in the center of the chin is a small mole. 'See?' says the human—he turns around and shows Blade his other face—no mole setting on that chin. The chin without the mole is fat, Blade digs, and the chin that got the mole on it is flat, like something drawn it inward. Otherwise, the faces are the same. Blade, he don't know what to make of it. He's peering and muttering and cussing and they laughing at him, 'You some silly bird, ain't you?' they saying—and one say, 'The threadmole is the knot at the end of the thread that winds through our bodies and holds us together. That's why the threadmole chin is flat; the thread done drawn it inward.'

"Blade, you can imagine: he's thunderstruck. His feathers up and down his back are wilting and unwilting with amazement. They done laid out their life-and-death secret before his very eyes; they done practically laid their souls down on his tongue. He so excited it all he can do to keep his mind on his plan, which is to invite fifty of them up to the Big House for a dinner and gala—So he flaps off, shouting after, 'Now don't y'all fight over who gets to go flying the first time, because you all getting a chance sooner or later'—He leaves them laughing and yelling up, 'Whatever makes you think we'd want to fly? We don't have no wings!' "

"You mean they accepted his invitation?"

"Why not? They jumping at the chance to meet this Massa God, because, damn, if it's someone like Blade they been sacrificing to, well ain't they been a pretty fool?"

He was silent for several minutes. She said finally, "So what'd Blade do next?"

Shifting, Gaylord stretched out on his back, interlaced his fingers beneath his head; he stared at the darkness among the beams. His voice seemed to him sudden and near in the heavy night silence of the dunes.

"It's evening, baby, and Mr. Blade, man-slayer hopeful to the Big House, fricasseer of loathesome plans, and genuine lay-wasting god, is hovering and fluttering and yap-yapping like a gorgeous pederastic sunbird over the preparations for the gala and the feast. Big House ain't never seen such Texas-rich hangings, of pure tenant-farmer condemned I believe they was, or such glowing plutonium settings, or such splendid lynch pyres of chandeliers. Miz V, she up in her dressing room squawking and screeching at her butterfly maids while they trying to plunk and latch onto her anyhow her most monstrous appointments and gowns. Stars all over the sky (remember, baby, I told you they were gods' houses) they emptying out each their bellyful of bird, and gods are gawkily swooping toward the Big House in such appalling numbers that astronomers say there never been such a night for shooting-stars as there was then. Only one ain't flapping out of his greedy skull with excitement is the Massa LG himself, who instead is scratching around fuming and speechless on finding he can't watch *Lucy* because all the current been diverted to the chandeliers. All the gods there, and everything ready at last. Blade gives a speech to the assembly, and lays out before them his unspeakable gold-star plan. I ain't going to tell you about that part, on account of how I'd just be making it up."

She laughed.

"Yeah. So Blade soars down to earth, in a swan dive, I believe it was, and as he nears, of course, he sees the people down there laughing till he thinks their heads going to all fall off their necks and his job going to be done for him—Fifty of them though, the soberest among them, recover enough to climb onto his wings. As he's starting to flap he say, 'Now don't be afraid, my friends'—That done it. They yelp like they was one,—'Whatever we got to be frightened of?'—and they all fall off of him guffawing fit to die again. Blade, he say nothing after that. He was only trying to be friendly. He shoulder them and fly them chuckling and giggling up to the Big House in the realm of the thunderheads and Tanzanian fields. He introduce them to the gods assembled in the ballroom, he introduce them to Massa LG and Miz V, who they bow down to, terrible disappointed in the Massa though they is, because they found he ain't nothing but a huge perfectly enormous pink bird who grumbles all the time and who wears two constantly blaring TV's like a pince-nez down to the end of his beak. Drinks is served. (Of the finest hog-soul puree.) Then the Massa say, all according to plan, Rantha, and he nod to the fifty humans sitting in a semi-circle at his feet, 'Missy?' he say, 'Missy? Which one of these humans you think is the most beautiful?'

"And Miz V say, she's trying to keep her voice below a screech, and she's failing: 'I think they all is equally beautiful, Massa'—here the humans smile and nod to each other—

" 'Mr. Blade?' Massa call—Blade, who's hopping around the tops of the chandeliers and coaching and conducting every inch of the way, Blade looks down and yips: 'Yes, Massa?'—'Blade,' says LG, 'Which one of these humans you think's the most beautiful?'—And Blade goes, 'I think they all of them is equally beautiful, Massa'—and the humans, they grinning pair of ears to pair of ears.

" 'Judge?' Massa shouts—and up waddles an old bird been chosen as one not likely to hand down a flighty opinion, since the star where he live is Sirius"—

"Oog."

" 'Now Judge?' Massa say, 'Which one of these humans you think's the most beautiful?'

"Well, Judge peers, he squints, he paces all around and rattles papers for a while, and then he say, 'I think they indeed is all equally beautiful, Massa, except'—here the humans start to laugh, but something all of a sudden in the air of that place makes their chuckles sort of creep off into nothing —'Except,' Judge croons, 'that the mole on the

217

chin on a side of each one of them is hideously ugly. I judge therefore that the nonmole fat-chin halves of the humans are a thousand times more beautiful than the moleagenous flat-chin halves they joined to.' And he waddles off and sets down.

"Now the humans you can imagine, they looking at each other, and looking at each other, shaking their heads, and bursting into tears, and blubbering, 'Ain't true, it ain't true.' And after a while they look around and bawl, 'Massa Lord God, it ain't true!'

"And Massa Lord God peeks up from CBS and NBC just long enough to growl: ' 'Course it's true. Sure as Eastern Time and Central Time and Mountain Time all three a dead bore, 'course it's true.' "

"Hey: that's actually pretty clever because—"

"Shh baby, because all the thousand gods are setting back real quiet, all according to Blade's gold-star plan, while the humans are babbling and bawling near gone mad with consternation, like one half saying to the other half: 'If I'm so ugly I ain't going to degrade you by being joined next to you no more'—

" 'You aren't, I'm telling you,' the other half answering, 'I always thought the threadmole was a real beauty spot on you—'

" 'How you know that,' first half saying, 'since you ain't never seen me?'

" 'I seen it on the others.'

" 'What you going around looking at the others for?'

" 'I'm not, baby, I'm only saying I—'

" 'You tomcatting around' (or pussycatting around, depending on which one had the mole, Rantha) 'You tom-or-pussy-catting around with the others, well I ain't going to degrade myself no more by being joined next to you—Blade! Mr.

218

Blade! Cut me off from this dog! (hussy!)'—And before long everyone of them shouting, since they ain't never had any arguments before and they don't understand that arguments get over and done, they shouting, 'Blade! Mr. Blade! Cut this thread-mole with your blade! Tear us apart and get me free!' And Blade, he flits down all a-worry from the chandelier he's on and he says real concerned-like, solicitously gliding out his hog knife, 'You sure of what you asking me, humans? Because you know, once it's been done it isn't never—'

"Miz V screeches, 'Shut up you integrationist trash you going to blow it again—'

"Blade, he paying no attention. His hog knife whirring like a fan on high on a hot day. Fifty strokes at the threadmole; fifty snaps of fifty un-leashed threads and they whip through bodies like escaping snakes, to be gathered by the lady-birds and by Blade's orders burned; fifty wrenchings apart by the two claws of Blade of the last human connection at fifty groins. One hundred half-humans, deliriously milling and squalling at their newfound lightness and separation, staring at each other, running up to Massa and showing off their new bellies, and their new moleless chins (though the ones that had the threadmole, they got clefts in their chins where Blade cut out the moles, and the clefts been handed down to this day)—'Take us home!' they yelling, 'We going to show the rest how we all of us beautiful now!'

"But now that those gods got the best evening meal of their whole eternal lives all trapped in their very crypt and sanctum, you think they going to let them humans go? They are, baby; because Blade, he's a clever bird. Besides, his life at stake. He takes them humans home. He follows them over the earth, whirring his hog knife and shouting along with them, 'We all going to be beautiful! We all going to be beautiful!'

"After that night, there wasn't one human left whole on the land. With the greatest of ease Blade popped before dawn five hundred human souls into his net, and he flew them on home to the realm of the thunderheads and Tanzanian fields to be devoured on spits by the residents of stars. He left the bodies to rot. And every night he, or rather his son, because Blade's gone now, visits the earth and dashes bodies to the ground and clutches the escaping souls in his claw and pops them into his net—or, if he can catch us asleep, he just lowers his beak gently down our snoring throats and plucks the soul out and leaves us to wake up and walk around dead for the rest of our lives—And before long, hatred, and envy, and distress, and war, and enslavement, and death, and all the rest were words flowed in rivers off the tongues of men, since now everyone a half, half-full and half-empty, everybody always wanting something else of somebody else's, hoping that at last that'll make him whole once more. Not a month had gone by after the night of the Big House before the cleft chins and the fat chins were dividing up the earth and fighting till they dead. It got so the only time they ever forgot where they were and remembered where they'd been is when they laid down together and made—hey, Rantha?"

He opened his eyes and looked down his chest, where Amarantha lay, with her limbs flung over his, fast asleep.

xii

Marian sat in her brother Mandus's kitchen and played with her hands. A stew muttered on the stove beside her chair. Beyond the open doorway, Mandus and his roommate Sam were gathering from a long table what seemed to Marian to be blueprints or large-scale maps, which lay curling among a dozen chair backs and a forest of ashtrays and beer bottles. She said loudly, "Those for the buildings you going to bomb, or the cops you going to ambush." She grunted: "Huh!" as Sam scowled in answer and her brother grinned, neither speaking. Together the two men eased the rolls of paper into a laundry bag and surrounded them with faintly reeking linen. "You tell John you going to use your coin-laundry for a commando-base when he helped set you up in it?"

Sam hefted the bag to his shoulder and Mandus studied it and punched it once where a roll hinted at its outline through the linen. "Well, sister, he said he only going to fund us indirectly."

"He never said any such thing."

Her brother mimicked in counter-tenor: "He never said any such thing." In his own voice, patting the laundry bag: "The other set, Sam. Ten o'clock."

Sam jerked his head sideways toward Marian. "Think we can dispense with this sideshow by then?"

"Why, Sam!" The men walked down a hall, her brother's voice fading: "Thought you liked being reminded of the pleasures of bachelorhood?"

She stood up and plucked the lid from the stew: her spoon herded the various lumps, which jostled like sheep. Simmering eruptions resumed, and minutes passed as with lowered face she let her thoughts linger in the salt and carnal steam. Her skin was heat-prickled and concealed in a small cloud.

Steps were behind her. "So what the fuck am I going to do with you."

Not looking up, she said quietly: "Your language, little brother, you aren't with your hoodlum friends just now."

A heavy frown gathered on his face: "What am I going to do with you?"

She smiled a moment. "Why don't you sell me, put the proceeds into gun belts or something."

"Yeah, bullshit." He turned away and stood looking out the window, which was rattled against its disoriented frame by the mendicant hand of the rainstorm. On the other side of the back lots, rows of lighted windows struggled from the buildings against the consuming darkness. Behind him, she slapped the lid onto the stew and said, "You glad about me and John being finished?" She turned to the sink to wash greens.

"Ease up, will you? Wasn't me that walked on you."

"Father would have been glad."

"That your opinion?" He turned round and regarded her face, low and studious over the greens; his frown relaxed. He said gently: "I can't see him being glad over it, Marian."

"You can't?" Her thumbs rubbed at grit in the

troughs of white stalks. "I don't even know if he ever come around to liking John, because he never would talk to me once I got to be a woman."

"He did like him though, sister. Respected him. You had to respect him."

"Father always made me feel I done him personal wrong by everything I decided on."

"Forget it, all right?"

"I used to think he was glad I didn't have any children since it proved what he'd been saying all along, and everybody sort of waiting for me to come through with a child, and each time I conceived it was as if there was coming another worse test I was bound to fail, until even John gave up on me."

Mandus walked back and forth, impatience touching his voice: "I can't see this as having much to do with the breakup, sister."

She loaded a pot with the dripping leaves and shook out her hands. "It did, though, and it was meant. I don't know why we ever even bothered, since he got it all planned from the beginning, like Father'd say, down to the last little minute in a little life, like you and me standing here now, brother"—The pot ticked over a fire. "Isn't he ever going to lift his hand from us? I don't see why we always have to be tried, is all. Over and over and over; I don't see."

He stopped pacing. "Sister, you married a white man, so it was going to end this way. Suprise is it took so long. My opinion—"

She interrupted: "What'd you tell him that night he came over here?"

"What night?"

"Don't give me that 'what night,' I'm telling you he come back from here a different man and he ain't hardly moved a finger toward me since that time, and that was April." She waited till the darkening greens collapsed into a mat; she closed the flames. "Give me plates, brother." She said sullenly, "I don't know what kind of political voodoo you used on him but you done froze his blood, and now he's talking about being ostracized and emigration and race war and Guernicas, and there's only one person he knows who got such a high fever in his head, that's you."

He laughed at her a moment. "I'm not taking blame for this. He asked me what I thought. I told him."

"That's right, brother." They sat down with the food. "You knew sure as you sitting here it's going to make his life impossible if he believe in your war predictions but you climbed up on your devil's pulpit anyways, you persuaded him best as you could since you can't resist tearing down everything you see including your sister's marriage"—He winced and turned away and waved his hand across his eyes as if to banish a fly; her lowered voice went on, "It wouldn't have cost you nothing to encourage him instead of threaten him, if he asked about your ideas you could have lied. Far as I can see you were just plain wanton."

"I don't know where you coming from or going to, Marian. John and me talked politics that time and nothing else. Wasn't no occasion for threats or lies or tearing down of any marriage. If he's scared, it's because any man who knows what's going on in this country is scared out of his skull."

"That's just what I'm talking about, don't you understand it isn't most people who enjoy tossing ideas of civil war about as if it was inevitable—"

He shrugged. "We got to speak a language the white man understands or he's not giving us the time of day."

Her voice rose: "You aren't talking to any white man now, brother, and you think I care for your maps and guns and thugs and any of your black revolution if it takes my husband from me?"

He screwed up his face scornfully. "You don't know what you're talking about."

"*You* don't know what you're talking about, yelling black power, blacks only, black states, black black at him till he afraid to touch his wife because she's black—"

"Bullshit, hear? Reason he ain't touching you is he sick of Mrs. Tom who left her mind back in Sunday School."

"What are you talking about, brother, you think he's one of your gunmen? He told me he scared out of his mind that the race hatred which people like you stoking up going to run him out of his clinic and spread to everywhere including his wife till he got nowhere to go except back to his lilywhite past—"

"That's what you're afraid of, sister. It isn't what he's afraid of."

"It *is* I'm telling you, what should I make it up for? He said between the government we got, and people like you, he and I going to be pushed and shoved apart and run back into our separate parts of town and that's near a quote, hear me? And you got to spill gas on the flames."

He scraped his plate gratingly, licked his fork, studied her. "So now he has gone back to his part of town, that what you're telling me?"

She waited, then let out breath heavily, pushed her own plate of coagulating food away, nodded.

"Besides which," he said, "the whole thing being my fault."

She closed her eyes. "I don't know, brother, I don't know who or what I'm supposed to blame."

He tipped his chair back and laced his hands behind his head, smiling broadly. "Yeah, you never can tell. One of the things we were saying when he was over here, I told him since this country's going to fall apart, and since it ain't going to be too nice for your integrated couple here, best thing for him to do would be to take himself and you and his medical equipment out of this country right now and set up in some already black state where the two of you going to be tolerated." His chair rapped forward. "Told him to try Jamaica. Go down, look it over. Thought you might like the beaches."

She looked at him with contempt. "We're Americans, Mandus."

He grinned at her. "That's all right. Nice people down there, they'll forgive you after a couple of years." Leaning back again: "Now, if he decides he isn't going to take you someplace that's safe like that, but instead he's going to walk out on you cold and run straight into the arms of the pigs, like you're telling me he's done, then I was right, isn't that a fact? This country is falling apart and it looks like your poor fool marriage is one of the bricks tumbling down, since as soon as your husband sees what's happening around him, he's off and running to save his skin, that's his white skin, sister, I'm talking about his white skin, because that white skin of his is one lot more precious to him than his marriage to you, Marian, since you've got a black skin, and when it's time to be counted he stands up as a racist, just like all the rest of them." She began to answer and he overrode her: "If that isn't true and he isn't a racist then what did he leave you for? You're the one told me that's just what he left you for, sister."

She gazed down blinking at her lap, where her hands worked at squeezing each other rapidly. With amusement he cupped his hand behind his ear as if to hear her better: "What'd you say?—Oh, you aren't telling your brother how he's talking like a hothead right now? Know why that is? Because you don't know any more whether he's a racist or not, do you." Still gazing at her hands, she shook her head fretfully. He mocked: "Poor big sister, she's always been afraid of it and now it's happened. Well that's a shame."

"He don't know what to choose, brother. Now with everything all going off the rails, he's just lost his presence of mind, since when he got married in the cause of brotherhood in this country and—"

Hands on the table, he pounced foward at her with an expression of delighted astonishment. "What'd you say you got married for?"

"He's been working for fifteen years for brotherhood, Mandus, and our being married is part and parcel of what he's been doing, and I've been a help to him, I have been, until you and your thugs started tearing everything down he's been trying to build up—"

"Is that a fact." He nodded his head with satisfaction. "Is that a fact. And I always thought you two got married to find a place to hide in, just like anybody else." He shook his head, "But no, you got married in the cause of brotherhood, well what an interesting thing to do, sister. Especially in a country so set and devoted on making a perfect system of racism, now that's really something intriguing. Here they been feeding you promises of assimilation and brotherhood and the coming day of the dream come true and you just didn't know that the promises were nothing but words to keep you quiet and a slave, no, you swallowed it all, hook-line-and-sinker, lock-stock-and-barrel, pap-nipple-and-tit, the complete package, and you based your grand little marriage on it. Is that all that goes into your marriage, sister, or do you happen to love this pig too?"

She shouted: "Shut up, brother, you shut up—"

He went on: "So it looks like you've got some thanks owing to your husband for waking up and realizing what his real interests are, which is to go back to his part of town"—his arm shot out pointing towards the north, and he shouted back, "which is the white part of town, Marian—"

She said, clenching her eyes, "He belongs with us—"

He jabbed his finger with a series of raps at the tabletop. "And your interest is to stay right here where you came back to, back to your own people."

"I've been with my people, I have been—"

"Oh you have? Then what did you have to come to my place for? Why didn't you stay in your own house? Because the truth is, what you've been doing is turning yourself into a white woman in a white man's house, denying the hatred you feel and denying the pride and denying your sisterhood with the people who are your sisters and brothers, and where's all that denying got you to? Nowhere. You listening to me? You've twisted and wrenched and beaten yourself into some gentlewoman shape that's got no use and that isn't your own, I don't see why you don't fall apart right here right now in a pile of limbs and tits you living all them lies."

She jerked her head away, her mouth turned down. He leaned forward and lifted her plate up, clacked it down again. "You eating this?" She twisted away farther, her gorge rising. He walked with her plate to the window and quickly ate the cold remains. He said swallowing: "Now our father, what he did is he ran"—he pointed his fork at her reflection, against which raindrops toiled on the dark pane. "You ran to the white man's bed, he ran to the white man's religion." His flat hand took off. "Vroom! Run sinna man. He figured if he stopped anywhere he just might wake up to the dream and then he might have to fight and so end up in a cell, like Gaylord Jackson's father—Yassa boss, Atlanta, Greenville, Springfield, Boston, run to the Lord. Way Aunt told it, it'd make her boil sitting there watching Father preach to his black congregation about what sinners they were, and she'd ask him after, what you telling them they sinners for? You tell them who the real sinners are, brother.—But he wouldn't. Oh, no. He figured he'd love the white man into brotherhood, transform everything around him by some kind of golden radiation. Isn't that what the Lord said? Love thine enemy? Big mighty Christian black man gets the Nobel Peace Prize and ends with a bullet in his mouth? Your father spent a lifetime talking about loving the people that he hated with all the guts they left him with. Faked him out when his daughter heard what his mouth said and married one of them. Maybe he should have come out with his rage in the first place instead of living like a man cut in two? Maybe he should have come out and told his black sheep who the sinners really were? Maybe he picked up on his white man's Christ so he could tell himself that he wasn't a coward not to go back home, and run everyone of them rapist crackers off the land his fathers made?" Mandus sang suddenly shouting: "Lord, won't you hide me? Our people been yelling it for three hundred fifty years and maybe that's why we still in chains?" He walked back to the table, where Marian sat hunched and twisted away over the back of her chair. "You're the same as him, sister. I used to stand by the kitchen door shaking in my shoes watching you sit by the stove glaring at the floor working your hands for hours while you plot some revenge, and Aunt would say 'How's that child going to find a man she don't send him running to Jesus for shelter'; and what've you done with that rage, Marian, you're sitting down on it and it's eating your life away. You don't think your husband knows that? You don't think he knows your love of him is built on quicksand and somewhere in your heart you hate him?" He leaned over her, squinting, saying between clenched teeth: "Hate him with every inch and coil of your guts? You don't think he knows how you killed half yourself so you could survive in this country? Your America? What the hell you think he left you for, what for in the name of your priss-ass Lord do you think he wants a woman who hates him and hates his people with half of herself and hates herself and her people with the other half? You think he wants a woman with the brain of a slave? No wonder he's out looking for some action, would have been ten years ago if he wasn't such a dried-out priest—"

The room was still. She said after a moment in a quiet voice, "Grant me, brother, I've got the privilege to go on denying the hate in myself and go on trying to be as decent a woman fit to live on this planet as I can, and go on trying to love my husband and the Lord howevermuch you hate them both and though they may be set against me, and trying to love my country sick as it is, and you, brother, though Jesus knows you're making it uphill going—"

He laughed at her. "You fucking saint, is that how you talk to John when you say you love him? You hate every one on that list, hear? Only thing you care one shit for is the tragic soap opera of your black-skinned self. The rest of it is nothing but speeches and posturing in front of the bathroom mirror."

She took in breath and held it; then said deliberately, pressing the palps of her fingers against her eyes, "I got no respect for this, brother. I don't hate my husband the way you say I do." She turned on him: "And I don't care about you and your bachelor ideas. You don't know anything about the love you scorn so. Only thing you know of is hate and war and degradation, that's all you have and it's where you're going to end."

"We've been at war since 1607, sister. People dying in that war every day. All I'm doing is suggesting we fight it in an organized fashion, using weapons on the enemy instead of on ourselves. You got something to lose? Good for you, the rest of us don't." He walked past her and into the living room; she followed quickly and said bitterly in the doorway:

"The man you want to fight got a million troops and H-bombs, and all our people got is Coke bottles."

"That's why we're slaves." He swept butts and

ashes from the long table into a trash can. "Thing about this country, though, it doesn't know what threatens it. All the missiles guarding the border against Russia and China, so much paranoic mania boarding up the windows against the madness in the head. Think what a couple of those fancy bombs or chemicals well placed and ready in the ports and the heartland could do for that man we're fighting, hm? Think of the debts we could collect, Marian"—He stood up and looked at her a moment, his jaw trembling. "Half the world begging to give us some, including some true-blood and blue-eyed, crackerjack cop-loving Americans who are itching to be rid of us and get themselves in power."

"You don't know them, brother, and you don't know what they'll do; they will get in power and then they'll put us in camps until they find out it's easier to gas us—"

"What if we use gas on them first?" He raised his eyebrows and smiled at her. "Think of that?"

"You're crazy."

They did not talk for a long time. She paced round the living room, aimlessly trailing her fingers on the walls. A nearby firehorn bellowed through the rainstorm, bringing forth sirens. She listened as the trucks clanged and snorted below, then failed to linger and revved onward, their wet wheels hissing. She said finally: "Can I stay here, brother?"

"Stay here?"

"Yes—"

He crouched, sweeping ashes into a dustpan. "I don't know. This ain't a safe place. How long?"

She said distractedly after a minute, "What? What did you say?"

"How long?"

"Brother, I don't know, how am I supposed to know—"

"That a fact?"

"I thought maybe he'd come looking for me—"

"Looking for you?" He stood up again. "Yeah? I thought you were finished with him?"

She looked at him fearfully. "Well I don't know, I—"

He lay the dustpan down on the table with a clatter and walked at her. "I thought you said he'd gone over to the pig? I thought you said that?"

"He's my husband, brother"— She said in a weak voice: "I want him, if he wants me—'

He grasped her head tightly in both hands, his fingers spread over her temples and her ears, the sides of his thumbs stroking her cheekbones, and he stared at her. She squirmed; he shook her. Tears of fright started from her eyes. He said through his teeth: "He doesn't, and they don't, will you get that through your head? They don't want us."

● ● ● Marian lay in her brother's bed in darkness, counting for sleep with the pulse of the rain. Blurred men's voices coursed outside the door, and in exasperation she pressed shut her ears, flung her head back and forth; the voices shattered out into laughter. She gave in to waking then; her eyes lay open to the timeless stillness of a strange room in night. She stretched her arm up, studied its length, aligned it to parallelograms of street light that swung up misshapen from the panes and trembled on the walls. Outside, with a last sown splatter on the pavement, the rain died.

Right now   Right now   This very moment
If you could stop time and look around the
world   You'd find every kind of thing ever happened all still and together like in a book of
photographs—every one of them sounds out there
got a life to it   People dying with their heads
split open   People seeing God   People rasping
out of breath exhausted with love   You lie in
your bed and someone giving birth in a bed like
yours on the other side of the wall   Beneath you
some girl finding her first blood, and above you
some man been middle-aged stumbles on nothing
and feels it crash on him he's old, remember, one
dinnertime, 'Father, how's the Lord keep all them
people in mind, he must be going out of his head'
'We are his head, child'—She chuckled and wavered
her fingers before her eyes. What that pope don't
understand is no one needs birth control more
than his Boss up there—Know what I'd like
to do? Like to stop time screech, a car in an
accident, and stroll down before every one of them
frozen moments like a general reviewing his army,
you there I'll take you   And dive in   Let the
world crank on again, what do I care what Brother
says about dreams, they're better than his nightmares   I suppose he'd choose a nuclear bomb
going off   Sploosh goes the world   I can't figure
what one I'd choose though—something peaceful I
guess, something you never want to get up from—
the Lord got all those moments in his pile, by the
time you decided on the one you want, it's already passed you by.

I ain't looking at my watch   It don't matter
what time it

She saw midnight on the green dial. Yeah, well I
don't guess he's coming now.

Maybe Mandus is right though

Maybe he is right   Maybe John does think I'm the one who turned against him   Out of hate Maybe he's holed up somewhere his own self because he couldn't bear going home with me not there   Don't make no sense though   He must know something about me

They're out there though   I don't know what they're buzzing over   But that grim Sam cat already whipped the door open twice coming in for something   I know he's checking to see if I'm listening in   As if I cared about stocking my ears with their cow manure   I can see why John still reeling from a night in this place   Chemical warfare   Bombs in the heartland   Any man wants power he's going to be a criminal   I don't want his black nation   Haven't we got governments enough   You ask me for a rundown of Satan's works, I'd put them on the top of the list

It's only the crazy people got an idea of what to do now   You got any kind of balance you know nothing's going to work way it seemed   I don't hardly blame him for staggering around   He used to be so sure   Ain't his fault what's happened   That don't mean he can't love me   I got nothing to do with what's happened outside Politics never stopped a man from wanting a woman   If he wanted her   And I begged him I begged him

And what did you tell him when he begged you back   I can't   That's what   I don't care   He got me riled   Yes so you gave him nothing so what do you expect from him.

I don't know what I feel about color   I always said there ain't no good in looking up too close into yourself and sifting in the garbage   He's

always saying the worst things about himself   Tor-
turing himself   He always got to tell me his
garbage and ask my forgiveness   I don't want to
hear it and I don't want to know mine either
Yes and he knows both   He knows you don't forgive
him or why'd you leave anyhow   Why not   I
got a right   He didn't trust me   He got no place
to think I'd turn against him   And you just made
it worse by walking out on him   That's just
fine because I don't care   If he's going to
think I'd cheat on him   So what because you
thought he was cheating on you.   He is cheating
though   He is   You did   You cheated and you
lost your ring   I love him though   I love him
I'm not made of hate   It's not true what
Brother says   How can John think I turned
against him   You did though   He turned   He
turned   He said he wanted to go back across
town   And you went back   You didn't trust
him   You ripped the marriage down well as him
I didn't   No I didn't   He's the one   He
started it with his crazy ideas   He ripped it
Him being so scared   What kind of man is that
What kind of man is that   You told him that
You don't forgive him   You want him to be
perfect all the time   You want some grand kind
of force holding you up every minute   You make
him feel like nothing for being weak here and
there   You make him hate you   He wants you
to love who he is   Not some dream   What does
it matter if he done what he done   He isn't
nothing but a human being

I don't know, I don't know, how are we ever
going to find each other, how am I going to keep
from telling him what I done   I'm never going to
find that ring and he never failed yet to catch me
lying   Why must you John   You'll never trust

me now   If you think you've been uptight   Just
wait till I start sitting around watching you and
wondering when you're going to ask me to bed
I know I won't be able to help it and it going
to drive you wild   You going to think I'm
chanting to myself   White man   White man   I
was out of my mind to say that to him   He's
crazy to think I meant that   I did though   I
know I did

I do have color feelings   I know I do
Brother's right   I felt I won something by
marrying a white man   I don't know what I won
though   I look down on his people same as I
look down on my own   Like he got to measure
up   Oh yes Marian your husband got to measure
up because he got the gold star lucky piece of
being white so he had better measure up and be as
worthy as the black people are   Or he isn't going
to be deserving of the great favor you bestowed on
him by giving him yourself   Because you done
him one tremendous favor by marrying him   You
took pity on the white folks and saved one of
their number didn't you, you beautiful Christian
woman

Oh baby are you one mess

He's nothing but a bunch of notions about color
to me   I don't know nothing about who he is
I wouldn't blame him a bit for cheating on me
If I was in his shoes   Shit I been stretching
him out between where I figure I want him and
where he's being forced to go by his own crazy
notions   I been pushing him around and setting
up standards for him   So he's trying to get out,
what do you expect   He's trying to tell you this
yesterday and what do you do, you attack him,
and out he goes

I don't know   I don't guess there ever been a

237

man who understood a woman, nor a woman either who understood a man, you could live five hundred years with him   It wouldn't help   You don't learn   You don't change   You want to give him what he don't ask for and then you want to keep what he needs—A woman thinks   There's someone   He loves me   I'm not alone   I got a reason for living   Keep thinking it honey it's a pretty dream

Man sometimes I can see what Martha been doing with her endless string of arms and legs What difference does it make once you know they're all strangers   He's kissing my breasts for the thousandth time this morning   He couldn't find me   There was nothing there   Nothing I'm a voice in my head trapped in a nowhere How's he going to find that, once he's stopped pretending he isn't alone.

It's you John   You done it   You blasted it I still would've lied like I always done   I still would've touched you everywhere and believed it was you   And then it was John   And then it was

We used to talk of these things   At least talk of them   I thought I could see him and him me I don't know when we stopped   We've forgotten all of it

I don't even know if he wants me again   I don't even know   He obviously isn't bothering to come looking for me   For all I can tell my walking out was just what he needed to set himself apart from me   What if I go home and I find he don't need me   Like Brother said   He doesn't want me   Brother said they don't want us What am I going to do if he wants to end it How am I going to start again

I love him though   Outside of all the crazy
things   Outside of all the crazy color things   I
love him   That's where Brother's wrong   He's
right but he's wrong   He says color's everything
which is half-true and he sets it up into politics
and tries to make it all true   And then it's false
     It is false   If we love each other, color doesn't
have to matter   It does matter now but it
doesn't have to   If he wants me again, then we're
not going back to the beginning again like I was
asking him to do   We're starting over just on the
basis of ourselves   Nothing else   No crusade
     No color   No faith   No politics   Nothing
else but ourselves   I'm telling him   I'm not thinking color any more   I'm through with the Comm-
mittee   I'm through with all of it   There it is
again   It's such a lovely thing the rain
     He used to love it when it rained   In the
summer and the spring   Once he said the only
time I feel a religious feeling Marian is when that
first rush of the rain comes like a divine hand
sweeping through the night   It was night   Like
now   Lying in the dark, he didn't know if I was
awake, Marian? He never calls me anything else but
Marian, Marian, Lord, I feel like I can hear every
time he ever called me coming back coming down
out there   Every drop is the sound of him calling
my name   I wish that sweeping hand of the
storm would snatch him on up from wherever he
is and land him down here beside me   Standing
here all in a warm light   All gentle   All made
of the rain   Come down for loving like that story
of a god   All changed into a shower of gold.

xiii

Amarantha!

Amarantha, you're going to listen to me

Look, Amarantha, I'm sorry to have to do this but that's no reason to

She stopped walking. Will you just forget it please? Forget the whole thing. She turned and stepped into the road.—Listen, Amarantha, can't you have a little patience? Try to understand that if you pressure me like that—She ran. Hey, Amarantha? He chased her under the streetlamps, into the middle of the roadway, up the rise; their steps rapped out into the night. Cones of approaching headlights waved at the top of the hill, and nearing her, he shouted: Get back on the sidewalk, are you crazy? She ran with closed eyes and pressed shut her ears. I don't care, I don't care—air brakes gasped. He caught her neck from behind and flung her aside onto the curb. She heard a thump; his body flew backwards. Their eyes met. Silence rang down.

Gaylord swung off the bunk while her rapid breath shook her in her sleep. She woke and sat up in a rush and coughed. Her breathing slowed. For a moment she seemed to stare, then began touching round the base of her skull with her fingertips. "Hey Rantha?" She turned her face up in surprise, and flushed hotly. "Oh. Christ."

"Yeah." He shook his cheeks and picked at congealment by his eyes. "So what the shit you moaning and groaning at."

"I wake you up?"

"Naw."

"Well I had the dream; I always do at night. The one I told you." She pushed back her hair and frowned. The window wrapped her shoulders in a gust of dawn. "I'm sorry if it bothered you."

"Yeah. I got needs." His steps slapped off, infuriating the floorboards, while she muttered:

"He's lucky I didn't screech as usual." She sat on the bunk, said after a moment: "You know something? I'm bored with that crummy dream and I'm not particularly curious about how it's supposed to end either." She considered a minute, then said: "Gaylord?" She heard his step in the doorway, where he had been watching her and listening; she said, "Oh." She trotted after him: "That's the point, why should I bother to care about him, I mean the person who got killed, my fiancé? since you're a lot more interesting than him? He was really sort of dull, if you bother to think about it."

"You're the only chick I know who can stand around expounding affairs of the spirit while a cat's trying to take a whizz." He suddenly spattered the sand.

"Okay, but don't you see this is sort of significant?" She gripped his bicep and shook it, and he said angrily,

"Fucking leave me alone a minute, will you?"

"Hey all right"—she retreated, and fumbled at the bedtable, then circled the room, brushing her hair. "No the thing is if we go together, even for a short time, I think that whole stupid affair with David is going to be a lot less important, do you see what I mean? The same as with you and your wife, like you were saying last night"—she grunted briefly as she tugged at a snarl—"because half the reason anyway I'm still stuck on the accident and all that ridiculous guilt about him is at least it's been something to hold onto, even if it hurts—are you listening?—but now that there's something to replace it and to be in between, no matter how soon it's over—do you think?"

He walked past her and clattered at the stove. "I got no proper thoughts before coffee." A box of kitchen matches sent out a muted rattling in his hand.

"Oh."

A match croaked and hissed. "You want coffee?"

"Okay—because that story you told is true, you do forget things, sort of begin again a little bit, when you make love and undo the damage that Mr. Blade did—"

"I thought you slept through half of that."

"Uh-uh, I did not, are you kidding? Just right as you finished, and you shouldn't be insulted because you've got a beautiful soothing telling-voice, did anybody ever tell you that?— Jesus there're a lot of snarls in my hair—even if I noticed you are sort of tone-deaf."

He stood in the open doorway, not answering, looking out to the brightening dunes. They hid from his sight the already risen sun, and left the sand-grass clumps by the shack still somnolent in shadow. Above the valley mists, whose gauzy fingers wandered over hills, a flight of gulls squalled, reminding them of stillness. He reached a pot from the stove. "Stay more than a couple days down here, you'd have them gulls' brains." He flung handfuls of water, slightly fizzed from staleness, over his chest and face. "Nothing to do but copulate."

"I like copulation."

"I didn't notice."

"Didn't you?" Still brushing, she stood behind him. "Listen, Gaylord, I've been thinking, the doctor might actually let me stay over with you sometimes—like on weekends maybe, because it's obvious what improvement there's been already, and what, well not caused it, but sort of liberated it, and he's always said that in a sense the treatment won't really have begun until I've decided I don't need the watcher and the dream—" her voice trailed off.

"You've been doing fine, Rantha."

"Do you think he'll say I can, though?"

"You don't know what he'll say. He's going to take his time, probably. I think you best not send your hopes any further than you can reach." He stood at the stove again while she said:

"I do, though, I feel much more confident, and if it turns out he won't cooperate we can always get a lawyer like you said."

"I don't know where we'd get the money, Rantha."

"Hm? Oh there're all sorts of legal-aid type things, aren't there?"

"I don't know that kind of thing." He fussed with powdered coffee and boiling water.

"Well, if—"

He interrupted: "I'm not too willing to take charge of that."

"Well all right then no one's asking you to, I'd be perfectly capable, I'd just need help in a couple of things and—"

Again he interrupted: "You'd need someone to

vouch for you. Someone to support you and answer for you."

"No, I can get a job, all right?" He made no answer and she said, "You want to stop futzing around with the coffee and tell me what's bothering you?"

"Look, Rantha." He turned round to her.

"Okay, out with it, will you?"

"You're talking about a job but you don't have no skill, understand? And what I'm saying is like maybe that doctor of yours is slow but you'd be out of your skull to walk away from the free check-days and medical and therapy and Braille lessons and they going to teach you some job when you ready, and you told me they planning to give you a skin-graft operation for free after a while? shit. Maybe they own you like a dog like you say, but they feeding you with steak, hear? Ain't no black sister on that kind of roll."

"That has nothing to do with me so what are you bringing her up for? You threw out the black sister you had and I'm not keeping her or anyone from anything—"

"I didn't say that, Rantha, because you aren't, I believe you aren't, I'm only saying you—"

She interrupted loudly: "Because what was all that talk last night about getting me out if you think I ought to stay inside? if you don't mind telling me?"

"It was something I said, see? You were feeling depressed and I wanted to cheer you up, that's all."

"Well thanks a million."

"I'm sorry, baby. I felt it at the time."

"And now what do you feel, please?"

"Your nightmare scared me, Rantha." Cups and saucers clanked in his hands.

"All right but I'd told you about it, I'd warned you? Gaylord?" Behind him, she lay her forehead on his shoulder blade. "That isn't it, is it?"

"You aren't cured yet, Rantha. You're a good chick but you aren't cured and I can't take charge of you."

She sidled round him, her hand on his upper arm. "Okay, you don't have to, because listen, I could still stay inside and if he lets me out to see you on the weekends, then—" she paused.

"We'll see what he says, Rantha. I don't know."

She said after a minute: "No, you haven't been listening because I never even thought of all that stuff about a lawyer until you mentioned it last night anyway, and forget all that, okay? Since I even think you're probably right? All I'm talking about"—her voice cut off.

"You promised not to ask anything of me, Rantha."

"Gaylord, all I'm talking about is something absolutely temporary—"

"You're going to try to make it permanent. Aren't you."

"Well I'm not going to hold you responsible, not for anything, that's what I promised in the water—"

"I'm going to feel responsible, Rantha."

"Well that's your problem then—"

"If it's my problem then I've got to deal with it, understand?" He faced her and held her by her upper arms. "See what worries me, baby. If we get going on this any much further, I'm not going to have any room to move around in, since what if I have to pull back, or pull out even? Rantha? I'm going to land you back in the hospital soon as you hear the first word about it." He dropped his hands from her and she gazed downward, saying nothing. He added: "I'm not going to feel free in this thing, little one."

She said after a moment in an undertone, "I'm letting you be free, though."

"It wouldn't end up that way. Seeing where we already are, Rantha."

"It would so end up that way because I promise you nothing will happen to me if you want to leave, at any time, Gaylord"—she rested her fists loosely on his chest. "Like this whole watcher thing I told you, it's about my father, and then it got pasted onto David, well it just doesn't fit my thing with you? We proved that last night? I'm really not crazy with you."

"Maybe so, Rantha, but I'm telling you, it's too late, don't you see that?"

"No I don't because I'm offering you sex and freedom and if you don't accept, it won't be because you're afraid of what'll happen to me, it'll be because you're afraid of what will happen to you—"

"All right, Rantha. You made your offer." He drank his cooled coffee quickly. "It ain't a risk I want to take."

"Well I don't see what risks have to do with this, we're not talking about anything but a couple of weekends."

"I don't want to get involved, all right? I just been through a shit marriage and I haven't got the stamina." He walked away.

She followed him: "*Who's* talking about getting involved? I'm talking about something completely casual and so don't you tell me I'm someone who can't control herself, just because you can't even sleep with a woman without thinking about something permanent and making all sorts of wild promises which you feel guilty about not keeping,

246

since no wonder your wife was able to walk all over you—"

"Leave off, will you? I don't have to do you no kind of service."

"No, mister, you don't."

He stood at the window, pressed his forehead against the sash, and began to speak in a quieter tone, "Look, Rantha, I don't want to—" She interrupted him sharply:

"Would you tell me where my clothes are please?"

"On the woodburner." He looked up. "One step to your left." Her hand slapped out. "You want your coffee?"

"No."

They stopped speaking. She dressed; he watched her body disappear.

He took his own clothes then and stood in the doorway once more. The top of the waking sun had crested the near dune. The sand's shadow line was flowing slowly in retreat toward the shack, ripplingly inching back over the hillocks, up the steps and up his body, stripping him of shade before the heat of the day. He shivered and perspired. She brushed by him to go out. As he turned from the door, the light strutted in after him and shimmered its stipplings over the bright floor. He collected the dishes and washed.

She said when she returned: "Hey?"

"Yeah?"

"I wanted to ask you, did you ever think of doing something with your stories? I mean like trying to write them down and get them published or something?"

"I was digging you for not thinking of asking that."

"Oh. Not even Mr. Blade though?"

"He belongs to me, understand? You keep your mouth shut about him, hear me?"

"Oh. Well one other thing."

"What."

"Do you think I should wear lipstick?"

They both laughed for a moment. "No, baby." She stood before him and he held her chin in the fall of light from the door. "Eye makeup; and your hair longer, see?" His gaze traveled down her and their muscles tautened. She moved away. He said, "You want to hit tbe beach before we go?"

"Uh-uh, not to swim."

"Too early. Just to walk."

"If it's just for a while, okay? Because I ought to get back."

"What you got for today." He batted their mattress back into place among the rafters.

"O. T. Occupational therapy. That's Braille lessons? At two. And also there's going to be about seventy hours of explaining to do."

"How you think they're going to take it?"

She cocked her head. "I think—Schleppstein's going to end up in favor. After some reproaches about procedure. You know? But as for Mrs. Linton; well, goodbye, it'll never be the same again."

"She a nurse or what."

"She's the housekeeper and she's not very advanced—Wait, Gaylord." She tensed. "There's a motor."

He listened. "On the road."

"No, it's turning."

"Fuck." He stepped quickly past the open doorway and stood beyond it. "State cop."

An engine died outside; a car door slammed.

Gaylord said, "He could have waited ten more minutes."

"Phooey because we didn't know it was private."
"Sure."

Steps thudded softly on the sand. "Mrs. Holbrook?"

She whispered: "Let me talk to him, all right?"

"Talk all you want. Secret is to keep him in circles."

"You watch." She stood in the doorway as steps halted before her.

"Friend of the owner, Miss?" A small wind passed by her arm as the cop looked inside; his eyes met Gaylord's in the shadow. "You read signs, buddy? Know what the fine is for tresspass around here?"

Gaylord said quickly, moving into the center of the room, "Yeah, but we just come in to warm up for a couple of minutes, you know? We were freezing out there sleeping on the beach"—he pointed—"With all that mist—it didn't look inhabited."

Amarantha backed up to let the cop in. He said, "The beach and the house are private and both are posted." His booted steps trod by her as he looked around the room.

"Yeah well the shack of course but I didn't know the beach was—we haven't made a mess, man."

The cop peered in a paper bag of garbage. "I could book the both of you for breaking and entering, did you think of that?" His steps stopped as he turned to Gaylord: "Did you think of that?"

"Yeah, but it was open, see, and—"

The cop interrupted, "It was locked when I checked it yesterday. Maybe somebody else got it open? Perhaps you think that you've got the right to bust into other people's—"

Amarantha interrupted him, "We tried to get

rooms in a motel down the road but they suddenly didn't have any vacancies, so we thought we had the right to bust into other people's."

The cop said gently, "Maybe the motel was full?"

"No, sir. We had a reservation. Sure but I'm sorry buddy I got nothing against your people but I got to think of my regular customers, isn't that prudent of him?"

The cop squinted at Gaylord. "That a fact?"

She said before Gaylord could answer, "If you look in his book you'll find a reservation for Dr. John Morrison. He figured that was all right over the phone."

His voice turned to her. "What's the name of this place, Ma'am."

"Quiet Nook, wasn't it hey? Yes, I remember."

"Come on," he said. "Let's have a look at him." He plucked up the garbage bag. "I'll take this."

She turned to Gaylord, grinning as the cop walked by her; Gaylord said, not moving, "Look, if you don't mind, officer, I'd rather we didn't press this."

The cop halted at the doorway, smiling. "Come on, doctor. We'll make it as short as we can."

"I'm not a doctor and we got things to do in Boston and I don't want anything to do with this, all right?"

The cop turned, hunching his shoulders. "Yes?"

She said, "Dr. Morrison's a friend of ours. His wife made the reservation. They were coming down in their car after us."

"They here?"

"We don't know. They never met up with us."

"All right, Ma'am. I'll accept that and if you don't mind we'll get down to the station now and get things squared away." He nodded once to Gaylord. "Come on then."

Gaylord said, "How about if we drop this, man. The thing happened like the lady says, but I just don't feel like going through this kind of scene."

"No, sir." The cop ducked out the door. "You file a complaint on him or I file one on you, understand? Get your things." He walked out and Gaylord watched him kick sand over the tracks left by the motorcycle. She whispered, "We don't have to go if we don't want to, Gaylord—"

"What are you talking about? Didn't you hear what he said?"

"Yes, well why don't we go then, it'll be fun to screw that little greaseball."

He spat. "Your fun."

"Gaylord, well I'm sorry but it's better than being arrested, at least it certainly is for me and I don't see—"

"You don't see nothing." He clenched her shoulder and hissed: "He wasn't planning to arrest us and you got to go play the fucking white crusader and drag my ass through court when I told you I'm on record—"

She turned and crossed the room to search for her pocketbook, muttering, "I told you I'm sorry, so we'll file the stupid complaint, it'll only take fifteen minutes."

He laughed loudly, then wobbled after her with oscillating knees, casting wide eyes upward and pressing together his palms in prayer. "Oh Lawdie Massa Judge sir how we been oppressed by that boss man down in that there Quiet Nook motel? Ain't letting none of us black folk in through the front door? but we shall overcome yes by the Precious Lawd with the help of your do-right

Honor sir we shall? Up your lily-white ass li'l Rantha?"

She shouted: "Then we'll tell him to arrest us is that all right with you?"

He said softly: "They're looking for someone of my description, Rantha. I'm not getting arrested."

"Then we'll have to file a complaint because I don't know what you—"

Her voice broke and he said sharply, "Smile," as the cop called, "Come on, people?"

He held her elbow tightly and said aloud, "Stairs now." They stepped out. "You got everything?"

She turned up her face, nodding. Yellow suns shone in her eyes. "Mm-hm—"

As they approached, the cop said, standing by his car, "You didn't stop here."

"Yeah, sure. We slept on the beach."

"All right. I'll ask you to ride with me, Ma'am." He said to Gaylord: "Use my tracks. Lead the way. I'm new in this county."

The car backed out of the driveway; the motor-cycle roared past. She listened to the police radio spit and she grabbed at the seat as they wove down back roads.

The cop said after a silence, "What's your name, Ma'am?"

"It's Miss. Jones."

She heard a smile in his voice: "Well, we'll get everything straight soon enough."

"My grandfather changed his name from Björnsson."

"From what?"

"Why do you think he changed it?"

The motorcycle's drone sunk and putted. Leaning out the window as his car stopped, the cop called to Gaylord, "How far is it?"

"Couple miles south on the highway."

The light was green and Gaylord turned, muttering, "He'll take care of her, fuck it." He pat the gas tank between his knees. "You going to come through now."

The cop said as they moved again, "You had this kind of trouble often?"

"What trouble?"

"Hey!" He honked his horn and said to himself, "Motorcyclists always speed. Always."

"Do we have to make some kind of complaint, or what?"

The cop said loudly, "Well what the hell's your friend think he's doing?" He honked again and the car leapt.

"Why don't you let him go ahead and I'll give the evidence."

"I'm afraid not. Well, he's slowing."

Gaylord rounded a curve and the car disappeared in his mirror. "Okay you cocksucker." He skidded as he raced up the rise of a side road that then forked; he turned left over the crest.

"I though he said the motel was on the highway?"

"Yes and it is so why don't—"

The car slowed and turned. A single rubber track ran left from the fork and the cop followed, reaching for his siren. He sat back expelling breath as the siren wailed. "Christ, these people, well excuse me Ma'am but you lean over backwards and next thing you know they're trying to push you over."

"You must have a problem."

"Believe me I do."

"I'm bleeding for you."

The highway was clear as Gaylord approached it once more. "Beautiful." He roared across the lanes.

Yellow dashes blurred as he throttled. The pines shimmered green. "See you around, Rantha."

The siren gurgled and moaned. For a moment she heard the motorcycle sound distantly as they shot squealing back onto the highway among braying horns; she was flung backwards as they sped on. The cop cursed, then excused himself. The car rattled and swayed. "Stupid fool, there he is, he must be doing a hundred."

She was sitting stiffly and tugging at her hair. "*You* stupid fool why don't you let him go and he'll slow down before it happens again—"

"Well Ma'am, he's going my way."

Biting her lip, she lunged at the wheel. With the back of his hand he rapped her head back against the seat. She sat up quickly. He muttered, "Try that again and I'll knock your face in." The car shook. "Put your seat belt on I told you!"

Gaylord's wounded arm seared with the shudder of the engine and he swore as the siren sounded in his ears. "This is more than I can chew, do something will you, Rantha?" He throttled up a hill and grinned suddenly, bent over the handlebars beneath the shouting wind. "My horse of the fucking gods." He yelled: "The fucking gods!" The distant sea swerved as he crowned the hill, he curved round a truck, he cried out and began to brake as railroad tracks leapt before his eyes. With rigid body he rattled over the tracks, and the motorcycle skidded, weaved, bucked him flying through a grove of pines. The motorcycle somersaulted over the truck and exploded in a tower of fire.

"Hold on, Ma'am!"

The seat belt slammed her stomach; her forehead thumped forward as the car shimmied to a stop.

Blinking, tearing at the buckle, she flung herself out the door and stumbled down the shoulder, waving her arms before her. "Officer! Officer!" She heard his steps slap on the road. "Down here!" His boots crunched, then padded beneath the pines. She ran down through whipping branches after his hoarse breathing. He shouted near her, "Over this way!" She tripped on a stump and fell on her shoulder. The cop said beside her: "He's unconscious. I'll get an ambulance. Are you all right?"

She nodded and sat up, closed her eyes. He said, "You remain with him." She listened to his steps strike off briskly into silence.

●●● John said aloud to himself: "Get out of bed. You can't stay here." He swung his feet to the floor and disengaged his trousers from a tower of children's puzzles and toys. "Thinking solves nothing, will you get that through your head?"

"I don't know where I'm supposed to go now." Looking out the door and down a corridor, buttoning, he spied and stepped out after a trotting pantless two-year-old, the youngest of his committee chairman Whit Whitney's six children. John had slept in her room. Overtaking her, he cleared his throat to speak, but she increased her trot and vanished through a door. "All these children, it'd drive me crazy." He walked onward, causing Victorian advertisements and derbied colored gentlemen to vibrate gently in their frames on the corridor walls. A woman's voice arrived: "John? That you?"

"Yes, good morning"—Having gained the kitchen, he leaned out a window and observed below, jailed through a fire-escape's iron slats, an undisturbed roadway, beside which a starched and bonneted family proceeded to Scripture through the rich light of a morning after rain.

"Hey there."

He looked left: Whit Whitney's wife, Alice, in African coif and bare arms, smiled from out a near window. She called along the brick: "The marchers aren't due for half an hour, that who you looking for, doctor?"

"How are they going to deploy people, did you hear?"

"Yes I did, there'll be a contingent going right here up Eliot, one up Dudley, one up"—her head popped from his vision, popped in again: "You put the fire on under the kettle and wait till I get something on, we've got enough yelling to do later."

Inside, fumbling with the stove, he muttered: "You'll never be able to explain it to him or her either if you don't go; you realize that. Wait, there's no pilot light. Even with what's happened; even more with it. Or to the others. Christ I don't even know everybody there now." He turned to cross the room, knocked on Whit's and Alice's door, but before he could speak she called:

"Matches in that blue box on the counter"—he crossed the room again as she concluded: "One up here, one up Dudley, one up Massachusetts Avenue, one down Massachusetts Avenue"

"Down Massachusetts Avenue though? Through Cambridge?"

"Yes, darling."

"Looking for students? On Sunday morning? And where are the soldiers?"

"Five hundred already in place at the plant. Whit's still trying to find out if they'll be more."

"I gather he isn't here?"

She swished from her room and bustled past him, tugging tight about her waist the belt of her floor-length housecoat. "That's the fourth night this week he spent at headquarters, I think he's moving in there. Haven't you got that lit yet? This being Whit's vacation; I'm telling you." She grabbed the kettle from him. "He hasn't been home once this week? I'm talking about coming home to be with his family?" Arms crossed wryly: "Well, hello?" she observed the two-year-old, pants now in hand, pad wordlessly across the kitchen, followed jingling by a large tan dog. The child halted before her mother's shins and held up the pants with one hand while enveloping with her lips the thumb of the other hand. The dog presented a wet and obsequious muzzle to John's groin. Eyeing the pants, Alice said: "Can you do that? I got my hands full."

John said after a moment: "Yes, all right."

"That's not to your taste, is it, doctor?" She crouched before the child, tugging the flaps of her housecoat to conceal her knees. "You going to leave it all to Marian if you have a family?"

"I'll admit I'd much rather if they were ready-made at twelve."

"Twelve? Twelve's the worst. Sonny's twelve." She rolled her gaze upward sardonically to him: "He's a *man* now." She slapped the child's now-panted buttocks, which produced the trot again, and she straightened, pointing: "I told Whit this one going to be that last one, and all of a sudden he's somebody who's got too much work to do to pay attention to his wife and children."

John dialed on the wall phone. "He's always worked harder down there than I ever did, when I was in his place."

"He don't have doctor's hours, darling."

"Yes, this is Morrison. Any calls." They waited; he said then, "Miss Jones?—Oh, her. No, tell them I've not seen her since nine A.M. yesterday.—That's right.—Never mind the appointments." He hung up and dialed a second number as she said:

"Whit doesn't have your hours so he's manufacturing them for himself, that's all."

"I'm afraid I made it harder for him by not going back last night; it was just—"

She interrupted: "It was just you and he both got stuck on the breeding and nursing process, and when that process gets over and done with, or when it don't come through at all like in your case, well you aren't to be found neither of you."

She circled the kitchen table, dealing out steel ware and cereal bowls. He hung up the phone again and said, watching her, "Are you the one put that idea in her head? Or maybe she put it in yours?"

"Isn't that the reason you two fell out, John? because you figured nothing come of your marriage?"

"It was her that walked out, Alice."

"Yes, darling. And that makes you blameless."

"I didn't say that or imply it."

"Didn't Marian tell me how much you want children of her"— she added with sarcasm, "for her to take care of, you always wanted them and as far as you were concerned that was part of the bargain of marrying her?"

"I wanted children, Alice, like anyone else, but that doesn't mean—"

"You wanted children, brother. But not for themselves. For their color. Leastways from what she told me."

He leaned out the window again. "Just what else did she choose to make public knowledge?"

258

"She got to talk to somebody, and it seems you aren't letting that be you? She told me how you two used to talk of children in the early times, especially you, how your kids were going to be in the flesh this blend of the races you and she were making in your marriage—that what you said, John? Isn't it? Some kind of living signpost to your political ideas?"

"Presuming this is any your business, just what's wrong with that?"

"Oh, what's wrong with that?" She laughed shortly and poured out juice from a waxed carton. "There's something obscene about it, that's what's wrong with that. About you and her both, did I ever tell you that? About getting some kind of satisfaction out of the skin-shade of the kids you produce. Maybe it's lucky you haven't had any, you'd have messed that kid's mind up before he was out of the belly."

"All right, Alice, perhaps we all have our problems—"

"Oh yes." She nodded exaggeratedly: "I guess we do. I guess we do. Since Marian was always a bit twisted in the head about color same as that whole family she comes from, and you go and give her a—"

He interrupted angrily: "We worked hard on that, Alice, as I imagine you know since she apparently keeps you well informed—"

"Enough for me to know that she didn't get no help from the complex you gave her by not letting a child be just a child, you had to make it some kind of liberation, and know what she told me?"

He said acidly, "What."

"Mm-hm, that sometimes she thinks she had all those miscarriages after your daughter died just out of nerves because she knew how she'd be judged if

259

she didn't come through." To John's reply she held up a flat hand: "Stop," and crossed the room to turn round by the shoulders a night-dressed boy who had been listening in the doorway. She pushed the child in a reluctant shuffle into the hall and shut the door on him.

John said, "She never told me that."

"Maybe you never bothered to ask her."

"That may be so but you just told me you've got your own anxiety and anger over—over this business"—he gestured to the closed door and the children behind it—"which you're taking out on me because you haven't had the guts to mention it to Whit, right? right? So now don't you—"

From behind the door: "Momma?"

"Just wait a minute, hear?"

"I need a drink of water—"

"Use the laundry sink, child, can't you think?"

John went on in a low voice: "If what you say is true, if she believes it to be true, then I don't know why she isn't relieved by my idea of adopting a child. I've been trying to get her to agree for a year at least."

"I know, darling."

"Yes I imagine you do. And if it's really anxiety that causes the miscarriages, which I think to be extremely unlikely, then my argument that adoption is often known to stimulate a natural family is an even more relevant one."

She regarded him with hands on hips. "If you were paying any attention to her, then maybe. If you were standing by her, to help her keep from feeling like a failure because she can't have a child then maybe."

"Goddamn it, Alice, I am, and I don't think I want to talk of this, I think you've—"

"I think I'm saying my piece, John. Since you and her can fight out your battles in any way you please, and come up with any ideas about white and black and race and children you please, but when they spill out onto meetings and you attack a man on account of his color in the name of the Committee, like you attacked that professor yesterday"—he looked up with surprise, and her voice rose:—"embarrasing every last person there, and then walking out two minutes after you came in, and leaving us to do the explaining about how our Committee which is supposed to fight racism in hiring just apparently got racism in its own membership, then you think that's our business well as yours and Marian's?" She paused for him to answer, but when, staring downward and opening and closing his hands, he began to speak in an undertone, she overrode him: "You know what Whit said? He said he believed what you really were was jealous of that man, because you want to be the only white member down there. What's he want, Whit says, to be our mascot? Come around wag his tail with his tongue hanging out?"

John shouted: "That's not fair, that's what Iannucci wants—"

"Iannucci's getting us one, two, maybe three hundred students for the march this morning and we don't care what color he is or they are or what their motives are so long as they fill the ranks large enough to stop that one'o'clock shift."

"That's a pipe dream, he won't get twenty students—"

"And how many are you getting? You even coming your own self? Are you?"

"That's my business."

She stared at him; he sat down heavily on the

windowsill and leaned forward, pinching the bridge of his nose, closing his eyes. "I don't know if I'm coming but I've gotten people too, I've done things."

"You've done plenty, brother, and it's time you got out of whatever bag you're in and did plenty again." She circled the table again, pouring out cereal and milk. "If it was for any other reason than this, John. If you wanted to drop out for a while because of your practice, because you needed a rest, or anything, you name it, but this color business. Because we've finished with that down there."

"We were trying to solve it down there. Now we've given up on it."

"What have we given up on? Maybe you've given up on something. I haven't."

"Alice, I believe you when you say that it's immaterial to you what color those students are, but you're telling me just by that that union between the races isn't a goal any more, it's a side-issue, a parenthesis." He passed his hand over his hair, letting out breath. "It's just I can't give up the idea of union."

"I don't know what union you're talking about, John."

"That's just what I'm saying. You don't even know what I mean any more."

"What do you mean then? Are we supposed to put on a dance of joy because some of our marchers got white skins? that your program? I'm going out today for jobs and nothing else, John, I don't know about you."

"All right, Alice, I'm not denying that but I'm talking about the feeling of union, the emotional bond of"—he broke off, and gestured with a circling hand. "Don't you know what I'm saying at all?"

"Only 'feeling' of union I know of is in the marriage bed, John. You lost that, and what, you want to find it again in the crowds?"

"I've lost it in the marriage bed because it's gone from the crowds, that's what I was trying to tell Marian."

"Did she understand you? I don't, one word, brother. What are you yearning for, a blood-brother-bond rite? a mystical orgy on the street? You ought to join some band of hippies if that's what you're asking for." With the kettle sloshing and puffing in her hand, she made a gesture of lifting with open palms. "Levitate the plant? Communal living two black couples and two white in the same house, mixing it up every night, that's your idea of where brotherhood is going to; sounds to me like what you really itching for is a new woman. That's all." She stood over him, arms crossed, head cocked. "You got a bit of the slave-owner in you, don't you, darling. Mind half the time down to the quarters, where mulattoes are in the making."

She waited; after a minute he shook his head in concentration and answered: "It's not a question of lust, Alice. I even wish it were, but what I'm talking of is a certain emotion—I don't know how to describe it but I used to have it often at work or at the committee or even walking down the street, and I'd feel that I was joined to everyone—"

"Joined after you got their skirts up."

"No, no, you don't understand. I felt it with men equally as much, I'd want to embrace them and sometimes I thought perhaps I was perverse; but I'd feel it with everybody, all the black people, and that's what I would express through love with Marian, and it gave me a sense of connection. But then it faded and lately it's seemed impossible; irrecoverable." He looked up at her earnestly. "There doesn't seem to be a sense of brotherhood in the community any longer, I'm not accepted any more, and this feeling I had has been left exposed and seemed ridiculous. So I haven't anything to bring to Marian."

"You've got to be accepted by the community before you can feel anything for Marian?"

"Maybe it sounds absurd but—"

"Mm-hm—"

"All right, Alice, but people accepted me because I was white and had believed enough to come down here, and I could express to Marian what I felt in return."

"Everybody thought you were just beautiful and that made you all warm inside, did it, darling. That's this feeling you had?"

"I felt gratitude—"

"And now things have changed and we're on our feet a little better and we don't have to accept a man except on his merits, and you don't feel any gratitude any more? You figure it's your right to be bowed down to just because of your color?" He looked downward, blinking and frowning. She went on: "That's brotherhood, accepting a person on account of his color without asking him any questions?"

"I don't know, Alice, I suppose it worked for me."

She nodded at him. "Everybody supposed to love everybody else indiscriminately. Is that it? And how about Marian, you love her indiscriminately? You love her any more than any black person you pass on the street and have this feeling of yours for? She just the one you happened to get with to pour your feeling into? Any reason you chose her above any other willing black woman, John?" He said nothing. She tapped her foot. "You like your wife for any reason, doctor? Any things you admire about her? Any things you two like doing together at all? You have any particular interests in common? You like to talk a thing over with her before you decide on it? When you make love to her, what do you think you're doing, making love to the entire population of Roxbury by proxy? You throw the South End in too? Angola, Mozambique, and the Belgian Congo? Why didn't you tell us before that you had all these important things in mind, John?"

He shouted: "She wanted it too! she wanted me to be the crusader and the great white father and she got herself loved for being black because that's what she asked for."

"Do you love her for being black any more, John?"

"I don't know."

"I bet that must have made her feel wonderful, being loved for being black. How about the bottoms of her feet, you love them, darling, since they're kind of pink, aren't they? How about the inside of her mouth, that rate?"

"Alice, I'm telling you I—"

"How come you had to spend the night here, if her color's all you care about? She didn't change it since I saw her last, did she?"

He sat stiffly on the windowsill with his eyes closed and his open hand shaking in frustration by his ear. "I don't know, can't you understand? I don't know any of these things any more."

She regarded him a moment, then with the bowl of a spoon banged the gong of a hanging pot: "Children?" She dragged a high chair beside her own and sat down. Children appeared and flowed into chairs in silence, casting large glances at their doctor. He stared back at them without moving.

"Sonny? John, you come on. I set you a place. You want krispies or the other? Sonny!" She plunged the two-year-old into the high chair. John stayed seated on the sill, gazing at nothing. Alice chattered at her offspring in an undertone, and called again: "Sonny, you going to eat?" Steelware clanked on china. Minutes passed.

"Momma?" Sonny's face was in the window; he was standing on the fire escape. "They're coming. I saw them from the roof."

"And how did you get up there?"

"Up the other stairs"—Seeing John: "They're marching right up the middle of the street, Dr. John, and no pig daring to try to stop them."

His mother said: "Don't you be trying to find out what they dare little brother, or they going to dare your manhood right off of you before you got a chance to use it."

The younger boy said: "Can I go up to the roof with Sonny, Momma?"

Sonny said with scorn: "No' 'cause you ain't old enough."

"All of you just eat your breakfast."

"They're here, Alice."

Younger faces crowded John's waist at the window and followed his pointing arm, as he leaned out. The first rank of bare heads and signs was topping the hill two blocks from them. "Let me see, darling."

Supported by the emerging upper half of a woman, a sign in black letters stating:

SLAVERY THEN
EQUALS
UNEMPLOYMENT NOW

strutted sidewise against the sky. The first rank stood on the crest; the letters J, O, B, and S, painted in day-glow on shirts, clung to the perspiring chests of men on the woman's either side. Cars and vans in the roadway slowed and swung to the side as the marchers trudged downhill. In doorways and beside parted curtains faces gathered to look out sleepily.

Alice said, "This is Sue and Pete Henderson's work, you met them? They're out of Springfield. Their idea is no sound trucks, no bull horns, any of that kind of thing. You've got to make it natural; wait on this."

"I'm going down, Momma. You coming, Dr. John?"

"Just wait a second. You've got a play to watch."

"Yeah but I want—"

At a seeming gunshot a small bearded man, the one with whom John had nearly collided on the street the day before, broke in an exultant run from the marchers' ranks. He was dressed as a field slave, and he held his burst chains high above his head. The chains dangled clinking from his wrists and bounced from the welts on his shoulders. With the huge voice John had heard, the slave shouted: "Freedom." As he passed below Alice's window, a second crack of sound startled the silenced street; the slave cringed. A lean black man floured over in white and nude but for a jockstrap leapt from among the marchers and with high-flung arched legs bounded in pursuit. His whip wriggled behind him on the pavement. The slave zigzagged on the roadway and shielded his face with spread hands. The bounty hunter, landing in stance, his tongue out, sashayed his whip gently over his head to touch the scarred shoulder of the slave. The slave jerked and cried out and fell. The bounty hunter stood over him, threw his head back and arms out in triumph. Then both men ran from the street and sat panting on separate stoops. Spectators moved round them.

Gesturing silence of their audience, the two actors pointed to a third, who, taking a lunch pail from a woman in the ranks, strode briskly across the front of the moving column. He wore a hard hat and blue overalls, which marked an X on his back. He approached two white men, one in business suit, one in blue shirt, tweed coat, and squashed felt hat, who stood up from behind a parked car.

"That's two of Iannucci's students."

"And Tom Hayes."

"Sure."

"They have four of these groups do they?"

"Two. Staggered. These ones are going to Cambridge at eleven."

Walking sideways ahead of the marchers' slow pace, the worker presented himself to the unionman and the capitalist, who crossed their arms and shook their heads in stylized unity. They said loudly in unison: "We never hire black men." They turned to opposite sides to spit. Then each gestured his departure with a backward jerk of the head and ducked once again behind the cars. In a self-embrace the worker gripped his shoulders and swayed. He was raising his hat and lunch pail above his head to throw them to the pavement, when a bent man in skull cap and white-face wound out from behind a car and offered a bottle. Grinning, raising thick brows, the newcomer pointed to the hat and the pail. The worker wiped his brow; the pawn was made. Twisting, the bottle held high above his mouth, liquid streaming down his neck, the worker stumbled to the curb and began to fall; then he too, with his companions, ran to a stoop and sat down.

The marchers halted beneath the watching windows. The woman with the title sign stepped out and rotated it; on its back was written: "JOIN US." The marchers turned outward to the tenements, white shirts winking. A banner was raised and bellied in the wind: "Help us picket the MacIntyre Company today and every day until it agrees to hire black workers." The marchers waited, then turned once more and stepped down the hill.

"Which is the Henderson fellow? He's splendid I think."

"The beard. His wife's got the sign."

"They going to join?"

"I don't know, darling. You're the one on membership. Sonny, you going to eat?"

The boy vaulted through the windowsill into the room, spilling milk from glasses on the table with the jolt of his landing. "I'm going down to dig that slave cat."

"You'll need something to eat."

"No, thanks."

John said, "We'll catch them up, Sonny, hold on a minute."

"You going, John?"

He sat down at the table and ate quickly. "Yes."

"What for?"

"What?" He looked up, chewing; looked down again. "Who's the bounty hunter."

"The tall one, that's one of Henderson's friends."

"Whit find them, or what?"

"He put an ad in a black drama magazine to see if anybody was interested in this kind of thing. Lo and behold, on Tuesday this whole group of them, all full of bare chests and gold earrings, you know?, shows up at the door, here, not at headquarters, just while I'm giving Pamela a bath, so I"—she stopped, seeing him lay down his spoon and stand up from the table. "All right, darling." She cocked outward her cheek, which he kissed.

"Listen, thanks." He slapped his pockets. "Did I leave anything?"

"You coming, Dr. John?"

"If you see Whit, tell him to call me—"

He stepped quickly down the stairs after Sonny. With a hand on the banister the boy pivoted in a leap around the landing and called, his voice hopping among the registers: "I heard Momma giving you a toke of shit? Man, she always handing it out."

"Yes I'm afraid it's her specialty."

"Momma's all right I guess. It's all them kids what does it."

"You think so?"

"Sure. No wonder Dad stays out. You think he's cheating on her?"

"No."

The boy paused and looked up as John descended; nodded and wrenched open the street door. "Yeah, I guess. Let's go."

● ● ●   Gaylord and Amarantha stood silent at the stern of a trawler, which for two hours had been putting toward Plymouth across Cape Cod Bay. She had said nothing to him since they had left the county courthouse in Barnstable, where Gaylord, with bandaged scalp and restitched arm, had refused to allege discrimination against the motelkeeper and had pleaded guilty to charges of speeding and trespass. He had been fined fifty dollars and released. At Barnstable Harbor, in a dockside cafe, he had bought their passage to Plymouth from a fisherman, who now slouched among his sodden nets further aft over the wheel.

Gaylord leaned over the sun-caught shoulders of the trawler's wake. His bruised skull ached, and as he studied Amarantha standing apart from him, regret and amusement changed places back and forth across his eyes. Weakly humorous, he described, to coax her into speaking, the shimmering spasms of the silver mackerel that floored the deck round their heels; the hundredfold schizophrenic stare of their fishy expiring eyes; the vast Yankee inwardness glaring from beneath the fisherman's moss tufts of brows, which flourished beneath the shade of an oilskin cap. Amarantha said nothing. Gaylord approached her, and watched while the wind draped her dress tightly behind, then before, then filled it wide from her bust like a sail, blowing his glance down within, along her familiar skin. Smiling, landing two fingers gingerly on her shoulder, he said: "Rantha, will you listen, taking off on the 'cycle like that was nothing personal, I would've done it to anybody. I just was—" She touched the fingers; pushed them. He shrugged and let them fall.

A dark tape of land lay distant on the port sea, and Gaylord, staring out at it, was startled by a bell buoy's clang just beside him. Tossing its head like a bird in angry courtship, the buoy defended a concrete breakwater. Plymouth Harbor lay beyond. The motor's thudding slowed. Amarantha said, not turning to him: "This the place then finally?"

"This is the place. Plymouth with the Rock."

"Any hope for a bus to get us back in time for the march?"

"What march is this?"

"What do you mean, what march is this?"

He reared back dramatically, in private mockery of her peevishness. "You mean John's thing? You going to that?"

"Aren't you?"

"Hadn't thought about it, baby." He took out his house keys; picked studiously at his nails. "We could go, though."

"I'll be perfectly okay by myself, thanks."

He dangled the keys before his eyes. "And how are you planning to get around?"

"Listen, a couple more hours, you put me in a taxi,

you're done with me, all right?" She dabbed nervously at her ankle where a mackerel's scale had scratched her; she licked the blood thoughtfully. Her expression cleared. She said, cocking her head a moment, "It's easy to find someone to lead you at a thing like that anyway, and getting helped crossing the street is the only chance I have to meet new people from the outside."

"I'm taking you to the march, Rantha."

"I'm sorry, but there's no point in prolonging something that's finished."

"It isn't finished."

"Excuse me?"

"I'm telling you, baby. If you're going to march, you're going with me. We're staying together, Rantha. Little spat as to what to plead in court doesn't change that."

"That's what you're calling it? You left me in the lurch, mister—"

"I'm sorry about that, Rantha; I'm telling you. It was forced on me. It had nothing to do with what we're doing together."

"Is that so, well I'm so sorry, I didn't notice we were doing anything. Maybe you'd better set up a buzzer system for me, like two short rings when you've decided it's off between us and a long and a short for when it's going back on—"

"I've been trying to get an audience with her ladyship for two hours now but her ladyship just wouldn't—"

She interrupted: "Because I'd like to know what makes you so conceited as to think I'm ready and panting every time your crummy mind changes, after dropping me like that? for a second time? Well I'm not ready, mister."

He frowned after her as she padded off among the

fish and ropes, hand over hand slapping on the gunwhale. He called: "Bzzzz-bzt, long and short is for on, little one."

She yelled: "On till you get laid again."

"No, Rantha. Longer than that."

"I don't believe you, shit on you, you aren't going to use my stupid lust to pull me back and forth like a Yo-Yo—"

"I want you to stay with me, Rantha."

"I don't care what you want, will you get that through your head?"

Terns exploded from the breakwater near them, detonating screams. At the stern just above their heads, the birds rose to hitchhike on the breeze in a greedy cloud, flapping, dipping, their close-seen bodies shapely and unclean. The trawler, heading into the harbor channel, swung its stern round beneath their feet with the time-stretching glide of a car skidding in snow. Waves ceased their hammering on the hull; the engine's drone separated into a putting. The moving boat seemed still. Gaylord approached her and leaned over the gunwhale where she was bent far over toward the water, flushing hotly. Her hair was dumped forward so that it ambled on the dying wind. She said after a while: "You said you didn't want to be responsible for me, and you've got to stop this back-and-forth, it's just too confusing—"

"Thinking it's a question of whether I should look after you, that's what was confusing us, or me at least, Rantha. It isn't hard for me to look after you. It's something interesting, and I'm always looking for something interesting. Question is, whether I'm going to look after myself or not." He leaned over beside her; their forefingers trailed in the water, causing hairpin waves that crossed. "Like that chase on the 'cycle, it was a bad idea, understand, it was the last

273

one of a year's worth of down-and-out jive ideas I've been hobbling around with. Turning you out is one bad idea more than I need."

She moved her trailing finger in figure eights. "I don't think you can do it. Every time we come to a problem there's going to be a new crazy routine to hide from the problem with. It's all got to be stories and routines every bit, and it isn't going to change."

"You've got routines yourself, Rantha. That whole watcher scenario on the beach yesterday and your little white crusader bit this morning, now that isn't going to change?"

"Yes it is, it'd better, because I'm trying to get rid of the problem, but you're trying to make it into an art, Gaylord—I mean, I like the stories, and it fills me up to be wanted by someone who could probably get anybody he asked for, with all these brains of yours to throw around, but you've got to come through absolutely plain and straight and direct without the stories when it comes to me, are you listening? or I just won't be able to do it."

"I'm talking to you straight now, Rantha. I know what I'm telling you." Standing up, he stretched out his arms to study his hands against a background of raised spars, nearing wharves, green trees. He said after a minute, "See, baby, a storyteller is like a foxy dresser, except with words for clothes: the dresser, just by hiding part of what she has, reveals more than she ever could reveal if she hid nothing at all. See what I'm saying? She's a chick turns heads in the street way she wouldn't begin to turn them if we all went nude. Same way, if I hide some things from you, not telling you what I'm doing at such-and-such a place, or where I've been to at such-and-such a time, it's only to dress the place and time and show myself to you as better than I'd be if I told you dull and straight what it was. Except this dresser, she has to know what to cover up and hide, how thick to lay it on where and where, and what to leave frank and open to the air, if she's going to have style. Same as me: running from you and that cop this morning, and not running from the other cop yesterday soon as I heard his siren, looks like I was trying to use stories to cover the wrong places up and get myself destroyed in a fit of bad style gone haywire. That's out, Rantha. I don't need it, now we got something going together."

"All right, Gaylord, that's all right for you but the trouble is I can't compete with it. I don't have any style and I don't want any, and furthermore I'm an absolute dowd, is what, and don't contradict because I never could wear clothes or makeup even in the seeing-time, and I'm better off without any."

"Who's going to contradict? Now guess who's a dresser."

"I don't have to guess. Your wife."

"Always editing herself body and soul so no one can get to her. She always was a disappointment when her clothes came off, though. Who wants a wife like that?"

"Oh."

"Chick like you, always looking to rub up to something, and notions all the time bubbling and streaming out of your head before you know which ones they are, style and clothes are nothing but clutter on you."

"Oh."

"You let me do the dressing, see, long as I promise to take all the decorations off whenever you ask it, and I'll arrange it so you can run around in the skin like last night whenever you please, long as you promise to go to your shrink regular."

She stood straight also. "That's our deal, is it?" Her

face considered him a moment with an ironic corner of her lip turned downward; she stuck her tongue out at him. "Blah."

He laughed. "So are you agreeing to the deal?"

"No."

He watched her stamp away towards the stern again, her retreating head surrounded by the sparkling breadth of the bay. Beyond her, an unstable shimmering band of sunlight stretched on the water as if in some charmed ship's wake. Gaylord called after her: "You're obviously going to have to go in with me, you got no choice, that's the fine thing—"

Her voice wandered back: "I don't care because I'm going to make you suffer, you watch."

"Oh yeah? How you going to do that now?"

"I have ways." She nodded briskly. "I'm going to keep making you feel guilty for this and that, which will get you angry, so you'll rough me up a bit, and then feel even guiltier." Her open hand wrote a spiral in the air. "My father and I used to get that one going."

"That so?"

"Mm-hm, and think of all the routines you're going to have to go through each time to get out of it and conciliate me."

"This ain't part of the straight and open deal we were talking about."

"You were talking about."

"If we don't make the deal, see, then I'm not playing."

The slowing ship floated on a hiss through the channel. "Phooey you aren't, because you obviously have to."

Ranks of squared-off trawler's sterns, early docked for Sunday and bearing green names, glided past. Standing behind her, he stretched his arms forward past her either side and held the gunwhale, fencing her in, his hands outside hers. He rested his loins against her buttocks quietly. They were silent for a while. He said then: "Did I ever tell you about my father at all?"

She answered after a pause: "You told me where he is now."

"Oh, yeah."

"When did it happen? Do you remember him?"

"When I was four or five—" The stern drifted sideways once more; the smell of black dank piles touched sweetly on the salt air. She said;

"Hey, are we getting there?"

"Yes, baby."

She leaned back against him slightly. "When you were four or five—?"

"We went North right after he was sentenced, yeah—he killed a man with a knife."

"Was it a white—"

He interrupted: "No, a black man. I don't know anything of the circumstances; but they knew it was him." Leaning forward, he reached down beside her to trap some slicked water in his hand, and tipped its iridescence to the sun as he went on: "There was a tree by our cabin, Rantha, a big elm, with a lot of Spanish moss drooping off of it. He'd been hiding up there. You couldn't even see him from right underneath. He slept up there for a long time, or so it seemed to us anyways—it must have been five or six or eight days. We'd eat under the tree and my mother would tie food to a rope he'd haul up when the guard—they had a cracker waiting round for him to show up home—when the guard had gone off to have a whizz. They found Poppa out, though. I always thought my mother told them. Maybe she couldn't stand the strain, maybe they told her they'd give her money to go North on if she talked, I don't know. I asked her a couple of times if it was her, and she always denied it; but when she was sick for the last time, she said: 'It wasn't over me anyhow.'—That's the first I knew that, Rantha. I forgave her then."

He watched the water slide from his hand and drop, to form new indigo meanderings on the green wash round the hull. "I never got old enough to climb that elm, or anything much but sumac then, but I remember thinking, like little boys going to do you know, when I get to be seven I'm going to climb that tree. When I understood it was Poppa up there, and he was hiding, from the white folk—well I'd never heard of anything so fine. They didn't have to coax *me* into keeping no secret. Him covered up with moss, and all those leaves, just hiding up there, living up there, and seeing out? Shit you couldn't even see him at all from below, even standing right underneath. But I remember watching that food-haul rope appear from up there, and disappear once she'd tied a bag of hocks or something to it, and how we'd panic when the tree would shake or he'd make a branch rustle—of course they must have thought it was the wind, if they ever thought at all. But one day a troop of men comes up, bossed by a man who twice had been around to talk to Momma and Elizabeth, she's the oldest, she's in Newark now—I remember feeling I was about to die when this man at the head of the troop strides on up to that tree. He yells, Jackson we know you up there, nigger, and you don't come down we going to burn you out—all right then, boy—way I remember it Rantha, he doesn't give Poppa any time at all, he just sets that tree afire.

"Well he's down and out of that tree and running across the yard before the first swatch of moss burnt out—I suppose he wanted them to shoot him, it being quicker, but they aren't about to, I don't know why; just one of those crackers lassoes him around the neck and I remember the jerk that rope stops him with, and the way he wheezed and clutched when he came down on the woodpile on his back. He didn't put up no fight. I don't remember any more, Rantha—except when I went down home with Marian's brother Mandus, and saw Poppa in his cell, and he was old, and hoarse, and scared, and dead bald."

Gaylord shook his hand out dry in the sun. "They came the next day with a chain to saw that tree down, I guess for the lumber, since they must have made some kind of deal with Momma, knowing she was going to move on. I put up such a squall about the sawing that one of them had to take me by the collar and lock me up in the outhouse. I remember how that thing cracked as it fell. I told myself I was going to find such a place to hide then, Rantha—"

Suddenly quiet, the trawler glided on still water; it overtook a parked row of pleasure boats, at which the fisherman spat briefly; then it roared in reverse, and the cloud of terns that had followed at the stern screeched past their ears and collapsed on the fish round their heels. Hysterical sqawking wings patted their cheeks and brushed their clothes. Gaylord whirled his arms and bellowed; Amarantha yowled. Taking up an oar meanwhile, the fisherman chopped about briskly at the feathered shoulders. He flung over the side two crushed corpses, and the cloud deafeningly swooped in pursuit. The fisherman took off his hat; grunted at Gaylord and Amarantha. His brows shot gray hairs in all directions. "Peck out your eyes if you let 'em." He wiped his hands on his pants. Amarantha wailed, shielding her face with her hands and running in place on fish, "When do we get to Plymouth?" The fisherman stared at her, his mouth turned down. He scratched his left temple and mounted the wharf that creaked hard by the hull. "Come on, Rantha, we're here. Foot on the gunwhale, okay? I'll pull you up." They followed the fisherman. "Hey, he turned the engine off."

She stamped on boards; water whacked beneath. "All right, so where's Plymouth Rock?"

The fisherman slowly swung his gaze down the littered beach to a small fane of slate-gray columns. A stone peeked from inside. Gaylord said, "Hey, no shit, I thought it was a cliff, or a boulder or something."

"Plymouth Rock?" she said, "it's this cliff, or a boulder or something."

"Ain't but the size of a small chest of drawers."

"That wasn't the size it was in my history book."

Gaylord asked: "Explain it to the lady?"

"Since how do they know it from a hundred others like it, after all this time, if it's just a stone? because I think it stinks."

The fisherman, while his hands wove a knot round a cleat, straightened slightly and swung his eyes round again. On the waterfront, souvenir shops, chain restaurants, and layer-cake motels shone their colors, chiefly bright orange, to the sun. Opening doors gasped nearby. "Hey wait, Gaylord, that the bus?"

He looked across the street. "Yes, baby."

"Come on then if we're going to march?"

"If we're making our deal."

"Goodbye, Mister fisherman." They tramped down the wharf. "Never."

● ● ●   Touching the windowshade slightly aside, Marian gazed down from her brother's apartment at a dormant Sunday avenue, empty now of the troop trucks and the jeeps fronted with barbed wire that she had watched rattle past at dawn. Where she had seen them turn in to a sidestreet toward the picket and the plant, shouts now drew her glance, and she leaned out: latecoming clumps of striding marchers, their fists raised high on rigid diagonal arms, were hurrying across the intersection and down the side street toward a hidden crowd. A chant rode faintly on the stillness to her ears.

"Those fists—"

She muttered silently under her breath, "Up against all that firepower, I don't know, stuffed in with all those people and ain't one of them barefoot either. You figure one pop of tear-gas and people get trampled, they do I'm telling you—

"He could've come by, at least he could've called—If he expects me to show, he knows I don't like these—"

The advancing surf of the chant broke upon the latecomers, who with upward-pumping fists suddenly bawled: "Freedom! Now! Jobs! Now!" Their mouths shot open with the words. A nearby churchbell, startled by noon, tolled the hour. "Get going if you're going. You're already in trouble trying to find him in that crowd. You don't even know if he's even going to be there or who he's going to show with either if he shows, you ready to go back home, well maybe he isn't interested in what you ready for. How do I know what he's been doing? For all I can tell everybody's fully informed as to what's going on except me—Those darling looks of pity, oh yes I know, I've given them myself. You're going straight home, hear? If he's giving you your walking papers, he's giving them in private."

"Get away from that window."

She leapt backward; the shade snapped up. Her brother hissed behind her: "Pull that down, goddamn you"—

The yellow shadow moved once again over his

armchair, where he had slept and where he now sat forward with clasped hands, windily breathing. He said furiously: "I told you, you stay here you obey the rules of the place."

"I'm going, brother."

He looked up. "Going back?"

"I don't know. Home."

"Fine. That's what you deserve." He leaned back in his chair, hands tucked behind his head, eyeing her with a sudden pleasure. "Better phone him up let him know you're coming, he maybe got to change the sheets."

She crossed the room to take up her pocketbook: "Are you leaving town or am I coming to a funeral?"

"Just keep your eyes on the headlines."

"You're useless to talk to." She walked out. "I don't think I'm going to be asking to see you again, brother."

"Then don't forget your book."

"I didn't bring a book."

He rose a moment in his chair and slapped a blue pamphlet lying on a table. "That."

"It's my address book." She stepped back in and grabbed it from the table. "Where'd you get it."

"Walter brought it up. Said you left it on the stoop when you were yapping at him down there."

"I couldn't have. I never carry it." She opened it, then cried out as she noticed the check marks John had made in the book the day before. She leafed through it at a quickening pace. "John came here—"

He snorted. "John came here. Scumbag." He closed his eyes. "Get home."

"Listen, this is his fountain pen"—she pointed to the checks in the open pamphlet. "He came looking for me, brother, he came looking for me—"

"He ain't been here."

"No just tell me what he said, it isn't going to change things, I'm going home anyways—"

He shouted: "I haven't seen him I'm telling you"—His eyes shifted up to her as she leaned over him, doubt and disappointment invading her face; he said with disgust after a moment: "Walter maybe could've shoved him off without telling me."

As she ran out he reached quickly to grab the hem of her skirt in his fist. "Walter's off and Sam's down there, and he ain't a nice man, so will you mind not fucking with him? Now get home?"

"Goodbye, brother."

They stared at each other; he let her go. She walked silently down the stairs, along the hall and out past Sam, who dozed in a tipped-back chair with a truncated shotgun on his knees.

Marian, looking back every few steps to see if she were followed, ran on two blocks to the intersection that late marchers still hurriedly crossed; jamming the address book into the belt of her skirt, she whirled round one last time, hands cluthing her opposite shoulders in a self-embrace; she turned the corner into the crowded side street. With shortening breath she slowed to a walk and held the address book up before her eyes. "I know these checks weren't here before yesterday." She flipped to the first page and thumbed through, saying aloud, "That's just his kind of crazy methodical way of doing it. He ain't omitting anybody, nosir." She squinted at an entry: "He's calling the notions shop and checking it when they answer, and when he finds out it's a shop, he crosses out the check; I can't believe him."—She had stopped and had turned sideways to the current of pedestrians that flowed past her without her noticing. "Of course he doesn't know if I left town or what, probably thinks, Lord shield me from what he thinks. I'm not going to be able to serve his precious stomach anything but mashed turnip after this holy weekend."

The book once again in her belt, she raised her eyes while a trio of young men in feathered felt hats bore down on her. Murmuring and whistling, they swung their shoulders sideways, to bump her mildly with their loins as they sashayed past. She shivered and grinned. "You go ahead see if I care, I'm reserved for him, he looked for me and he isn't cheating, not now anyways, and I don't care about before"—she looked up the street above the heads of the advancing latecomers. "I don't care about any of the things brother says." She gazed at the sunlit buildings, her vision suddenly mystified by a jagged bolt of light which climbed the wall of a townhouse to its fluted cornice. Her eyes followed a row of ornate knuckles which protruded from beneath the cornice as if in evidence of fists buried in the walls. The pointed corner of the roof, from where she stood, led to the similar corner of the building beyond, to a rank of corners down the block, each emerging from the one before, each framing the last; in the brilliant stare of the summer noon, the receding corners appeared as shapes without substance, mere rich surfaces, whose edges were defined by the rain-washed air with such clarity that she thought they might explode.

"We're going to have no regrets, you can't if you want it to begin again, what difference does it make who's been touched by who? I'm not even going to lie about how I lost my ring. I don't care about the past. I don't want the crusade and I don't want the Committee and I don't even want to go down to the Cape anymore."

Bright clothes were moving through the sunlight; the houses contained between them thickening crowds. She walked on again toward the picket, watching her feet jutt forward on the sunned concrete as other bodies brushed urgently by. "I know it is. It's going to be stronger. I know it is." She looked up as from a stoop nearby two well-timed hoarse voices bawled: "What do you want?"

A group of men passing her shouted at her ear: "Freedom!"

"When do you want it?"

"Now!"

The neared voices overrode, to her ear, the dimmer reverbrating response of hundreds. She ran up the steps to a building and looked down the street. A block ahead the roadway was filled to its full width with an uneven surface of heads, caps, banners, and raised arms. They were not advancing.

"How'll you get it, brother?"

"Jobs!"

"When?"

"Now!"

The plant that was the object of the picket squat in red brick against the street yet five long blocks further on from where she stood. She climbed up on the banister: the crowd ceased abruptly one block short of the plant. The march's advance was clogged by soldiers who stood facing the crowd shoulder to shoulder in a brown line. The plant itself looked out through its closed gates on to an empty roadway, which had been cleared of cars and was lined with jeeps. On the sidewalk before it, what seemed to her to be not more than twenty, marchers were trudging a picket with hoisted signs. Another line of soldiers stood guard on them at the sidewalk's edge. Their bayonets, and those that pointed at the crowd, winked at her.

She could not make out the picketers' faces. Jumping down from the banister, she ran along the street until the crowd closed round her, and looking about, she chose a tall man with a two-year-old on his shoulders to ask: "How do we get in to the picket? I thought there was going to be a march?"

The man's hand sprang quickly to spread on the child's small thigh at his neck; he looked down at her. "They let the first fifty in. Then they closed off the street."

"I know but can't you get in? if you know someone in there?"

A woman standing beside her said: "My sister's in there."

The tall man said: "Fifty picketers. That's all they said."

"Pigs they afraid of more than fifty brothers," the woman said.

"Right on."

The woman went on in a quiet voice: "They got five hundred in there to guard them, ten to one, that's what it's supposed to be for jungle fighting; that's what we are; jungle people; Viet-Cong. They figure we just might get the union men to sit down with us unless they come around armed to the teeth and make it look like it's a war."

"That's right."

"Yes."

"They want a war, they looking for it, they maybe going to get it."

Marian had ceased listening; she was muttering to herself: "He's in there, I know he is, and far as he can tell I'm sleeping off some kind of crazy night out—He's going to get put in jail and this is going to go on and on"—Biting her lip, she stared round, gazed absently at one of the two-year-old's feet, which hung down his father's shoulder; toes in miniature twitched upward from the base of the sandal, a few inches from her eyes. "Look at this. You can't believe how little kids are put together out of rubber"—She squinted up closer along the side of the child's foot at the line, straight to the casual eye but to her close-studying eye slightly serrate, which separated the colors of the upper and the sole. Her eyes moved up; the crowd's uncertain launching of a song was struck by the boom of the father's voice, startling the child so that he grabbed the father's thick hair at the crown, his peach nails disappearing into the tufts:

Deep in my heart, I do believe

The child's hair grew in larger curls, bespeaking to Marian a mother of lighter skin: the woman, perhaps, the flare of whose skirt was just visible beyond the husband's knees. She watched the dark holes of the child's nostrils widen to ovals and his round eyes stare as he rode with fright the vibrations of his father's voice. At each phrase she could hear the last note linger in the forward crowd, as if in his echo.

We are not afraid

The child with a sudden eagerness began to kick his father's collarbone with his heels; tunelessly, audible when his father took breath, he caroled: "Ba, der, da—"

The woman Marian had supposed to be the mother set hands on hips, revealing bare arms; they were white. Startled, and curious to see her face, Marian sidled round behind her and began to peer, then jumped as someone suddenly said in her ear, "We been looking for you."

"Lord, you scared me." It was Gaylord, against whom she had sidled up without seeing him; the white woman was Amarantha, who turned around saying "Hm?"

Gaylord said: "It's Marian, baby."

"Oh great, is John here? I thought you were coming down to the Cape, hey?"

Her eyes were oddly wide in the glare. Marian said nothing, observing in puzzlement their costumes: Amarantha was dressed in a nurse's uniform, Gaylord in full whites, with a cap tucked down on his temple over a winding of gauze. The girl demanded of her silence: "So where's John?"

Marian asked Gaylord, "You haven't seen him this morning, have you?"

"No, baby. You didn't come with him, huh."

"I was going to meet him."

"He must be up front in the picket then, ain't he?"

"No, I'm asking you—"

Amarantha said, "Didn't he say where he'd be, though?"

"I don't know—I don't know where he is—"

"Well *now* what are we going to do please?"

Gaylord said, studying Marian's face, "You figure he's in the picket, though?"

"Yes—"

"Then we're going in up front, Rantha, see?" The girl said: "I still say they won't let us through, though; you watch."

Marian said, "If you're acting as medics, though, are you? Won't they let you through?"

"That's what I'm telling you, Rantha."

"Yes but we *aren't* acting as medics, would you please remember which is a routine and which isn't?"

"You have to play a routine like it's real or it doesn't get off the ground."

"All right but there's a difference between routine real and nonroutine real and—"

He interrupted: "Not while you're in it there isn't."

Marian said: "Look I don't know what this is about, but if you think we could go up front, Gaylord—"

He said, "I had this shattering idea of picking up some whites and one of these"—he exhibited to

Marian a stretcher, which he held rolled-up, and on the vertical like a staff—"and plowing through the lines supposedly to fetch some old mamma who'd have fainted, see, and then we could picket, and this bitch whose idea it was to picket in the first place is giving me gas on the irrelevant grounds that we might get arrested, which is preposterous and in the second place it pisses me off those fucks telling me what street I'm going to walk on—"

Amarantha retorted: "That's just what I'm saying because how about yesterday? Because they're still looking for someone"—her voice jerked silent, and she added after a moment—"for something to make an issue out of."

People had cocked their heads to listen, half-smiling. Marian, said, smiling also, "All they can do is turn us around, honey. Isn't any harm in trying."

"Yes but what I'm saying is—"

"It's two to one; we're moving out." He unfurled the stretcher. "Rantha's at the back end. Excuse me, people." He lay the stretcher on the pavement and marched her backwards by both elbows: "Phooey, phooey"—"Yeah, yeah;" halted her, and raised the wooden handles against her palms: "Look, now all you do is—"

"I know what a stretcher is, blah."

At the stetcher's front end, saying: "Follow next to Rantha, all right?" Gaylord blew a shriek from a toy whistle and stomped forward, yelling: "We got to make a pickup, now move aside, will you?"

Layers of doubting listeners allowed grudging space for their passage and closed round behind them again. They struggled forward in silence through the muttering crowd. The marchers' song thinned, scattered, died out. Marian halted as a sudden voice thudded from ahead through a bullhorn; the voice shuddered indecipherably back and forth betweeen the buildings. It was not John's. She caught up with Amarantha, who herself had stopped and was yelling at Gaylord; Marian watched the unblinking and angular face with suspicion and a sudden touch of dislike. She smiled sardonically and shook her head. Turning round, Gaylord said sharply: "What are you smirking at?"

The girl said, "Who's smirking?"

Stepping onward again, Gaylord called back with annoyance: "I always did think you don't approve of miscegenation, Marian. Except as a religion, of course?"

Amarantha said, "Hey we scratched up your motorcycle a bit, is the thing."

"It doesn't matter, honey. He don't ever use it now."

"Well he won't ever use it now."

"Why what happened?"

Somebody said, "What's the problem, brother."

A woman called, "They already brutalizing up the brothers in there—"

Gaylord bellowed to turning heads, "No problem, hear? Heat got to somebody." He pressed on and called back again, "Like marrying a cat to cure him of his color, that isn't really miscegenation anyways." He paused. "Hey, Marian?"

Amarantha said, "Will the real miscegenation please step forth? That's not very nice, Gaylord. She can smirk if she wants."

"I was just kind of surprised, Gaylord; you know?"

"Let me through, will you?" He called back again: "Oh yeah? You figure we going to take this thing seriously enough for you?"

"It doesn't have to be serious; come on."

"Why it's got to resussify the great American fiddledeedoo, now don't it? that ain't serious?"

"Leave her alone, silly."

"No baby, now this isn't to be trifled with. If we don't realize what great job lots of high-priced humankind we representing in this thing, we're liable to beat about, undersell, and put the wrong address on the whole beautiful package, ain't that right, Marian? And all just for a couple of laughs and good lays? Perfectly shocking."

Marian yelled at him, "You leave off, I don't have any feelings like that—"

Gaylord said, "She doesn't have any feelings like that, Rantha."

"Leastways I know what feelings I have and when they're wrong, which is more than I can say for some people I know—"

She frowned at her trudging feet, biting her lip and muttering to herself. After a minute, Amarantha's feet beside hers stopped short; Marian looked up to see Gaylord already jawing at a soldier in the line. The soldier made Gaylord no answer and stared past him, his pale eyes blinking beneath the lip of his helmet. While Gaylord talked, the soldier twitchingly shrugged and coaxed along his shoulder the heavy nubbed belt which hung down and festooned his chest. Various leathern boxes clung to his waist. While he moved, the tip of his rifle, which both his hands gripped, wavered gently. Marian moved forward. As she hopped on tiptoe there sprung in and out of view the nearly empty roadway before the plant. Beside the wire fence she could see the languid placards of the picket and a dozen unhelmeted heads, none blond, circling slowly.

"John! John!"

No one looked up; her voice did not carry. Gaylord was saying: "Now listen, friend, this lady's a registered nurse, understand? We got to get in there and administer first aid, and you aren't going to stand in the way of that, are you?" The soldier shifted his feet; sweat dripped from his chin. Someone called: "They aren't going to say one word to you, brother, you're wasting your breath."

Gaylord said: "That your orders son?"

Another man yelled into the crowd, "They aren't even letting the medics through, hear? Someone could be dying in there and long as he was black, they wouldn't budge."

"Right on."

Gaylord muttered: "Where's your C.O., soldier."

"Far as I'm concerned we ought to walk right over them if they don't let us through, we've got them surrounded I'm telling you—"

The soldier moved nervous eyes to Gaylord's right, and Gaylord jerked away. Amarantha shouted as she followed at a trot, "Gaylord, this is crazy I mean it, you're getting to the point where you'll do something dumb—"

"Excuse me, all right? Excuse me."

Marian hurried after him: "Gaylord, you don't have to do this, John'll realize I couldn't get through—"

"I'm not doing this for you, see?"

Scattered calls of "Let them through" gathered into a precise shouted chant: "Let! us! through!" which spread back through the crowd while Gaylord worked across the roadway. Marian and Amarantha followed him. The inner group of picketers began to leave the sidewalk in front of the plant and to approach the other side of the soldier's line. Jumping up and down again, Marian could not find John's face among the nearing signs. Gaylord stopped before a large man with wings. He announced: "Mass. General Hospital Badge Number 153478-A, received call at 12:23 P.M. reported heat prostration, request permission to proceed."

The noncom regarded him mildly. "I didn't send for any ambulance, pal."

"Believe it came from MacIntyre and Company."

"That so?"

"Yessir."

"Yes?" The noncom considered; then said; "When I need an ambulance, I'll send for one. Let's hope that isn't any time soon, pal."

"Gaylord, will you please—?"

"Let! us! through!"

Marian suddenly shouted again: "John! John!"

He was approaching her in the file of picketers that was now circling just beyond the line. Her shouting was inaudible over the chanting crowd. He did not look up from his abstracted stare at the back of the picketer before him. The crowd, pressing in, kept her from working down the line towards him. She waved the address book over her head, yelling hoarsely, and as he passed her, its fluttering pages caught his eye.

Stopping, unable to hear their own voices, they faced each other across the gap between two still helmets. The chant flowed out into a roar, and in an advancing wave of curiosity people turned and stood on tiptoe to look toward the furthest edge of the crowd. The soldiers's line had broken. Gaylord and Amarantha had disappeared. John pointed with a questioning look to where a trickle of shouting men in colored shirts had already squeezed through the break and were joining the picket. Marian shook her head; she could not move. He swung his arm into the gap between the helmets. Wary of the bayonets, her stretched-out hand could not reach his. She withdrew it, brought it forward again with the address book held out, which he grasped, and their forefingers failed by an inch to meet on the outside page.

She mouthed: You take it, and backed away slightly from the soldiers, who were eyeing her and roasting silently. Dark floral splotches of sweat widened on their uniforms. The crowd, intent on moving toward the break, let the chant fitfully die.

In the coughing and confused stillness they looked at each other, still silent, till she said at last: "You left it on the stoop of Brother's building—"

He frowned, dropped his eyes. She said: "Brother didn't tell me you'd come till an hour ago, John, but I was there all the time—"

He cleared his throat. "I came round about six—"

"I was there, baby, waiting, just Brother didn't tell me you'd come, that's all—"

"I thought we might still go to the Cape"—he looked up at her: "I came straight on back as soon as I got to headquarters, I thought I'd been wrong, but when you left the door open, I was afraid you might have left."

"Don't tell me, John, I was angry, I was angry, I only stayed out because I wanted you to come—"

"I was there at six, had you—"

"I told you, baby, yes—"

"That goon of his didn't let me up."

"Brother didn't know you'd come until later, John."

"Yes, well the damned thing is we still could have gone down to the Cape."

"John, I didn't want to go down there, it was just a stand-in thing for wanting to go back to the beginning and begin all over again, and we couldn't go back, that's what you were telling me in the argument, we can't—"

He nodded: "Yes and all the while that I was telling you we can't I was still blaming myself for not being able to."

"You're blaming yourself for not wanting to, John"— She shook her head, half-laughing—"You don't want to go back and I don't either, we've just been keeping up the appearance for each other—"

He said after a moment, "Maybe so, yes I suppose that's so, but—"

She interrupted: "I don't want the crusade any more, John, I don't care what I said in the argument, I want all of the color-struck things out of our marraige and I don't want you winning any wars, I just want a man."

"Do you feel you have one?"

"Yes, don't you see, John, yes—"

"Even though I couldn't—" he stopped short, looking angrily at the motionless guardsmen and at the stymied crowd.

She said, "Yes, John, even though."

"The thing was—"

"The thing was I was asking you to be something you can't be any more."

"What if—curse these bastards,—if with what we've been talking of, what if I have trouble will you realize what it's from and not suspect I'm running off with some woman—"

"There isn't going to be any trouble, John."

"Will you help, then?"

"That's what I'm trying to tell you, baby—come on, let's go home."

"No wait, maybe you can—" he looked down the line as a shout went up; the break was closed. Men were yelling in argument in the distance. "Damnit, I'm afraid they've—"

"John, come on, come home, I'm sure they'll let you out, they aren't going to stick on that—"

He swung his arm across the line again, smiling. "I want to stay, Marian. This is still something decent for me to do. We're going to try to stop this one-o'clock shift."

"Baby, I know, and it's all right about the shift, but

one man isn't going to make any difference, with all this crowd"— Smiling still, he raised his sign, which said 'JOBS' in large red printed letters, above the soldiers's heads. She went on quietly. "This is where we began it yesterday, John, letting the politics stand in between us"—She held her fists at her chest and said shaking her head, "Don't you see we've got to get that Committee out of our house every bit or it's going to ruin us like it come near to doing, I know that, John."

"Why don't you quit the Committee, then. You've never liked the work, really."

She began to speak; stopped short. She said in an undertone, "Baby, don't be angry, I—"

He interrupted, "I'm not angry. No really, the only reason you've come down there is to keep the politics mixed in with the marriage, isn't that so? So if we're going to unmix them, fine, quit the Committee and don't come down there any more than you would to my office. I just do this for myself, all right?"

"You won't care if I don't"—she left the thought unfinished, and he said:

"I don't want you to bother with this. It's something separate."

"Baby, that's fine with me, that's all I'm asking, but—"

"And I'll try not to get arrested so I can get back early and we'll have some time together, all right?"

"All right, John, all right"— She embraced herself and grinned at him.

"After all it's"—he raised his turned wrist to exhibit his watch to her.— "Sunday and not yet quarter to one."

Appearing beside John, Gaylord overrode her response by yelling at her: "What the hell are you still out there for after all that work I done for you?"

She called, "How'd you get through, though? I couldn't move."

Amarantha, on Gaylord's arm, shouted, "Because of our uniforms, and I think it was mean of you not to stick with us, since I need help in keeping this person from getting shot."

Gaylord said cheerfully: "Coming to this was your idea, not mine."

"I don't care because I'm tired."

"Good morning, Gaylord."

"Good morning? Not congrats? You realize it was us got that line to break?"

"You did?"

"Hey is this John?"

"Hello, Amarantha."

"Good because I need you to intervene in something, do you know a doctor named—"

A bullhorn crackled and bellowed just behind them: "All you people who got through the line please move this way—please move into the picket you can see circling at the end of the block."

The din of the crowd rose, and John shouted: "I should be back by three, and if I'm not home by four you call headquarters to ask for the arrest list, they should have it by then."

"I will—"

Gaylord had been unwinding a length of gauze from round his head. "Look, Rantha, I'm going to tie our wrists together so we don't get separated."

"No listen I'd prefer to be free, because if I fall?"

"I'm not letting you out of my sight." He grabbed her unwilling arm and locked it against his chest with his elbow. She tugged and pumped and yelled: "Since what, you think our little arrangement gives you some kind of state powers or something?"

"Remarkable way you got of putting things."

"I'm joining women's liberation; you watch."

The bullhorn thudded from a distance: "Everybody wanting to picket come on down now toward the line."

"John, don't get hurt—"

"Don't worry. I'll be home soon."

"Yes"—She reached across the line, past the soldiers's blinking eyes and after him as he strode off with Gaylord and Amarantha. He raised his sign; the shirttails jumped from his belt and rippled in the wind. His blond head was covered by the crowd.